TWO THOUSAND MILES
FROM OMAHA

S.D. Goldman

TWO THOUSAND MILES
FROM OMAHA

S.D. GOLDMAN

S.D. Goldman

Published by S.D. Goldman 2024

Cover art courtesy of Emily's_World_Of_Design
@Emilys_world_of_design

ISBN: 979-8-9912018-0-3 (PPB)

S.D. Goldman

To those still searching.

S.D. Goldman

Chapter 1
179 Miles to Omaha, 2018

Ryan heard his phone vibrate before he opened his eyes. To his left, on the nightstand, he heard it ramble as he reached to grab it. He opened his eyes as he pulled it close to his view.

5:00 a.m., it read.

Sliding the alarm off, he set it back on the nightstand and gazed upward to the large fan in the middle of the popcorn ceiling. He watched as it turned, though it provided no relief from a warm April night.

He did not remember where he was.

He blinked a few times before glancing to his right, and instantly he saw the slim shoulders and tanned skin facing him. Sheet pressed to her mid back, she lay peacefully, unaware of his awakened eyes, her red hair cascading onto the pillow like a fiery fountain of bliss.

Ryan turned back to center before getting up from the bed. On the floor, he found his pants and put them on. Exhaling, he opened the bedroom door and walked into the hallway as he began to recall his location. To his right, a door stood ajar with a roommate sleeping inside. He walked past and moved into a bathroom on the left.

Shaking his head, he turned on the water before splashing it onto his face. Raising up from the basin, he saw himself in the mirror.

His face was boyish despite being thirty years old, and charming in its own way, from his faint freckles to his firm jawline and symmetrical hazel eyes. His hair was longer than he liked, but it flowed across his forehead in a manner that indicated more surfer than popstar. As he stared, he began to focus on the bags beneath his eyes and the small bruise on his lower neck.

How did we end up here? he thought.

He sighed before turning back to the bedroom.

She continued to lay tranquil on her bed, unaware of his motions. For this, he found himself thankful. He didn't need any distractions so early in the morning. Finding his shirt on her side, he put it on before he turned to her.

She was petite and beautiful, from her small nose and moderate lips to her high cheekbones and thick, luscious hair. On any normal day, Ryan would have loved to continue gazing at her.

He recalled the night before, when she had been as alive as ever. Their dinner and drinks had been peaceful, and in each other's company, they found someone that seemed to understand the other, at least for the night. Ryan remembered the band playing to the right of the bar, and he remembered how beautiful she had looked in the neon lights. He found himself having a good time. He always did with her. She seemed content with his company, and she never asked for anything more than he could provide. He liked that most of all. As the night had progressed, drinks moved to a lakefront walk, and before long, a ride back to this apartment. It had moved so quick, but it always did with her.

He moved back to the nightstand and grabbed his phone and watch. He didn't want to be in the room any longer. Taking another long exhale, he pulled the door closed behind him. Shortly thereafter, he was out of the apartment.

He found his Toyota in the parking lot of the complex, and as he stepped inside, he closed his eyes.

He should've left a note. He should've woken her up. He should've explained himself. But he didn't. He couldn't find the words. There was nothing that could help.

He liked her but could give her no more.

She was not *her.*

He breathed out as he opened his eyes, and suddenly he saw snowfall.

He gazed through the windows and realized he was no longer in his Toyota. He was in a Jeep, the same as he had been years ago. His gaze moved outside the vehicle, where the snow continued.

It surrounded him, as though it had no other purpose. His focus deepened as he could see he was no longer in the apartment parking lot. He was no longer in Iowa.

He was in South Dakota, parked alongside a country road. The lights from the nearby town of Shannon glistened off the snow around him. Staring out from the driver's side, his eyes focused ahead as he saw a vision he had dreamed many times before.

She was there, just outside the front of his parked Jeep.

Blonde hair pulled up into a stocking cap, her face was turned skyward as the snow continued to fall. Her eyes were closed as she remained peaceful in the moment.

A low country song played on the Jeep's radio. It was a melody he had committed to heart, and it reverberated throughout the vehicle as he stared ahead.

He watched as she tilted her head downward and turned to him, serenity and warmth etched across her face. He held his breath as she walked around to the driver's side door. He could feel her presence as she leaned in, and he could smell the wildflowers in her perfume as she brought her face to his.

He closed his eyes, knowing that her kiss, this moment, was all he wanted.

"Mel—," he heard himself say.

He opened his eyes. There was no snow. There was no *her*. The vision was gone.

He looked out the driver's side window to see the apartment.

The woman inside would never understand how his heart belonged to another. The woman inside would never be the one he dreamt about day after day, and night after night.

He knew it, and he hated it. The dinner, the drinks, the walk; it was always the same. Her room, his room; it was always the same. Him leaving, her wondering why. Him never able to explain.

He never planned to end each night like this, but his plans meant little. It was an endless cycle of moving on and moving back, of trying and failing. Same story, different girl. Same fun night. Same regretful morning.

He never wanted to break hearts, but despite it all, he always did with her.

***

"Don't worry, Stein," Jim Reynolds said with complete apathy, "we're just waiting on you."

Tyler Stein entered the conference room looking just as labored as his boss did in addressing him. Taking his seat four down from Jim, he set his legal pad on the table.

"We missing anyone else?" Jim said sardonically.

Around the room, the male-dominated team of managers for the Spirit Lake division of Central Plains Ethanol sat around the plain conference room.

Ryan sat at the end of the table, the only person clad in a work uniform instead of business casual clothes.

"Alright, let's get started," Jim said. "Stein, where we at?"

"Grinding corn as of 7:15 a.m.," Stein responded.

Jim turned to a man to his left. "Joe, what'd your guys find?"

Joe, the maintenance manager of the group, leaned forward as he spoke . "Found a dead possum in the bulk elevator."

"Poor bastard," another man across the table muttered under his breath.

"He took a while to get out," Joe continued, "and he broke a few buckets, but we got 'er done."

"How'd he fall in? Conveyor lids off?" Jim turned back to Stein.

"We're looking into it now."

Jim attempted his most professional eye roll. "You don't know yet?"

Stein exhaled. "No."

Jim looked down the table. "Not sure why I even bothered. Ryan, your crew is on today, right?"

Ryan's ears perked at his name being mentioned. "Yes sir."

"Can you answer the question I posed to your manager?"

Ryan cleared his throat. "During shift change, my guys went out and took inventory. We found three lids off the grain conveyors. We shut them down to put the lids back on."

Jim smiled in approval. "Thank you, Ryan." He turned back to Stein. "That's how he got there. Your shift supervisor knows the answer."

Stein cowered.

"What else do you have?"

Stein took another deep breath. "New enzyme company showing up today looking to trial product. Other than that, we plan to keep making booze from corn."

"Great idea," Jim replied unenthusiastically as he turned toward the man across from Joe. "Aaron?"

Ryan watched as the safety manager next to him looked down at his notepad. "So far so good."

"Finally," Jim replied. "I'm glad someone here has some good news."

The meeting concluded less than ten minutes later, and as they all filed from the conference room, Jim called out, "Ryan, can I see you in my office?"

Ryan stopped in the hallway, suddenly dreading his decision not to rush out sooner. He turned back around and made for the door across from the conference room where Jim's name hung over the title of Plant Manager. Palms clenched, he entered as Jim sat at his desk looking at a piece of paper.

"Get the door, Ryan," Jim said.

Ryan nodded, knowing he was in the only place in the plant he feared.

"You've been with us," Jim looked down at a piece of paper as he spoke, "four year? Is that right?"

Ryan nodded as he stood behind a chair.

"And one year as a supervisor?"

"Yessir," Ryan said.

"You like it?"

Ryan nodded. "Yessir."

Jim smiled. "You don't like it."

Ryan tilted his head. "Excuse me?"

Jim leaned back. "You don't like it. You don't."

"I'm not sure—"

"Why are you here, Ryan?"

"What?" Ryan felt his breath hold in his throat. "Am I in trouble or something?"

Jim shook his head. "Just be honest, Ryan."

Ryan managed a chuckle. "Last time I was honest in a manager's office, it didn't end well."

Jim continued looking at the paper in front of him. "I assume that was at...hmm...Gibson's Department Store in Florida?"

Ryan realized that the paper was his own resume.

"Last job listed before here."

Ryan nodded, though he was still perplexed.

"I got to admit," Jim continued, "this is the most eloquently worded resume I've ever seen for an ethanol company."

"Thanks?"

"The format is a bit messy, however."

"I typed it at the public library."

"Your margins are out of whack. It's like you typed it up and gave it to a four-year-old to edit."

"The library's Microsoft Office was from 1985."

Jim smiled. "All this doesn't answer my question."

Ryan allowed himself to breathe. "I'm not sure what you're asking me."

Jim leaned back. "I want to know why you're here. You've got a great resume with internships and a bachelor's degree in journalism. You have work experience. Why did you come here? Why have you stayed here?"

"Why did I come here?"

"To Northern Iowa. And to an ethanol company."

Ryan looked down to his feet.

"You're a perplexing guy, Ryan," Jim continued. "No family here anyone knows of. No connections. Yet you have the skill set to do pretty much anything. And in four years of knowing you, you've barely mentioned anything outside of work."

"I enjoy the work."

Jim smiled again. "It's fine if you don't want to answer."

Ryan took a deep breath. "Honestly," he heard himself say, "I'm here because you hired me."

Jim cocked his head.

"Jim, listen, I—" Ryan paused. His secret had to come out. He stammered as he spoke it aloud. "I've got a record. I'm—I'm a felon."

Jim sat back in his chair. He nodded as the silence between the two increased. Finally, he breathed out. "And?"

Ryan blinked his eyes. "And what?"

"And what does that matter?"

"And…" Ryan became very confused.

Jim stood up as he moved to his coffee machine behind the desk. "Jesus Christ, Ryan, you live in Iowa. Everyone here's a felon."

Ryan swallowed. "You…knew?"

"Of course. Hell, I'm more surprised yours wasn't for meth, honestly. Everyone else here seems to love that shit."

Ryan remained silent.

"Ryan, listen," Jim began. "Do you know where our company's plants are? Norfolk, Nebraska. Clarenda, Iowa. Saint James, Minnesota. Any of those sound like big cities?"

Ryan continued to remain quiet.

"God, no," Jim continued, sitting back down. "They're all in BFE. If we didn't hire felons, we'd have no one to work for us. It'd literally be me and the guy we hired seasonally to mow lawns, and to be honest, he's a random stop away from a DUI charge." Jim paused. "I want to know why you are *here*?"

"I don't know," Ryan stammered. He wanted more than anything to be out of the room.

Jim softened. "You really assault a police officer? I ask because that's what Google told me."

Ryan didn't respond. He had already known what Google said about him long ago.

"I'm not saying that's cool." Jim shrugged. "But it is unique. Still, forty-five days in jail plus two years' probation seems like a harsh charge given your first offense."

"I wasn't particularly helpful to the police."

Jim chuckled. "I imagine they didn't like you assaulting their fellow officer."

Ryan shrugged. "Probably not."

"Did you live in South Dakota?"

"No," Ryan replied cautiously. "I was just driving through helping a friend out."

"A friend?" Jim replied. "So you do know people in the Midwest."

"Bo actually wasn't from here."

"Bo?"

Ryan shrugged. "That's what I called him."

Jim nodded.

Ryan exhaled. "We were on a road trip across the country from Florida. And we don't really keep in touch anymore," Ryan replied. "For what it's worth."

Jim nodded as he took a deep breath. "So, after two plus years you just decided to come back? The Midwest must have left an impression for you."

Ryan smiled. "Florida wasn't for me."

"And Spirit Lake is?"

"It is now."

Jim returned the smile. "You didn't come here to work at an ethanol plant, did you?"

Ryan understood that he had tiptoed around the subject enough. "I came back for things that don't exist here anymore, and once I figured that out, I decided to make a life on my own." He paused for a moment. "I drove a little bit and found you all were hiring. I figured the cost of living is cheaper here, the weather isn't too bad, and most of all, it's hard to find a job with a record in Florida, believe it or not." He paused. "So I applied, was hired pretty quick, and the rest is history."

Jim nodded as Ryan finished the story. "Weather here sucks."

Ryan laughed. "I don't mind it."

"So, you came back here to find something."

Ryan thought about it. "Yeah, I did."

"Something, or someone?"

Ryan hesitated but then nodded. "She was a waitress at a diner in South Dakota."

Jim chuckled. "Of course she was."

"I don't think any of this really matters," Ryan said. "What I was looking for is gone and there's absolutely no trace of her."

"No trace? Did you check social media?"

Ryan squinted his eyes. "Yes, I checked social media."

"She have any family you could look into?"

Again, Ryan provided a labored answer. "A brother, but he wasn't around either. The whole family left. So, I found nothing." He paused. "But I've moved past all that."

"Have you?"

Ryan contemplated the answer. "Yeah. I have."

Jim returned to his upright position at his desk. "Do you mind if I ask you one more thing?"

Ryan shrugged as Jim logged in to his computer. After a few clicks, he pulled up the screen he needed. He stood as he turned the computer screen.

Ryan saw a screen full of production data.

"Do you know what this is?"

Ryan nodded. "Daily production totals."

Jim nodded. "Shift totals, to be exact. And your shift is far and away leading the pack."

Ryan continued to stare at the screen.

"So naturally," Jim continued. "I tried to figure out what the difference was. And after all my investigations, I found that the reason your team leads the pack is because *you* are leading them."

Ryan did not raise his gaze from the screen.

"You're the only supervisor who rallies his team. You're the only one who doesn't just sit in the control room and sleep. You're out in the field, and you're out developing your team."

"I'm just doing my job," Ryan replied.

Jim smiled, as if the statement was what he wanted to hear. "You got a gift, Ryan. You have a degree, and an innate ability to communicate. You inspire your team. They said as much."

Ryan became uncomfortable with the compliments.

"You aren't meant to be a shift supervisor. Hell, you're not meant to work at this plant."

"I'm not?"

"No Ryan, you're not. You're built for something better. And if the only reason you came back was to find something that doesn't exist, then you don't have many reasons to stay."

Like a dealer turning the river, he pulled out another piece of paper and laid it before Ryan.

Central Plains Ethanol is calling for any professionals with communication skills and ethanol knowledge to join a special team of facilitators leading the discussion on ethanol's sustainability and marketability. If selected, you and the team will travel to conferences and meetings across the country to represent Central Plains on the national landscape. As expected, the right candidates will hold exceptional skills in communications, facilitation, personal marketing, and the ability to speak in front of large crowds. High travel and performance bonuses on top of an adequate salary can also be expected.

Ryan set the paper down. "I'm confused."

"About?"

"This." Ryan indicated the paper with the word "Facilitator" on top. "You want me to apply for this?"

Jim snorted. "No," he said. "I don't want you to apply, I want you to do it. I've already prepared my recommendation to be sent to the CEO. I just need you to tell me yes."

"Whoa." Ryan sat back. "I'm sorry, but this is a lot…"

"Ryan, what's there to think about?" Jim replied. "You just told me you have pretty much nothing here and you have the tools for this sort of opportunity."

"I've never *facilitated*. I don't know enough…"

"Sure, you do."

"I don't," Ryan repeated. "I don't even know what they're presenting on." He grabbed the paper from the desk. "'*Facilitators leading the discussion on ethanol's sustainability and marketability*'? What the hell does that even mean?"

"They want you to sell," Jim explained.

"Sell what? Ethanol?"

Jim shrugged. "The idea of ethanol."

Ryan set the paper back down and continued staring ahead.

"They want you to go into places and introduce or sell the idea that what we're doing is a big deal, that it's saving the planet, and that they should get involved. Either to buy it at gas stations or plant corn for ethanol usage. There's a script I'm sure."

"Jim, I don't know—"

"Ryan," Jim leaned forward. "People *believe* what you say. You have that gift. Whether it's your team, or an audience of prospective buyers, you can win them over because I've already seen you do it." Jim paused. "This is a once in a lifetime opportunity. You'll travel the country for free. You'll develop visibility and exceptional skills. Who knows, some CEO could be listening to you talk, and you might end up hitting it big. At least consider it."

Ryan exhaled. "Then what?"

"The initial meeting is at corporate in Omaha tomorrow. They'll explain the program there and then you'll have a better idea of what you're getting into." Jim turned back to his computer. "But there's only so many spaces for the initial meeting, so if you want it, I'll send my recommendation off, and you'll be guaranteed an interview."

Ryan considered it all. "What about my job here?"

Jim chuckled. "Ryan, this is bigger than your job here. Sure, it'll suck to see you go, but you have too much talent to stay here." He paused. "This is a huge opportunity. A huge promotion."

Ryan mulled the word over. *Promotion.*

"That's what it is." Jim turned back from his computer. "Listen, good leaders develop their employees. Some employees, like Joe and Gabe, are comfortable in their positions, and that's good. Others like Stein have great potential, which is why I'm so hard on him, because he can be so much better. You, however, don't need that. You just need a push out of the nest. You said it yourself; you came back for someone who isn't here, but that doesn't mean she doesn't exist out there somewhere," Jim added as he indicated the window and the world behind him.

Ryan looked up, and the weight of the honesty in the man's words grew heavy.

"Maybe out there in that huge world, you can find what you're looking for. But if you can't find it," Jim said as he smiled with a nod, "find something better."

***

It was after work when Ryan found himself walking towards his car. As he moved, he pulled his phone from his pants pocket.

Missed voicemail.

He pressed play as he walked to his truck in the lot.

"Received ...this morning at...7:18 a.m."

He then heard another voice more familiar.

"Hey...it's Caroline." The voice was tired, labored. "The, uh, walk of shame routine is becoming a habit, I guess. You could have woken me up at least. You know I actually believed you when you said it'd be different this time." There was a pause. "I feel like a broken record." Another pause. "Listen, Ryan, it doesn't have to be anything serious, but this can't just be nothing. That's not what I need." He could feel her pain through the words. "Call me back if you want this to be something, but if you don't..." She paused. "Then please, don't. I can't keep doing whatever the hell it is we're doing." There was more she wanted to say, but he could sense the words would not come. "Bye." Click.

Ryan took a deep breath as he reached his car, then deleted the message. He gripped the door handle and paused. He closed his eyes and felt his hand shake. Then, after only a moment, he opened his eyes. A few seconds later, he was in the Toyota as he pulled onto the main road, singing along as the radio blared.

Chapter 2
In Omaha

The downtown Omaha headquarters for Central Plains was a modest building for a Fortune 1000 company, although the entrance was large enough to suspect the interior would be more elegant. As Ryan stepped inside the doors, he saw giant murals on either side of the glass vestibule, one of Mt. Everest and one of the Riviera coastline. Eying them in their entirety, he appreciated their size and scope, even taking time to read the caption on the bottom of each.

Climb your toughest peak.

Live to find your beach.

Ryan stepped into the atrium as he removed his sunglasses. Approaching the front desk, he spied the receptionist staring at a pad of paper in front of her.

"Good morning," he said.

"Morning," she replied. "Who are you here to see?"

He rested his hands on the counter. "Ryan Collins for the facilitation interview."

She nodded as she moved to another piece of paper. "You'll be upstairs." She motioned to a glass staircase behind her. "Room 203. Have a seat outside the room and wait to be called."

Ryan nodded as he followed the instructions, taking care to walk slowly up the stairs, knowing his loafers had little traction on the shiny steps. Reaching the top, he peered down a long hallway and saw a small group of chairs sitting in front of a door. Sitting in these chairs were what appeared to be three men, each with a chair between them.

Ryan approached and saw the room marker before he took a chair at the end.

He noticed the three men each staring at him as he sat, and he nodded hello, realizing the nervousness he felt.

"Here for the facilitation job?" the man across from him asked in a higher voice than Ryan expected. He appeared to be in his late twenties, with glasses and a full head of brown hair. In his tie and suit jacket, he could have passed for a gamer turned stockbroker, and Ryan found it unlikely he had ever worked at an ethanol plant.

"Yeah," Ryan replied.

"It's a great gig," the man replied, tapping his feet. "So much travel."

Ryan smiled, knowing he had picked the wrong seat.

"Which plant do you work at?" the man asked.

Ryan looked to the other two men, who each stared at their feet. "Spirit Lake," he said.

"Nice," the man replied. "Corporate office for me. Accounting."

Close enough, Ryan thought.

"Steven," the man said as he stuck out his hand.

Ryan obliged. "Ryan," he said.

"That's Donovan." Steven pointed to the man seated to his right. "And that's Mike," he said, pointing to the person to Ryan's right.

Ryan gave a courtesy wave as each man tried to make the introduction as short as possible.

"Family typically goes to Spirit Lake at least once a year," Steven continued. "Great fishing there."

Ryan nodded. "It's a nice place."

"Hard to find that type of fishing around here. I mean, I love Omaha, but if it wasn't for the wife, I'd be up in Minnesota or somewhere."

Ryan's ears perked at the *wife*, but he said nothing of it.

Just then, the door opened, and a woman exited, taking a seat between Donovan and Steven.

"Steven," another woman said from the doorway. "You're up."

Steven's eyes went wide. "Wish me luck," he said to Ryan as he stood.

Ryan smiled. "Good luck."

Seconds later, the door closed, and Steven was gone. The silence that followed was tangible as the four of them sat.

"You all get to know Steven?" the woman new to the group said.

Smirks formed on all the men's faces as they continued to sit.

"He's got a lot to say," Donovan said. "I'm glad Mike showed up."

Ryan saw him roll his eyes.

"Try working every day near him," the woman said.

"Accounting too?" Mike replied. It was the first words Ryan had heard him speak.

"AP, yes," she replied, as though also surprised to hear the man speak. "Maria."

Each of the men responded with their names, and as they spoke, Ryan was able to survey the group.

Maria appeared to also be in her late twenties, with brightness radiating from her persona. Clad in a vivid red and pink flowery top, she commanded attention, with dark brown hair as large as her aura.

Mike was perhaps the youngest of the group, and his conservative clothing choice of pressed white shirt and pressed black pants indicated he may have had dressing help. No more than twenty-four, he was a subtly handsome young man, with a thin beard and a strong jawline.

Lastly, Donovan was the picture of style in a full suit with a rich purple undershirt. His dark skin and deep brown eyes were soothing, and he appeared to always have some form of a smile on his face. He appeared to look more model than anything else, and Ryan was curious as to how he had ended up in the Midwest over L.A. or New York.

"He isn't really that bad," Maria said, "He just loves to talk. This job would be great for him."

"He seems qualified," Mike added, with laughter from the group.

"What plants are you all at?"

Donovan looked up, as if suspecting their eyes on him. "Norfolk. Safety manager."

"Clarinda, lab," Mike continued.

Their eyes turned to Ryan.

"Spirit Lake, operations."

"Nice," she replied. "A lot of variety."

"I wonder how many more people will show," Donovan said after a moment.

"Hopefully not too many," Maria responded. "It'd be better odds if it's just us."

***

It was just them. After nearly an hour of waiting, Ryan was called in, and he found the panel more intimidating than the questions themselves. In a formal round-robin-style approach, each suited individual asked generic questions, such as his personal background, his interests, his role in the company, etc. Ryan was safe in answering them as well. Smiling responses such as, "Florida. Majored in journalism. Needed a change of scenery. Able to adapt to any situation." He gave them the answers he knew they wanted to hear.

After about twenty minutes, he was beckoned back into the hall, where the remaining individuals sat in relative silence, save for Steven, who asked about each person's interrogation.

"You all can come in," the lead interrogator said as she opened the door towards the five in the hall. In hushed silence, they filed in and stood in the center of the room, Ryan last among them.

"First," the lead woman said from the center of the table after a few moments, "we want to thank you all for interviewing for this position. As you may be aware, we are looking for talented spokespersons from our company to help promote our business ventures in areas we are looking to reach. Our goal is to raise not only awareness, but sales in these areas. With that said, this is a new opportunity, and always subject to change. After careful consideration, we feel you five are best suited to meet our needs, and therefore, we would like to extend this promotion opportunity to all of you."

Ryan could hear exhales and excited murmurs from the four to his right.

The lady continued. "We would like to celebrate your achievement by a luncheon, if you're able, but first we'll go through the necessary HR paperwork with you individually. Please return to the hallway and we will have HR representatives meet with you shortly."

"Thank you so much, Mrs. Anderson," he heard Maria say, and he wondered when she had said her name.

Ryan stood silent for a moment, unsure of what to do next. After a second, Mrs. Anderson glanced at him, and he knew he had to do something. Smiling, he turned as he walked back out the door, wondering how many times he would have to walk back and forth.

"This is so exciting!" Steven exclaimed seconds after the door shut. Handshakes and high fives were passed around as Ryan took a moment to breathe out, though uncertainty gripped his body. He had not expected to suddenly have his life upended, and he struggled to process it all.

"It's pretty cool we get to travel the country," Ryan heard Steven say as he attempted to continue processing his thoughts.

How long was this going to be for? What was he going to have to sell? How would he survive living hotel to hotel? It was all too much to consider.

"Ryan?" he heard Steven ask. He turned to see all four of his new companions looking at him.

"Huh?"

"Have you ever done anything like it?"

Ryan stared at them. "Done anything like *what?*"

Steven laughed. "You know. This. Travel the country. Be on your own. It's crazy, right?"

Ryan smiled as he considered the question. "Yeah, it is," he said. "Once in a lifetime experience."

***

"I'd like to introduce you to your team," Kim Anderson said as Ryan entered a large conference room sometime after noon. He looked around to see his four teammates already taking their seats opposite more unfamiliar faces. From left to right were two girls and a guy, all of whom appeared to be around Ryan's age. Attempting to blend in, Ryan took his seat next to Donovan.

"Let's go around the room and introduce ourselves, say what we've done in the company, and offer up one random fact about ourselves," Mrs. Anderson said as she took her seat next to the guy. "I'll start. I'm Kim Anderson, leader of this project. I work as the director of marketing here at the company, and I have a dog named Turtle, along with two kids and a husband."

"Lead with the dog," the guy said next to her. "Classic."

Kim laughed as she beckoned the man on.

"Mark Schwartz, marketing IT. I'll be putting together your materials for each session. I also do regular IT, but don't tell anyone." As he spoke, Ryan realized he was younger than initially thought, and perhaps haughtier as well. "I'm a devout Huskers fan and have attended at least twenty games. Even met my wife at Memorial."

"And she still puts up with you," Kim responded with a chuckle. "Allison, next."

"Allison Jennings. Marketing coordinator. I'll assist with sales and any other areas needed." Ryan could sense she was intense in her job. "I've lived in the area all my life and have a cat named Ken. I also love *Jeopardy*."

"She has a daily calendar of trivia if you ever want to test her," Kim said with a laugh.

Ryan turned as the last unknown face spoke.

"My name's Emma Kelle," the woman began. "I'm originally from Tennessee and have lived here for a little under a year. Oh yeah, and I'm also a marketing coordinator. I...I'll be responsible for your schedules and travel." Ryan smiled as she stuttered through her introduction. He could sense her nervousness, but he also saw an underlying sweet nature about her. Perhaps it was her bright blue eyes that adorned her rounded face, or maybe the innocent green headband she wore across her straight, dark blonde hair.

"You don't have an accent," Steven said after she had finished. Ryan could tell he had been waiting to speak.

She smiled and shrugged. "Guess it just skipped me."

Kim leaned forward. "Emma is also going to be in and out during the next few months because she is getting married…"

"Aww congrats," Maria said, followed by similar messages from the others. "When's the big day?"

"Still planning," Emma replied. "It's a lot of work."

"I'm sure!" Maria continued. "Will it be back in Tennessee?"

"I think so," Emma responded. "That's where most of my family is."

"Well, good for you. Keep us posted," Maria added.

A brief silence followed before Kim turned to the new arrivals. "Now on to you all. Who's first? Donovan?"

Ryan sat back in his chair as he wondered if any of this would ever feel normal. Looking around the room at all the excitement and jubilation, he felt more out of place than ever before. He wanted to be back in his plant. He wanted to be back in his solitude, alone with his thoughts. He wanted all those things, but knew they were long gone. This was his new life, and these were his new people.

Like it or not, this was his new reality, and there was no going back now.

Chapter 3
In Omaha

Ryan was falling asleep.

Sitting in a small conference room with the lights dimmed, he watched through lowering eyelids as the PowerPoint continued. The current slide was numbered forty-two, but it felt like six hundred.

The most important questions, namely where they were going and what the travel would look like, remained unanswered. Instead, they focused on the sales pitch itself, much to Ryan's annoyance.

He found himself looking around to his other teammates and saw Donovan's eyes continually droop. At least he wasn't alone, he thought.

Looking at Mike and Maria, who sat next to each other on the other side of the table, he saw them alternate between taking notes and focusing on the screen. They seemed interested. He wished he had that level of attention.

At the front end of the table sat Steven, and in him Ryan saw an unparalleled level of interest, ranging from furious scribbles in his notepad to questions on every other slide that seemed to make the already long presentation even more droll. After each answer was presented, he then returned to his notebook to continue the frantic scribbling. Before long, a page would turn in his notebook and the scrawling would begin again. He must have had at least twenty pages of notes.

Ryan looked to his notebook and saw only once sentence.

Ethanol sales pitch.

He took a deep breath. He never anticipated he'd be a salesman.

Maybe this was a mistake. Maybe he was not cut out for this type of job. What did he know about selling? Or ethanol? Sure, he had been making the product, but it was a paycheck, not a known commodity. All he knew was that it was made from corn, and it smelled like moonshine. He had no idea how it worked in a combustion engine, or how it was going to save the fossil fuel crisis.

He exhaled again, and before long, his eyes began to droop. Shaking his head awake, he sat up and attempted to start taking notes, but it was not long before his head lowered again.

Christ, man, get it together, he thought as he cracked his neck. He sat upright, attempting to maintain focus. He looked towards the slides, wondering how much further they were in the presentation.

Slide forty-three.

He gritted his teeth. He needed a break.

He stood up, unnoticed by the group. Slowly, he moved towards the back door and pulled it open. Stepping outside the room, he took a deep breath, thankful to be out of the dark and sleepy space.

"You looking for something?" a voice said to his left.

Ryan jumped at the noise and turned as he saw a familiar face staring at him from the end of the hallway.

"No—I mean, yes," Ryan said as the girl with the green headband approached. He struggled to remember her name as he stared at the pop of color on her head.

She smiled at him. "Bathroom?"

"Yes," Ryan replied, though he wondered why he was lying. "Actually, no."

"No?"

Ryan smiled. "No, I mean, I don't need a bathroom. I just—" He paused as he searched for the words. He turned back towards the room. "That presentation is so boring."

She laughed as he smiled.

"I mean, seriously, I was falling asleep. I had to get out."

"It is boring," she said after her laughter died down.

"You had to sit through it?"

She sighed. "I created it."

Ryan felt a lump in his throat. "Oh God, I didn't mean…"

"I'm kidding," she said as she sensed his discomfort.

Ryan's eyes went wide. "Really?"

"No." She shrugged. "I really did make it. I don't know why I lied there."

Ryan couldn't move.

"It's a boring topic," she said. "I did almost fall asleep creating it though."

Ryan admired her honesty.

"I'm also not sure if the people in this office should be teaching you all how to sell ethanol. I mean, I haven't even been to a plant."

"The…color scheme is…nice though," Ryan tried.

She smiled. "Thank you. I was pretty pleased with that."

He could sense an innate compassion within her, albeit covered with an adorable awkwardness.

"You know what," he said, "I may take you up on that bathroom location."

She nodded. "Down that hall to the right."

"Thank you," he said as he trailed off on her name.

"Emma."

"Emma," he repeated. "I'm Ryan."

"I know," she replied as she turned, adding even more to his discomfort.

"You're—" he struggled to find words. "You're going to keep my sleepiness a secret, right?"

She turned back around, steps ahead of him. "As long as you keep it a secret that I created it…"

"Deal," Ryan replied.

"Deal," she repeated before turning back around without another word.

Ryan stood in the hallway a moment longer before turning. He had never been happier to have an awkward conversation end, yet somehow there was a sadness there as well, as if perhaps he enjoyed being confounded more than he originally thought.

***

The remainder of the training crept by.

What began as an endless barrage of PowerPoint presentations and unending situational discussions turned to the weekend, and before long, Ryan found himself staring at his closet with an open suitcase placed precariously on his bed. He sighed as he looked out his window to see a bright spring day. Packing was the furthest thing from his mind.

His gaze returned to his schedule, printed out in bold font with a folder of travel itineraries behind it. He perused through them as he considered his road ahead.

Elgin, IL – Monday thru Friday, April 23-27
Madison, WI – Sunday thru Wednesday, April 29-May 2
Rochester, MN – Thursday-Friday, May 3- May 4
Omaha (Corporate) – May 7

He noticed there were no dates after May seventh. He didn't know what to make of it. Was his life now scheduled in two-week intervals? Were they expected to fail after two weeks? Uncertainty was never his strong suit.

He returned to his closet. He needed more clothes. Looking at the wall of T-shirts and jeans, he sighed. One pair of khakis and a polo was not going to be enough.

He looked back at his travel folder, now sitting on top of his three-inch binder of selling spiels and guides. He needed to practice more.

We are a company on the brink of a new revolution.

"What revolution?" he mused aloud. "Turning corn into booze? How unique. There aren't thousands of guys doing it in their garages, are there?"

We are powering the future. And you have the great opportunity to be a part of it.

"Please, give us money." He pulled shirts off their hangers. "Actually, please give us your land. We don't want your money, but we want you to make *us* money."

We have unlocked the power of agriculture.

He pulled more clothes from his dresser. "We have created Frankenstein vegetables."

We have reinvented the corn kernel.

"We have made corn inedible."

He continued musing aloud as he packed. Before long, his suitcase was filled to the brim, leaving the rest of his room and closet bare. He sat on his bed as he looked around, realizing just how little in the way of furniture and décor he had. It was almost as though he had not embraced the space.

"Four years," he breathed. *Where had those years gone?*

He needed an escape. He needed to not focus so much on the blandness of his living space. He pulled out his phone.

Rubbing his eyes, he saw a few unread messages, and upon opening the app, he saw several from women he barely remembered. He read them but stopped upon sensing an angered tone in some. He knew he would not respond.

He scrolled further down his message list and saw another he had yet to respond to, this one under the name of "Bo". His mind instantly returned to the days spent driving across the country with the man alongside. It seemed so long ago. And all that was left was a message he had yet to respond to, and the memories of a South Dakota stop along the way.

He shook his head as he tried to dislodge the thoughts from his mind.

He flipped to his Facebook and was bombarded with posts from family. The first was of his mother and father sitting at their pool, drinks in hand. It looked peaceful. He smiled at the thought. The next was from his cousin, Brandon, though it only showed his hand embraced with another. Ryan read the post. *Celebrating two years with my love at the place where it all started, Forest Park.*

Two years, Ryan thought. He couldn't recall seeing anything about the relationship before. He clicked through Brandon's profile and saw very few recent images, though some depicted him with groups of friends.

Ryan clicked his own profile. The last update was from a year ago, a simple picture of him in a hardhat at work. It had four likes. The last time he had checked, there had been six.

He clicked the search bar. He typed the letter *M* and stopped.

The first search that popped up was recognizable. The name was plain as day, a call back to the endless nights Ryan had spent typing the name just to see if a profile showed up. None ever did. The name didn't exist. She was not there.

Why did she matter so much?

Ryan shook his head as he closed his eyes. It was a question that bogged down his mind far too often. On the one hand, he had survived just fine without her for the past years. Yet on the other, he recalled just how alive he had felt in her presence. She was his equal in personality, full of cynicism and wit that allowed him to feel alive and full of vigor. Her view of the world was as disheveled as his, and he knew she would hear his thoughts and never find him boring or obtuse. She listened to him, even if it was to make her own point. She understood him.

He recalled sitting in her father's farmhouse and staring at her wall of books. Never was there a place where he felt so alive. He recalled seeing her own manuscripts tucked into the shelves, and he knew he had never seen her more nervous than when he read her words. It was intimacy unlike any other, and he had never experienced it before.

Three days. That was all it was. And yet in that time he had found a connection he had never known before. And as for the final evening, when he watched her from the driver's seat along some country road before she climbed inside and pressed herself to him, it was a memory he could not shake.

He recalled laying together with their clothes thrown onto the floorboard, a teenaged mentality packed into adult bodies. He promised he'd never leave her. It was a promise he knew he'd break.

He remembered it all too well. She made him feel seen. She made him feel like he mattered. She mattered because *she mattered*.

Taking a deep breath, Ryan exited the app and put his phone away. There was nothing there but heartbreak. There was nothing there but pain.

He glanced around his room.

No matter where he went, it was all the same. Everywhere was empty, and he had no idea how to make it feel whole.

Chapter 4
463 Miles from Omaha

Ryan stared at the clock on the bedside table. Grinding his teeth, he waited until it changed from 6:59 p.m. to 7:00 p.m. Once it did, he stood up from the hotel room bed.

It was time to head downstairs.

To his right, his suitcase lay on the floor, flipped open. He had attempted to pull out his toiletries, but nothing else. It all lay as haphazardly as it had when he'd packed.

Stifling a yawn, he moved to the door and stepped into the hallway. Soon after, he was in the elevator, heading down the twelve floors to the main atrium and the hotel restaurant.

Stepping inside, he noticed more patrons than expected for a Monday night. Scanning the tables, he spotted familiar faces.

"There he is," Donovan's voice called out as Ryan approached. "He can settle this debate."

"Hey guys," Ryan replied as he took a seat. "Sorry I'm a bit late."

"No worries, I just got here too," Mike replied as he shook Ryan's hand from across the table. "It's been a thrilling discussion."

Ryan smiled at the comment as he sat between Steven and Maria. "What discussion am I coming into?"

"Well we're—" Steven began, but a glance from Maria silenced him.

"He just got here," she scolded. She turned to Ryan. "How's your room?"

"It's good. Twelfth floor."

"Same," she responded.

"It's a nice place," Steven interjected. "A little fancier than airport hotels."

"Also cheaper than airport hotels," Ryan said as a waiter brought him water. "But it is nice." He took a sip from the glass. "So what discussion did I walk into?"

"Donovan wants to go clubbing," Maria said.

Donovan's face turned to shock. "It isn't *clubbing.*"

Ryan looked at Maria.

"It's clubbing," she confirmed.

"It's a bar in the city," Donovan explained. "And they play music."

"Live music?" Ryan replied.

Donovan exhaled. "Some nights…"

"Tonight?"

"No…"

Ryan shrugged.

"It's a bar," Donovan explained. "It's got a nice rooftop patio and drinks."

Steven laughed. "A bar that people go clubbing at."

"It's a Chicago landmark," Donovan continued. "It was an old historic place and it's a staple for celebrations." He paused as he turned his phone so Ryan could see the screen. "Look, it got a 4.9!"

Ryan laughed. "Sounds fun."

"I want us all to go," Donovan responded as he surveyed the group.

"Hence the discussion," Maria concluded to Ryan.

"Ah." Ryan nodded. "Who doesn't want to go?" He knew the answer before he asked the question.

"I don't think we should be going out the night before a presentation," Steven's voice echoed first.

"Fair," Ryan said.

"And I said," Donovan snarled, "that we're all adults, and one night won't hurt."

"True," Ryan countered. He grabbed a dinner roll from the table.

"So, would you go?" Donovan asked as Ryan took a bite.

Ryan chewed as he thought. Nothing sounded more unappealing than loud music and a night out, but it was hard to ignore the stares of his companions.

"Why not?" he replied.

Donovan hit the table in approval. All eyes turned to Steven.

"Don't look at me," Steven replied. "I already said my thoughts."

"And they were noted," Maria responded. "But what you fail to consider is the team building this will do."

"Peer pressure," Ryan muttered as he buttered another piece of bread. "This should work."

"Come on, Steven," Maria continued. "You don't want to leave us hanging."

Steven was clearly annoyed, yet his mouth spoke despite his facial arrangement. "Fine," he said. "Fine, I'll go."

"Yes!" Maria exclaimed.

"But we leave at a reasonable hour," Steven stipulated.

"Fair," Donovan replied.

Despite his agreement, Steven still seemed flustered. After only a moment, he arose, claiming he needed the bathroom.

"I can't believe you convinced him," Donovan said after a moment to Maria.

"You just got to talk to him in terms that make sense," Maria replied. "Like the team stuff. He's big into it."

"Smart," Donovan replied. He turned to Ryan. "Good thing you showed up when you did."

Ryan smiled, outwardly expressing indifference. Inside, however, he reasoned he may have more in common with Steven than he had originally thought.

***

The bathroom was dark. Lit by blacklight, Ryan could make out the spray-painted musings on the walls around him, but little more. His own reflection scared him as he found the sink and mirror. He cursed as his heartbeat settled down.

Ignoring the certainly empty paper towel dispenser, he wiped his hands onto his pants as he took a deep breath. He ambled through the door as another patron entered and was forced to squeeze past.

"You'd think they'd make these bathrooms bigger," the man said with a half-drunk laugh.

Ryan smiled. He was not nearly drunk enough to find humor in the situation.

The entire establishment was dark, though the main entertainment space was full sun compared to the twilight of the bathroom. Adorned in all matter of wood and 1800s-type industrial fixtures, the whole of the space reminded Ryan of an aged whiskey barrel turned into a room. Even the workers seemed prepared for a return to the nineteenth century. And yet despite the music that played incessantly overhead, it did appear to be more of a bar first, music second locale.

"You couldn't be more wrong," Maria said aloud as Ryan approached their table near the bar.

"It's basic facts," Donovan responded, drink in hand.

Around the group, there were quite a few patrons scattered throughout, with most belonging to a large gathering of men towards the back corner of the room.

"Your facts are crap," Maria countered with a laugh.

"What'd I miss?" Ryan asked Steven, seated to his left.

"Donovan's trying to argue that coincidence isn't actually coincidental," Steven replied. He reached for his water and took a sip.

"I heard a song when we came in here," Mike began. "And it was a song I remembered hearing at a Bull's game when I came to Chicago in the late 2000s. I remembered the song because it was super catchy, and I merely said…" He tried his best to show innocence. "'*How coincidental I hear the same song on a return trip to Chicago.*' Then asshole here," he playfully indicated Donovan, "tries to tell me *coincidence isn't really that impressive.*" His voice attempted to mock his counterpart.

"It's not," Donovan replied. "I'm not trying to ruin your connection. I'm just telling you the truth."

"How so?" Ryan inquired.

"How so what?" Donovan replied. "How is it not impressive?"

"Yeah."

"Well, for starters," Donovan began, "we place way too much importance on coincidence, when in reality, the odds of the coincidence happening are better than the act happening in the first place." He paused. "I tried explaining that to these pagans, but they wouldn't listen."

"Explain it again then," Mike replied.

"It's easy really." He leaned forwards and adjusted his cuff link. "Tell me this, how many songs are there in the world? Ballpark it?"

The group thought about it.

"Okay, seriously, don't give yourselves an aneurysm," Donovan said after a moment.

"A billion," Maria said.

"Surprisingly, no," Donovan replied. "About ninety million."

Steven raised his hand. "And you know this how?"

Donovan turned to him. "I Google shit."

Steven seemed to accept the answer.

"Okay," Donovan continued. "So, ninety million, give or take. But that's every song in the world. We're talking Indian music, African, etc. So, adjust our ninety million for the twenty percent of the world speaks English and we're at roughly eighteen million English songs. Now, considering you were in a public place in America, that means the song must be mainstream. And from every music album, only two or three songs out of twelve or so become mainstream."

"So, we're down to a million," Ryan acknowledged.

"Exactly. One million. But that's every genre, and considering you were in a sports arena, I doubt Conway Twitty or Miles Davis was playing, so we need to remove country and hardcore rap and jazz and all other genres that don't fit that setting. Realistically, I'd say your chances of hearing your song the first time were maybe one in fifty thousand."

"Okay, that's not great," Mike replied.

Donovan rolled his eyes. "Yeah, thanks for the clarification. So, what's the odds you'd hear that song again on your next visit to the same town?"

Steven shrugged. "One in one hundred thousand."

"Wrong."

"No," Steven countered. "It's basic statistics. One out of fifty thousand each time."

"Sure, the math says that," Donovan said with a smile, "but in reality, that's where you're wrong."

"How so?"

Donovan sat back. "You already knew you heard the song here," he began. "So you know it's played in this region. There isn't some bias or something against that. Plus, you heard it in a massive sports arena, which means it's a wildly popular song. It stands to reason once you heard it, given *how* you heard it, it'd only be a matter of time before you'd hear it again, especially in a city that already has shown it love. You see?"

The group remained silent.

"How does that not make sense?"

Maria shrugged. "It's just, a lot."

"Well, don't get it twisted," Donovan replied. "My point isn't to say Mike hearing the Spice Girls twice isn't unique."

"It was the Black Eyed Peas." Mike glared at him.

"My point," Donovan replied, "is hearing the song the first time was even more impressive. Two? Alright, that's cool. But the first time was without any evidence or criteria. It was a one in fifty thousand shot! We don't respect that!" He paused. "When something unique happens, like hearing a song for the first time, you should enjoy that and know it may happen again, but it won't nearly be as impressive odds-wise the second time around, despite what you may think."

"Well, it isn't interesting unless it happens twice," Mike argued.

"Every encounter is interesting," Donovan replied. "That's the point. It just isn't interesting to us unless it happens twice. Then we start talking about fate and all that bullshit when it's just physics, or life, or something."

"I don't think that's physics," Steven chimed in.

"Let's say..." Maria sipped her drink as she sat up in her chair. "Let's say we finish our jobs and return home, and you and Mike see each other at a bar. Isn't that coincidental and unique?"

Donovan nodded as the statement was said. "I mean, sure, it's *coincidental*, but that's not the point." He took another sip of his drink. "Consider this. We both live within a couple hours of Omaha. Mike here," he motioned to his subject, "he seems like a classy guy. He likes his whiskey, which I more than appreciate. He has a sense of style, which is also something we both have in common. Knowing those facts, if he were to go out to a fine bar in the city for a good time, chances are it'd be a location I'd go to as well. Given Omaha has tons of bars, but only a handful we'd probably be at, the odds are on a given Saturday night, we'd have a decent chance of running into each other." He took another drink. "But what were the odds we would meet the first time, here on this trip? I mean, come on, of all the people in the country, what are the odds? What about all the people in our company? Furthermore, for us to meet, we both had to be at this exact moment in our lives, working at Central Plains at the same time, we both had to apply to this position, *and* we both had to follow through with the process to accept this job." He looked over to Mike. "It's a damn fluke we'd ever meet! A once in a lifetime chance! Pure, unbridled happenstance."

"I'm happy to know you too." Mike smiled.

"That's my point!" Donovan exclaimed. "We have to celebrate this shit. The fact we five people are here at this moment. The fact we made it here at all! I mean, doesn't it just get you all riled up?"

They all smiled as he filled the room with vigor.

"I mean, sure, I'll see you all after this given what I just said." He looked to Steven, and then down at his outfit. "Except you, Steven. We'll probably never see each other again." He turned to the rest of them. "But regardless, let's celebrate now!" He turned to the bar. "More drinks!"

While he was gone only a few minutes, the group sat in silence, as though each was processing his entire belief system.

"I'm never saying the word 'coincidence' around him again," Mike said to laughs.

"I heard that," Donovan said as he returned. "You can say whatever you want. I just think we use the word 'coincidence' too much. It's all about odds. Some are better than others. What one person says is a coincidence is probably just the result of good odds, like this song situation. Think about it. Ryan, have you ever had a song come back to you?"

Ryan sat in silence as the group turned to him.

"Well," Donovan reasoned, "have you?"

Ryan shrugged. "Sure."

"What was the situation?"

Ryan felt his pulse quicken, and a vision entered the back of his mind. It came upon slowly at first, like a gentle snowfall. "I was driving. I stopped for a quick rest, and I heard a song I'd heard some time before over the radio."

"And it was a special song?"

Ryan swallowed. He could almost see the snow of South Dakota. He could almost see her once again in the headlights of his Jeep. The vision was coming back to him, enveloping him in all its glory.

He blinked, and the vision was gone. He turned to see Donovan staring his way. "Yeah," he stammered. "Yeah, it was special. Just one of those 'know where you were' songs."

"That was very descriptive," Donovan mocked. "Maria, you?"

She nodded and started a story that Ryan began to tune out. He could feel the hairs on his neck rise as he considered his past vision. No matter where he went, *she* would always find him.

As their next round of drinks arrived, Ryan stood up. He motioned that he was going outside for a minute, as though to take a phone call. As he walked away, he could still hear his companions arguing.

"I'm just saying," Donovan concluded, "these are my beliefs. You don't have to agree. It's just what I know."

"I don't agree," Mike replied, clearly enjoying the effects of his alcohol. "Except when you said I dress classy. I agree with that."

"Common ground," Donovan replied. "We can build from there."

***

Ryan stepped out onto the rooftop patio sometime after the conversation. Adjusting his eyes to the change in light, he walked over to the railing at the edge of the space and stared out across the city. It was cooler here than inside, and he was glad of the relief. That relief, however, was short lived.

He gritted his teeth as his eyes focused on an unknown location. He wanted more than anything to rid himself of the thought that now rained torrentially inside his mind. What had started as a song recollection was now a flood of memory of the three days he had spent falling for a woman he had never known before.

It began as a detour, as a broken-down car and a chance encounter at a diner. Two souls lost in the ether of post-college and pre-life. On their last night, when passion had mixed with emotion in the front seat of his Jeep, he recalled on how he contemplated *forever*, and he wondered if this was the place to find it.

He had wanted to tell her everything; about how he was on a journey from Florida to Washington to return a man to a place where he could grieve the loss of his wife. He wanted to tell her that he had simply picked up the man alongside the road when he himself was at his own lowest point. He wanted to explain that the money he had was stolen in order to get the man home. He wanted to explain it all, but running away was easier. He never expected to get caught, and as a result, he did what he had to do, although disarming the suspecting cop was never in the plan.

Perhaps that guilt was also why he had chosen to run no further after the journey was completed, after he and Bo had made it to Spokane and the grieving was over. He could have fled or continued to drive on, but that would be too naive. He had to stop running. He had to admit his mistakes. He had to atone for his crimes. He had to tell her the truth.

He knew the consequences. He knew the cops would be waiting, especially after what had happened to one of their own. Yet none of that mattered. And so, he returned to South Dakota. He walked back into that diner. He told her everything. He told her the truth. He told her how she made him feel.

He shook his head as the memory flooded back. He recalled the roughness of the cops as they grabbed him at the counter. He shook his head as he remembered the look on her face when they tried to arrest him. He'd said all he could as he was drug away: *You know me. You know me. Remember that, and not these handcuffs. Remember the real me.*

Had it been enough? Could he have said more? Could he have told her how she made him feel? Could he have expressed that he was no longer the boy who had stolen money just to keep someone else's journey going so he didn't have to return home?

Or had she forgotten?

Why had she not waited for him? Why did he return back years later to find her gone, with no more than a memory left behind? Her brother? Her father? All were gone. Why?

He opened his eyes as he attempted to quell the anguish inside his head. It was the pain of nostalgia. It was the pain of an unfinished life.

"Hey, man," a voice said to his left. Ryan continued to stare out across the city in a trance.

"Hey, man," the voice repeated. "You got a light?"

Ryan turned at the sound. Blinking, he saw a large, well-built man standing at the same railing some four feet off. "Excuse me?" he said.

"A light?" the man said as he held out his hand to display a cigarette.

"Oh," Ryan replied. "Sorry. No, I don't."

The man nodded as he put the cigarette away. "That's fine," he countered, "I should quit anyway."

Ryan turned back towards the city.

"You out here to escape the noise too?" the man said after a minute.

Ryan half turned. "Yeah," he said after a second. "Something like that."

"That place is loud," the man replied. "Especially my group." He nodded toward the large group of men inside the windows that Ryan had spotted earlier. "The peace and quiet out here is nice."

Ryan could sense the man's need to talk, and although he wanted none of it, he knew he couldn't escape. He looked toward the group inside. "Bachelor party?"

"Yeah." The man nodded.

"Poor bastard," Ryan said with a laugh, turning back toward the city view.

"Yep," the man replied. "That's me."

Ryan felt his eyes go wide as he turned back toward the man. "Oh no, I just—"

"It's fine," the man replied.

Ryan cocked his head as he stared at the man. Although he appeared only slightly older, he seemed much calmer in disposition. He also stood a good five inches taller, complete with broad shoulders and biceps that filled his shirtsleeves. He wore a collared shirt and pressed pants, and his perfectly trimmed jet-black hair sat uniformly across his head. His black skin radiated in the light of the patio, and when combined with his approachable smile and confident stance, he painted a true picture of assertive masculinity.

"You married?" the man asked after a second that felt like a minute.

Ryan scoffed. "No," he said. "No, I'm not."

"Seeing anyone?" the man asked.

Ryan shook his head.

The man leaned against the railing. "You're lucky, man." He took a deep breath. "I've become envious of all you single guys. No cares. No issues."

Ryan considered the man's words. His mouth spoke before his head knew what he was saying. "No one to talk to," he said. "No one at home."

The man glanced to him.

"It's not all great," Ryan replied. "There's a reason everyone tries to find someone to spend their life with."

"Yeah," the man countered. "But let's be honest. It's all bullshit. Marriages nowadays end in divorce. It ends in unhappiness. Hell, my parents are divorced. My aunt's been married twice. The entire idea of 'settling down' is so convoluted now."

"Then why'd you propose?" Ryan replied. "If I may ask."

The man looked back to the city. "I don't know. I felt like it was the right thing to do. I mean, we've been together for a while. It just felt like I should."

"You aren't in love?"

The man shrugged. "What's love? You ever been in love?"

Ryan smiled. "Yeah, once."

"Just once?"

He shrugged. "Once for sure."

"Why aren't you with her then?"

Ryan chuckled. "It's a long story."

"But you knew it was love?"

"No." He took a deep breath. "But I knew it was different."

"Different?"

"Yeah," he replied. "Like I forgot everything else when I was with her. She consumed my attention. It wasn't about looks or physicality, though she was gorgeous. It was about us connecting on a deeper level. I felt good around her, like she was where I belonged."

The man remained stoic as he stared from the balcony.

"And if I had to guess," Ryan said as he leaned back against the railing himself, "you probably feel the same way towards your fiancée, but your nerves are just clouding your judgment."

The man exhaled, and Ryan could see the trepidation in his mannerisms. "She's amazing. She's so full of life. She balances me out and keeps me sane."

"And pretty too, right?"

The man turned. "Dude, don't repeat this, but our first night together, when I saw her, I cried. Straight up cried. It was like…wow." He shook his head as he recalled the memory.

Ryan laughed. "See? I'm fairly sure you're in love too."

The man clenched his teeth. "I'm just worried I'll miss being single."

"Miss what?" Ryan chuckled. "What's so great about being single?"

"Freedom," the man replied. "Getting to bang whoever you want? One girl forever does not sound ideal…"

Ryan contemplated it. "Okay, sure, now it may not sound good, but look at it this way, you'll be guaranteed one person."

The man laughed.

"And you know single life isn't just about sex."

"Yeah, but you get more of it."

Ryan smirked. "At what cost?"

The man stared at him as though confused.

Ryan breathed out. "It's never just about sex, even if it starts that way. You go to a bar or a club, and you pick up a girl, and sure, you may get lucky. But what about the next night? What happens then? Do you call or text? Do you answer hers? Maybe you develop feelings, or maybe she does." He paused. "Then there's walks-of-shame, and friends finding out. There's ex-boyfriends, or ex-girlfriends. There're families to meet, new social settings you get dragged to. What started as sex rarely ever ends that way, and when you move on, then it's the same thing with someone new. I haven't even talked diseases or pregnancy scares. Or the money you spend on the drinks. Is ten minutes of getting off worth all that, over and over, on repeat?"

The man laughed as Ryan finished. "You seem to know this process well."

"They don't hand out awards," Ryan replied with a laugh, "but if they did…"

The man gripped the railing as he processed the words. "I guess I never really thought about all that."

"Of course not," Ryan replied. "When you're committed, you always think you're one breakup away from being a porn star. But it never works out like that." He paused. "Finding someone to stick with is a whole lot better than that mess."

The man turned. "Forever is a long time."

"It is."

They remained silent for a moment longer.

Once again, Ryan heard himself speak. "Then don't marry her for forever."

The man stared at him. "What?"

"When are you getting married?" Ryan countered.

"Next Saturday."

"Forget about forever then," Ryan replied. "Marry her for Saturday."

The man shook his head as if not understanding.

Ryan took a step closer. "Marry her on Saturday. Decide to marry her for Saturday."

"And then what?"

"Then do it."

"I'm not following…"

Ryan shrugged. "You don't know what forever looks like. Hell, I can't even grasp that. How can you ever fathom doing something for that long? It isn't reasonable. So instead of all that stress, marry her on Saturday. You'll enjoy your day and wait for her to walk down the aisle. You'll see how gorgeous she is, and your stress will melt. You'll eat cake and take pictures. Then you'll spend the night together. Then, on Sunday, when you've come down from the wedding day, you'll look over and see her just as you saw her when you first met, and you'll choose to marry her again. Monday will be the same. And Tuesday, and so on. You marry her one day at a time, and pretty soon, a week will become a month, and then a year, and then fifty." He paused as he stared out across the city. "Don't marry her for forever. Marry her every day."

The man remained silent. He continued to stare out from the balcony, and Ryan began to wonder if he had said something wrong.

"That was some deep shit," the man said as he turned to Ryan with a smile.

Ryan nodded as he returned the smile.

"None of my asshole friends," he joked as he motioned into the bar, "none of them will ever say anything that profound."

Ryan shrugged. "I've had a lot of time to think on it."

"You've got to be swimming in women. You are, aren't you?"

Ryan laughed.

"See, I knew it. Damn, that was good. Marry her for Saturday. I like it."

"I also spend a lot of money on drinks," Ryan joked.

"You should say that shit to the girl you lost."

Ryan shrugged.

"I'm serious."

"Maybe one day," Ryan replied. "Maybe I will."

"Do it," the man replied. "If you can convince me to get married, then I can convince you to find that chick."

"Noted," Ryan said half-heartedly.

"You promise?"

"Promise?"

"Hell yeah, I want to hear it."

Ryan laughed.

"I'm serious."

"Fine, fine," Ryan countered. "I promise."

"Promise what?"

"I promise to eventually… Come on, man."

"You promise to find your lost love and make it happen."

"Fine, I promise to do that. Eventually."

The man laughed. "Good. Now Jesus heard it. You can't be breaking promises that Jesus heard."

Ryan smiled. "I won't try."

The man took a deep breath. "I guess I better get back inside. Someone's got to take care of those animals."

Ryan glanced inside the windows and saw the group of rambunctious friends dancing wildly. Their noise was audible from the patio.

"Good luck," Ryan replied.

"Thanks," the man began as he held out a hand.

"Ryan," he replied.

"Ryan," the man repeated as they shook hands. "I'm Andruw. Dru for short."

"Pleasure to meet you, Dru."

"Same. I mean it. Thanks for this. You've cleared my head."

"You'd do the same for me," Ryan replied.

Dru began walking away. "Maybe we'll cross paths in the future."

Ryan remembered the previous chat about coincidence and fate. "Probably," he replied with a laugh. He saw Dru's face become puzzled, and he realized that the man had no clue what he was referring to. "Hopefully," he corrected.

Dru nodded. "See you, man."

***

Ryan walked back into the bar sometime after. The bachelor party had since moved on to another location, and now the entire establishment was quieter and more peaceful. Ryan saw his party spread out between the dance floor and a few tables, and he knew that their night was ending. He took a seat at the bar as a slow ballad began playing over the speaker.

"Must be the mellow hour," Ryan murmured as the bartender prepared a drink.

Ryan turned in his chair as he looked out across the patrons, each in their own trance with the music playing overhead. The bartender brought the drink over and Ryan took a sip. He watched as Maria and Donovan danced while Mike sat at the table with a drink, clearly content. Steven had found solace with a group of businessmen at another table.

For the first time, Ryan felt at peace as he stared at his new family. Sure, he knew little of them, but they were his connections now. He had not chosen them, and he didn't know how long they would be together, but they were all there now, and that was all that mattered. This was his life. This was his purpose now.

A glint to the left caught his eye, and he turned to see a shorter blonde woman lean over the bar. Dressed in an outstanding black number, he found himself staring for much longer than expected. He turned away, but not before noticing her cast a glance at him.

"You look lonely," she said over the music.

Ryan waited just long enough to build suspense. "Just enjoying the song," he said as he turned to her with a smile.

"Are you?" She moved a bit closer.

"Somewhat, it's got a nice..."

"Sound?"

He chuckled. "Yeah, that's it."

"It's one of my favorites, if you can believe that," she replied, inching closer.

Ryan considered her words. "I'd believe it."

"The band came here last year and performed at the United Center," she continued. "It was insane."

He held his drink steady. "I'm sorry I missed it." He flashed her a smile.

"From out of town?" she asked as she gazed into him.

"How could you tell?"

"I'm Melissa." She stuck out her hand as the bartender dropped her drink off.

S.D. Goldman

"Ryan," he replied as he shook her hand. He stared at her blonde hair and then down to her rounded face. In the faded bar light, she could have been anyone.

"In town for long?" she said as she sipped her drink.

He smiled. "Only a couple days."

She considered it before smiling. "We better not waste any time then."

He took a deep breath as he pulled a twenty and a ten from his wallet. He set the bills on the bartender's side and stared at them. Thoughts flowed through his mind without end, yet he couldn't stop his actions. He took a deep breath as he motioned to the bills and then to both of their drinks.

He turned back to her with a smile, "I just hate wasting time."

Chapter 5
463 Miles from Omaha

It was past 7:00 a.m. when Ryan stepped into the restaurant the next morning. Seeing Maria and Donovan at a table, he approached.

"Morning," he said as he sat down.

Donovan let out a grunt from where he lay sprawled out across the table. "I'm never drinking again," he replied without moving his head.

"Rough night?" Ryan said as a waiter filled his coffee mug.

Donovan lifted his head up. "It wasn't rough until I stopped…"

Ryan smiled. "Well, there's the secret." He took a sip. "Don't ever stop." He paused as he turned to Maria. "Where are the others?"

"Steven already went to the conference room," she replied, looking as fresh and prepared as ever. "I haven't seen Mike yet, but I'm sure he'll be down."

Ryan nodded as Donovan let out another pained grunt.

"We did make an executive decision, however," Maria said after a moment, as though ignoring Donovan.

"An executive decision?" Ryan asked.

"Yeah, about the presentations." She leaned forward a bit.

"When did we make this 'executive decision'?" Ryan inquired as he took another sip.

She thought about it. "Sometime around last call."

Ryan considered it.

"We think that I should be the lead presenter for the first class. Mike will be my co."

Ryan nodded.

"In the afternoon, Mike will lead with Donovan." She paused.

"That sounds fine."

"And you and Steven will head the sales table."

"That's fine for today."

"Indefinitely."

Ryan's eyes grew wide. "Indefinitely?"

"Yeah." Maria took a deep breath.

"You don't want me presenting?"

"We don't want *Steven* presenting."

"Because?"

He watched as Maria turned sheepish.

Ryan sighed. "He knows his stuff."

"He does," Maria replied. "But putting our fates in his hands is like giving a child a machine gun. You see how he can be."

Ryan didn't respond.

"He'd be way too excited for these farmers," Maria reasoned. "No one will buy *him*, let alone *us*. He'd send a message that I…" She paused. "That *we* think won't be good for sales."

Ryan took a sip. "So instead, you want me to babysit him at the sales table?"

"If we just single him out, he'll suspect what we're doing. Putting you with him shows impartiality."

Ryan remained silent.

"Plus," Maria replied, "it's a great gig for you. You don't have to talk. You just take down names of people who want more info and hand out the brochures. It's pretty sweet."

He continued to sit, unmoved.

"You OK with it?"

After a moment, he spoke. "Yeah," he lied. "I'm good."

"Good," Maria said as Mike approached. "I guess I'd better go break it to Steven."

Ryan took another sip of his coffee. He watched as Maria got up and walked past Mike, and in the process, he saw them share a brief whisper of conversation. After unsuccessfully eavesdropping, he turned back to Donovan, who continued to lay on the table.

Exhaling, Ryan set his coffee mug down. It was going to be a long day.

***

It was around sunset when Ryan sat unmoved in the hotel lounge, his drink inches from his resting hand. He stared into the glass as the beads of water streamed down the sides. Silence filled the space as his companions sat around him.

"I'm going to bed," Mike said aloud from across the bar.

"It's 7:00 p.m.," Donovan replied.

"Yeah," Mike said as he stood. "I want to enjoy these nice beds while I can."

"Don't talk like that," Maria tried.

Mike glared back at her. "I'm just being real."

"It's a couple bad days," she replied.

"Five classes in three days and we've had how many responses?"

Steven stared at his notebook as he sat in the booth nearby. "Two."

Mike turned back to Maria. "Two."

"It's a bad start."

Mike looked to Steven. "How many people showed up, Steven?"

Steven looked in his notes. "One hundred and eighty-four."

Mike turned back to Maria.

"It's a really bad start," she explained.

"We aren't prepared for this," Mike responded. "The audience came for the free coffee. We aren't trained speakers, and most importantly, our presentation is straight up dog shit."

"We'll get better…" Maria tried.

"We don't have time," Mike replied, voice rising. "If we come back to Omaha with a response percentage of… what is it, Steven?" He turned.

"One percent."

"Jesus, really?"

Steven double-checked. "Yep."

Mike turned back. "We need at least seventy-five percent. Hell maybe even eighty! There's no way. Absolutely no way."

"We still have Madison," Maria argued. "We still have Rochester."

"And? Even if we got half signed up, it isn't going to put out this dumpster fire. *One percent*." He repeated the last line as if unsure it was true.

"We can practice," Maria replied. "We can at least—"

"I'm going to bed," Mike said, silencing her. He turned to Ryan and Donovan. "You all better enjoy these hotels." He turned around without another glance back.

Ryan heard Donovan sigh next to him. Soon after he got up and left the group. Steven followed moments later.

Ryan finished his drink and set it onto the table.

Maria took a deep breath. "You think we're done too?"

Ryan considered it. "I think…" He paused as he reined in his thoughts. "I think a good night's sleep will help everyone."

She nodded, though she didn't move. "We have so much at stake…"

Ryan heard the comment but said nothing. It seemed almost out of place.

"It'll be alright," he replied, not knowing what else to say.

She stood and smiled. "Good night, Ryan."

He nodded as she walked away from the table.

Taking a deep breath, he stared across the room as he continued to sit at the empty table. Before long, he rose, though his mind was still focused on her parting words.

So much at stake.

Perhaps there was a lot at stake. Perhaps their jobs, and maybe their careers, were in the balance. Perhaps it all should've mattered more than it did to him. One thing was certain, however—he was not about to start worrying now.

He was alone and alive in the city, and stress was a thousand miles away.

***

There was a knock on his hotel room door just past midnight.

Ryan got up from the bed and looked to the clock. He waited a moment before the knock repeated. Heart rate increasing, he moved to his pants and slid them on before turning to the door, taking care to look through the peephole. He took a deep breath. He opened the door halfway.

"Hey, Ryan," Steven said as he stood sheepishly in the hallway.

"Hi, Steven," Ryan replied. "What's up?"

"Were you sleeping?" Steven asked. "I'm sorry if I woke you…"

Behind Ryan, the sheets of the bed jostled around. Steven's eyes peered in before recoiling. Ryan followed his eyes before turning back.

"No," Ryan replied. "I was awake."

"I'm sorry," Steven replied. "I can come back."

"What's up?" Ryan replied.

"I just…" Steven thought about his words. "We're not doing so good…presentation-wise."

Ryan thought about it. "No," he replied. "No, we're not."

Steven took a deep breath. "I was thinking of maybe looking at some changes to help us out."

"Changes?"

"Yeah…some big changes."

"Like?"

Steven stared at Ryan. "The script."

"You want to change the script?"

Steven gritted his teeth. "I already did."

Ryan turned his head. "You did?"

"Yeah, and I wanted to run it by you and maybe get your opinion?"

Ryan considered it. "You want *my* opinion?"

Steven nodded. He pulled a binder from his bag that was draped across his back.

Ryan stared at it. "Now?"

"If you don't mind."

Ryan took a deep breath. Behind him, he heard the sheets move. He turned his head back towards the room and contemplated the offer. He bit his lip and turned back to Steven. "Tell you what," he said. "I'll meet you down in the lounge in ten."

"Yeah?" Steven replied.

Ryan nodded. "Yeah."

"You're serious? You'll help out."

Somehow, he heard himself agree. "Yeah, ten minutes."

"Thanks so much," Steven replied as he put the book back in his bag. "I'll see you down there."

Ryan smiled as his counterpart turned and sprinted down the hallway. Staring after him, Ryan breathed out.

"At least one of us is happy," he said.

***

Ryan found himself walking into the lobby shortly thereafter, now with a shirt and shoes to accompany his pants. Running his fingers through his hair, he spotted Steven at a far table in the empty lobby. The sound from the nearby television was barely audible as he approached the table and stifled a yawn.

"Quiet down here," Ryan said as the yawn subsided.

Steven looked up from his notebook and binder as though he barely heard the comment.

"So, what's up?" Ryan asked as he sat across from Steven.

Steven turned his binder over to Ryan. "I was thinking about the entire flow, from the initial inspirational aspects to the videos, and I just think it needed a retooling. I crossed out most of the dialogue and rewrote it with this." He turned his notebook over as well, and Ryan saw that he had rewritten most of the entire script in some way. It was an impressive feat.

"When did you start this?" Ryan asked as he glossed over the words.

Steven thought for a moment. "I did most of the rewrites today, during our second meeting."

Ryan looked up. "But when did you start this?"

"Start?"

"Yeah, start. When did you begin to make these changes?" He flipped through the pages and pages of notes that Steven had taken. "You didn't do all this today."

Steven remained silent.

"When did you start?"

"The first day we got the script."

Ryan remained expressionless. "You knew this was crap on day one?"

Steven shrugged. "I felt like—"

"You can be honest."

"It was...lacking."

"Lacking?"

"I don't want to put down—"

"It was shit. You can say that."

Steven shrugged. "No, I can't..."

"It was written by people who have probably never been to an ethanol plant, let alone seen what ethanol looks like."

"Maybe—"

"And furthermore, it was written by people who have never met farmers in their lives."

"I don't know about that..."

"I do," Ryan replied. "I do, because I know who wrote it, and she told me all of those things." He paused, sensing that Steven was uncomfortable. "Don't get me wrong, the effort they put in was top level stuff, but it just doesn't work for what we're doing."

Steven turned back to the binder. "I know, that's why I rewrote—"

"Why did you wait until now to speak up?"

"What?"

"If you knew this was bad, why did you wait?"

Steven thought about it. "I don't know."

"You care a lot."

"I do."

"Then why wait?"

Steven sat back in his seat.

Ryan leaned forward. He had no intention of dissecting the man's personality, yet somehow, the aura of his demeanor was poised for examination. "Listen, you're a smart guy, but there's more to you than you're letting on." He paused. "If we're going to do this together, you've got to give me something more than the 'aw shucks' polite guy act."

"It's not an act."

"It's not?"

"No," Steven replied. "I'm a jovial guy."

"Jovial?"

"Yes, as in happy."

"You don't seem happy now."

"Because I feel…" His voice trailed off. "I feel like you're maybe attacking me."

"There's no 'maybe,'" Ryan replied. "I just want to know who you are. You *did* come to my door."

Steven bit his lip. "I'm me. I'm Steven. I'm a God-fearing husband with three kids who volunteers from time to time-."

"And you can't say shit?"

"What?"

"Shit," Ryan repeated. "You can't say the word."

"No."

"Because of your religion?"

"Because it's not a nice word."

"Your words have feelings?"

"Can we get back to the script?"

"Why didn't you speak up when you saw the script was shit?"

"Why does it matter?"

"Because it does. It matters to me."

"It shouldn't."

Ryan leaned on the table. "I've found that the things that shouldn't matter are the ones that matter most."

"I just decided not to speak up."

"That seems unlike you."

"Well, it's true."

"No, it's not."

"Ryan—"

"Why didn't you speak up?"

"Ry—"

"Why didn't you speak up?"

"Please."

"Why…didn't you speak up."

Silence. Steven stared back.

"Why didn't—"

"Because no one cares!" Steven sighed as he leaned back in his chair.

Ryan remained silent.

"No one cares what I think," Steven began. "No one values my opinion. I'm the weird guy who doesn't shut up. I know what I am. I'm the guy who's put in the back of the room at the *sales* table so I won't be seen, just like you." He paused as he considered his words. "Our team considers me a liability. If I spoke, I'd screw things up, or make it more difficult." He turned back to Ryan. "So, I kept quiet because it's what they want me to do."

Ryan's voice softened. "So why speak up now?"

Steven took a deep breath. "Because we're failing."

"Don't you want to go home? Be with your wife?"

"I do," Steven replied. "I miss her like crazy."

"But..." Ryan sensed it coming.

Steven smiled. "I spent the last six years in the same cubicle on the same floor of the same building. Each year, I think I might get to move to an office, or maybe get 'senior' in my title, but nope. It always passes me by. I'm never quite as good as my colleagues." He paused. "My *flaws* are pretty evident. But then this opportunity came up, and I knew if I could do this right, if I could get this to stick, then my family, my wife, they'd all, you know, be proud of me." He paused. "I know they chose us five because we're all that showed up, but man, the look on their faces when I told them all...I was a *traveling man*. I was *official*. No more cubicles and covering up vents with paper to keep warm." He chuckled a bit to himself before becoming serious. "This job...it means a lot. I don't expect you to understand."

Ryan continued to stare at the man.

"Pride," Steven continued. "Pride is a stupid reason to give yourself to something, but I'm only human."

For a moment, no one spoke.

"What'd you mean 'just like you'?" Ryan asked after a moment.

Steven seemed confused.

Ryan turned. "When you said that you're the guy they put at the back table so you won't be seen. Like me. What'd you mean?"

Steven considered the question. "I mean, we were both put at that table for a reason. Me because of my talking..."

"...and me because I don't care." Ryan finished the thought. It suddenly made sense. He wasn't babysitting Steven. They were babysitting each other. They were both liabilities in the eyes of their counterparts. He exhaled as he ran his fingers through his hair.

"Look at it from their side," Steven reasoned. "There's a lot at stake for them. These jobs are important. They're just doing what they think is best."

"By calling us idiots? By saying I don't care?" He rose from his seat and began pacing.

"By minimizing their risks."

Ryan rolled his tongue against his teeth. "Well, they're doing a great job."

"They're stressed. We can fix it."

"Why are you defending them?" Ryan replied, hands on his head. "They put you at the sales table. They're literally saying you're not good enough."

"None of us are good enough yet," Steven replied. "But we can change that."

"Doesn't it piss you off?"

"Of course it does," Steven replied. "But I'm not going to change their opinions by being angry."

"So, your solution is to rewrite the script and prove them wrong?"

"My solution is to rewrite the script and help the team."

Ryan stared at him as he stared back.

"Listen, if I spent my energy on revenge," Steven said after a moment, "then I wouldn't have much left."

"That's noble of you," Ryan seethed. He continued to pace as he shook his head.

Steven sat back from the table. "What most upsets you?"

"That everyone thinks I don't care!" Ryan retorted. "That pisses me off." He paused. "Hell, even you probably think it."

"I don't—"

"Why did you ask me to help you? If you don't think I care."

Steven took a deep breath. "For the same reason you agreed to do it."

Ryan stopped pacing. His intensity decreased.

"It's not all black and white," Steven replied. "We're not all good or bad, regardless of how we view ourselves or the people we're around. Everyone's just a different shade of gray."

Ryan took a deep breath. The words cut deep, and he struggled to ascertain who they were meant for. Finally, he moved back to the table and took a seat.

Steven inched toward the binder on the table in front of him. "We good?" he asked.

Ryan's eyes moved back to the binder. "Yeah," he replied. "We're good."

***

The clock ticked toward three in the morning as Steven stared at the brand-new manuscript in front of him. Ryan continued to sit opposite, but now was accompanied by a coffee mug.

"We've met most of our goals," Steven said, staring at another sheet of paper with some hastily made objectives.

"It's still too long," Ryan replied.

"We've cut almost an hour and a half."

"We should cut another half hour."

"Why?"

"Because we don't need it."

"We have to present *something*," Steven countered.

"What's our objective?" Ryan replied.

"To sell them on the company and the corn seed—"

"No," Ryan repeated. "That's our job description." He paused as he turned the binder towards him. "Our objective is to get them to sign a piece of paper requesting to be contacted by a sales rep."

"Is that not the same thing?"

"No."

Steven sat back. "Explain."

"Our metrics are based on how many farmers fill out the paper. That's it. That's where our job ends. So, that's what our goal should be. Not selling clean energy or the company."

"And how do you propose we do that? Forge names?"

"No," Ryan replied as he laughed. "But I like how you thought of that. Maybe I'm rubbing off on you."

Steven smirked.

"All we need to sell is *us*," Ryan replied.

"*Us?*"

"We're one of them. We're in their shoes. We convince them that we're on their side, and the rest is easy."

"But we're *not* one of them."

Ryan scoffed. "Well, sure. But we can be."

"So, you want to fake it?"

"Not fake it," Ryan replied. "Just level with them. Take an interest in them."

"I'm not seeing the difference…"

"You've ever been to an early morning diner outside the city?"

"Outside of Omaha?"

"Yeah."

"No."

"Well, I have," Ryan replied. "I've been to quite a few around Spirit Lake. Do you know what all the farmers have in common?" He grabbed a pen and began to write on the bottom of the newly created script.

Steven considered it. "I don't know, what?"

Ryan turned the script back around. On the bottom, he had written large and clear words: *Central Plains Hats.*

"Hats?"

Ryan nodded.

"What does that mean?"

"It means we need to get hats."

"Hats? Like ball caps?"

"Yep. With our logo on them."

"And?"

"And we'll wear them. And give them out. All farmers love their hats."

"That's your solution? Give them free hats?"

"Yep. And pens too."

"And pens?"

"Yep. And we also take out the company video."

Steven reared back. "We can't do that."

"Yep. It's twenty minutes too long."

"It's eighteen minutes."

"And it's gone. Along with the trivia."

"The trivia is interactive engagement."

Ryan leaned forward. "We're selling to guys who watch *Andy Griffith*, not *Paw Patrol*."

Steven seemed to grow more nervous.

"Everything else is fine," Ryan replied. "Everything else in the script is good. Maybe more stories though. You know, analogies about farming life."

"I don't know any analogies…"

"Sure you do. Just throw in something about Marty Robbins or how politicians all suck."

"That may be too broad a brush…"

Ryan could sense he was pushing his luck. "Fine," he replied. "Use the new script then. It's still better than what we had." He paused. "Regardless, you'll do great."

Steven's eyes went wide. "*I'll* do great?"

"Yeah," Ryan replied. "I figured you'd be the one to give the presentation."

"I made it," Steven said. "I never said I'd present it."

"Why wouldn't you?"

"Because! I'm not ready for all that!"

"Who else would give it? You know it better than anyone."

Steven continued to panic.

"You'll be fine," Ryan replied. "Plus, I'll be your backup. It'll be great. I'll get the hats and pens tomorrow. We'll be golden." He sat back from the table, as if pleased with his work.

Steven didn't move.

Ryan smiled as he realized the coffee had likely increased his confidence. "Relax, man," he said after a moment. "What's the worst that could happen?"

"We fail," Steven replied. "We screw it all up."

Ryan shrugged. "Well, then," he said, "from where we are now, we've got nothing to lose."

***

Ryan returned to his room soon after their meeting ended. Taking a deep breath, he moved to the bed to find it empty.

He turned to the table across the room and saw a note illuminated by the only light in the room. He clenched his teeth as he read the words etched in a scribble:

All you'll ever be is a fuckboy.

He stared at it for a moment, then closed his eyes before opening them.

Behind the note he saw the ice bucket, complete with an unopened beer. Reaching inside, he found the ice had turned to lukewarm water. Slowly, he pulled the beer out and grabbed the bucket before moving to the sink to dump the water. He then moved outside his room and down the hall to the ice machine.

It was better this way, he thought, as the machine grinded in front of him. Anger was always better than disappointment. He was in no position to make long distance work. He was in no position to show love. It was better this way. It had to be better this way.

Returning to the present, he saw the ice had overflowed the bucket. Pulling the container back, he reached down to pick up the spilled ice, though it proved a difficult task. Abruptly, he heard a room door open from the hallway, and he scrambled to pick up the remaining ice. Standing upright, he moved to the edge of the ice room and peered into the hallway.

To his surprise, it was familiar faces that he saw, though they didn't see him.

Standing outside the room was Mike, having just exited. Still inside the room, with her head barely visible, was Maria. Ryan watched from a distance as the two shared a brief whispered conversation before a long and deep kiss.

Ryan's eyes went wide.

Mike pulled away from his lover after some time, and with a smile, he moved down the hallway towards the elevator. Maria, with a similar smile on her face, moved back into her room and closed the door, leaving Ryan alone and still undetected in the hallway.

He stood there stupidly for a few moments more, still processing what he had seen. Finally, after he judged the coast to be clear, he returned to his room with his now-full bucket of ice.

"So much at stake," he repeated from earlier. He smiled as he shut his door. "We all have so much at stake."

Chapter 6
463 Miles from Omaha

Ryan found himself more cheerful than usual as he carried a large box through the hotel lobby towards the conference room. Humming a soft tune, he rounded a corner and entered the room on his right. Stepping inside, he found a frigid environment.

Standing to the left, Steven was busy with a computer open that was projected onto the large screen in front of him. On the right, Maria,

Mike, and Donovan all stood reviewing a large binder that Ryan knew was the revised script.

"What the hell is this?" Maria asked as Ryan entered and set the box down.

Ryan played coy. "What the hell is what?"

"This," she replied, holding the script.

"Looks like a binder."

"You changed the script?" Mike asked, just as annoyed.

"Um, no," Ryan replied before motioning to Steven. "We changed the script."

"Why?"

"Because it sucks," Ryan answered. He began to pull hats from the box he had brought in. "And we aren't getting any sign-ups using it."

Donovan interjected. "What makes you think you made it better?"

"Honestly, nothing," Ryan replied. "But it is different."

"Different doesn't mean better," Maria retorted.

"But it does mean different," Ryan replied.

"Isn't it a little late to give this to us right before the class?" Mike asked. "How are we supposed to present on such short notice?"

Ryan turned from the table. "Well, you aren't." He motioned to Steven. "He will."

The three turned to Steven and then back.

Ryan turned to Steven. "You didn't tell them anything?"

Steven shrugged.

Ryan returned to his box. "Fine, yes. Steven will be presenting this time."

Maria stepped forward. "Do you think that's a good idea?"

Ryan turned from his task. "I do, and I'm a bit curious why you think it isn't? He's capable of it."

"I think this should be a discussion among the team," Maria replied.

"We're discussing it now."

"No, you're telling us what's going to happen."

Ryan motioned to Steven. "Yeah, because he didn't want to, apparently."

"What are you doing?" Mike asked upon seeing that Ryan was conducting a separate task.

"I'm organizing hats," Ryan replied.

"Where did you get them?"

"Marcy's Embroidery."

"What is Marcy's Embroidery?"

"It's an embroidery shop, owned by Marcy."

"You made hats?"

"I didn't. Marcy did."

"Why?"

"Because farmers love hats. And Marcy likes making them. So, I went and bought the hats she had so that we could give them away. Speaking of that, Donovan, at 11:30 a.m., you'll have to meet her associate in the lobby to pick up the pens."

"Pens?"

Ryan turned. "Yes. Pens."

Maria shook her head. "You got pens and hats made overnight? With our logo on it? From some random embroidery shop?"

Ryan scoffed. "Of course not," he replied. "That isn't nearly enough time to get them customized. Plus Steven only sent over the logo this morning. No, today we're doing blank pens and hats that she had available. But in a couple days she'll be FedEx-ing our stuff to wherever we are with crisp logos ready to go."

"This is ridiculous," Donovan said.

"No, it's incentives," Ryan responded as he tapped his head. "Give the people what they want."

"Blank multicolored hats with no logos?"

Ryan sighed. "For now, yes. But the plan is in place."

"The plan is ridiculous," Maria interjected. "Why not just use some online third party for this shit?"

"Farmers want things made here, in America," Ryan said as he leaned against the table. "It's not about the hats, or the pens, or anything like that. Hell, Marcy can't even make pens herself, she's ordering them in. It's about the message. It's about the optics. We work with small businesses. We care about country towns. We care about *them*. Marcy's tag is on everything we hand out. That shit matters."

"But it's bullshit," Maria said. "It's all just bribery. It's a t-shirt cannon at a minor league baseball game. What's next? Free coupons under their seats?"

"If you've got a better idea, I'm all ears," Ryan replied. "Seriously, please. Someone got a better idea?" He looked around the room. "Nothing's working. Nothing's going right. This may not be the best solution, but it's something." He paused. "Listen, we removed the bullshit from the presentation. The 'save your environment, sea-turtles, and all that' notion. It's all gone. Instead we're going to hit them with things that matter: their community and their pocketbooks. We'll let them know we're one of them. It's simple; we're going straight to the facts with a bit of civility and empathy mixed in, along with free hats and pens."

"Empathy?"

"Yeah," Ryan replied. "You know, telling them that Illinois was ruined by the governor and all that."

"Who's Illinois's governor?" Donovan asked.

"It doesn't matter," Ryan replied. "Just level with them. Tell them you loved how *Dallas* ended."

Maria shook her head. "What the fuck is *Dallas?*"

"Maybe not *Dallas* then," Ryan replied. "Listen, if this sucks, we'll go back to the script, but for now, it's worth a shot. Steven knows this stuff. He'll be fine."

"And I assume you'll be his backup then?" Maria asked.

"Not that he needs one, but yes, I will," Ryan replied.

"And what about us?" Donovan asked.

Ryan moved to the front of the room as he carried his empty box. "Well, Donovan, you'll be our supplier. Miss Marcy will be by, as will the Donut Prince, and someone will need to meet them."

"Donuts?" Mike said.

"What about us?" Maria responded, overriding Mike's comment.

"Us?" Ryan asked.

"Mike and myself."

Ryan shrugged as he pointed to the back table. "I guess you two will be at the sign-up-slash-hat-throwing table. Every time a farmer gets a question right or says something good, you'll throw them a hat."

Maria glared daggers. Mike remained confused.

"You're putting us at the sign-up table?" Maria said as she sighed.

"Slash-hat-throwing table," Ryan replied.

"You're joking." Maria glared.

"About?" Ryan replied. Knowing an answer was unlikely to come, he shrugged. "Come on, you're with good company." He smiled as he motioned to Mike. "Just keep your hands where I can see them."

***

"This is why we're here," Steven said rather coolly as he stood at the front of the room with the presentation projected just across his left arm as he spoke. "I'm not a salesman. He's not a salesman..." He motioned towards Ryan, who stood at four o'clock in the large room. "We're messengers. Errand boys. The difference is simple. Salesmen get doors in their face, and we give you donuts." The crowd of relatively older man chuckled.

Ryan watched intently and continuously stared at his watch. They were twenty-five minutes in, and already, the participation was significantly more engaged, albeit still slightly subdued.

"The fact of the matter is this," Steven continued, changing slides, "two-year average increase of three bushels an acre. You can do the math on that. Next fact is simple: fifteen dollars less per bag. Now listen..." Steven paused as he leaned on the front podium. "I'm not sure what you all constitute a deal here, but in Omaha, we call that a porterhouse for a sirloin price." The group laughed again, this time more audibly.

Ryan turned to the back table and found Maria rolling her eyes in disdain.

"Anyone done the math for their acreage?" Steven continued. "Anyone figured out how much more yield that is?"

A man in the middle of the room shifted in his chair. "A helluva lot."

Steven smiled. "That's absolutely right, and that gets a hat!" He motioned to the back of the room, where Mike and Maria continued to sit wordlessly. "Hat patrol!" Steven tried again.

Slowly, Mike moved to the pile of hats and grabbed one. With the look of a sideshow attraction, he made an altogether poor throw towards the center of the room. After some shuffling, the hat was finally given to its new owner.

"Mike," Steven yelled over the crowd. "You might want to hold off on your Cubs tryout. Maybe dream for the Kane County Cougars level."

This brought out even more laughter from the crowd. Looking around, Ryan smiled as he saw the good-natured attitudes of those in the chairs. It was contagious. It was a complete transformation. It was everything he had hoped and expected.

"I got a question," a man in overalls said at the opposite side of the room.

The room grew silent as Steven turned towards the man. "Yes, sir, you can have a hat too."

The man shrugged in his seat. "It ain't about a hat."

"Of course," Steven replied, smile fading slightly. "What is it?"

"Well," the man began, "I've been doing this now for, I don't know, sixty-plus years out in Elburn."

"I respect that longevity," Steven quickly interjected.

The man smiled weakly. "Thank you," he replied. "In those sixty-plus years, I've been to my fair share of presentations, though to be honest, most are in garages and elevators and not in fancy conference rooms." He leaned forward as he spoke, and his voice became blunt. "Needless to say, ten years ago, I bought into the pitch and planted thirty thousand acres of their shit. Funny thing happened in a year though. The company went under, and the local elevators wouldn't take their genetically modified crap. Turns out the company I had invested a year's work in wasn't all too eager to help me. I was told that I could take it to their storage facility for market price, but that was down in Decatur, three-plus hours away. I don't need to tell you that you don't make much profit hauling grain seven hours roundtrip. Now, that year was a rough year for me, all because I didn't ask the most important question." He paused as he considered his words. "What guarantee do I have that your shit will still be good next year? What guarantee do I have that ethanol will still be around next harvest, or that your company will still be around next harvest? I've done the research. Ethanol companies seem to come and go quite rapidly, and to be honest, I don't want to mortgage my farm again. So, tell me, what guarantees do you have?"

The room was now ice cold. Ryan felt a lump grow until it was practically blocking his throat. The silence surrounding everyone grew palpable.

Steven stared at the man with a blank expression on his face, and the lump in Ryan's throat grew even more. The lead presenter remained silent.

"Anything?" the man asked after a moment.

Steven swallowed audibly. "Well first," he began, though there was little confidence in the words, "let me say that what happened to you is unacceptable, and that should never happen."

"It's business," the man replied coldly. "There ain't a farmer here that hasn't been screwed over by some business somewhere. It's a part of the business." He took a deep breath. "I'd just much prefer to be able to prepare for the next one."

"Well," Steven retorted, "I can assure you that Central Plains has no plans to close up its plant—"

"Is that a guarantee?"

Steven stared back, clearly unnerved. "No, it isn't."

"You don't know, do you?" The man exhaled. "You have no idea. All you care about is me signing your contact form."

"That's not entirely true…" Steven stammered.

"But it is at least partly true," the farmer responded. He stood from his seat. "Your presentation looks great, and the free shit is nice, but putting lipstick on a pig doesn't change the bacon. You understand?"

Steven stood wordlessly at the podium, and Ryan could almost sense the panic in his soul.

"Say something," Ryan said under his breath. "Get him back…" He turned to the back table and could see Maria and Mike watching on. Surprisingly, they seemed just as shocked and worried.

The man began walking towards the back of the room.

Ryan felt his heartbeat through his chest. Sweat beaded on his brow.

"I can guarantee it."

The man stopped in his tracks. Turning slightly, he and everyone else in the room trained their eyes to the exact spot where Ryan stood.

"Excuse me?"

For a moment, Ryan wondered if he had been the one to speak. Calming his nerves, he opened his mouth. "I can guarantee it," he said more confidently.

"You can?"

"Yep," Ryan replied. "I can guarantee that your crop will be accepted at our plant this year, and for the years to come." He found his feet moving towards the front of the room, and the eyes moved with him. "I can also guarantee everything that my friend Steven has said about yield and price."

The man appeared perplexed as he still stood at the back of the room. "And how can you guarantee my corn will be accepted?"

"Well," Ryan began, "because there's no way it won't. Especially here."

"Here?"

"Yep, right here. Where you farm. Where you call home."

The man took a step back towards his seat, and Ryan could sense a slight change. He was still flailing, but no longer drowning.

"What's your name, sir?"

The man stood rigid. "Dale. Dale Gower."

"Well, Mr. Gower, the company that screwed you over," Ryan said as he stood on the opposite side of the screen as Steven, "it was Fieldman's Seed, wasn't it?"

The man's eyes narrowed. "It was."

Ryan shrugged as he turned to the group. "How many of you all were screwed by Fieldman's?"

A half dozen hands raised, some more animated than the others.

"Yeah, same as in northern Iowa," Ryan replied. "What they did, and didn't tell you obviously, was straight up thievery. They booked the fields before sourcing the terminal. They did it here, Iowa, Minnesota. Their plan was to secure the crops and use that for processing negotiations in Brazil and Argentina. But it turns out no one down south wanted the grain. It was too late to pull the plug on you, so they essentially did nothing. In fact, all your grain is probably still sitting in Decatur."

Ryan rubbed his brow as he continued in his words. "I could tell you that ethanol is a different beast, but that'd just be my words. Let me speak to the facts." He turned directly to face the man who had spoken. "Your grain, next year and the year after, will go to our Waterman plant, a plant that's been running for almost six years, and a plant that is currently building extra bin space for your corn." He paused for a moment. "But you're right. Ethanol is a fickle industry. How do we know that Waterman is going to stay open? Well, let me tell you." He moved away from the podium, and all eyes continued to be riveted on him. "Grain companies go under, or get sold, because there's a thousand similar companies all looking to do the same. It's competition, and that's not great for stability. In ethanol, it's the same way. You got your POETs and your Valeros and even Central, but can anyone tell me where the nearest plant is next to Waterman? Anyone?"

The room remained silent.

Ryan nodded. "It's a mom-and-pop plant, a forty-five-million-gallon capacity, and it's located in Kewanee, which, last I checked, is nearly two hours away." He paused. "That's it. Two hours of untapped potential and two hours of no competition. Waterman isn't going anywhere, especially with projections in the industry as high as they are. In fact, there might actually be *too much* potential for the plant. There's more corn in the fields than can be processed by the plant, which, quite frankly, poses a real issue if you're trying to move your grain next year. There simply won't be enough space, and you'll be forced to take your regular yellow corn to Kewanee or to the river, where they'll pay you less per bushel."

Ryan paused and looked down to his feet as his mind raced onward. He could feel a bead of sweat on his brow, yet somehow, he felt comfortable under the pressure. He looked upward to see all eyes on him, and he knew they were breathing in his every word. This made him even calmer. He loved nothing more than to be believed.

"I'm not a salesman," Ryan said. "And to be honest, I'm not the smartest of guys—just ask my exes." He began walking back toward the podium slowly as the crowd chuckled. "I'm a regular guy who spent his past days turning wrenches and working with corn. So when I see a no-brainer of a deal, let me tell you, it's a no-brainer of a deal. You all have an opportunity here to be first in line on opening day of some real good cash, better than you'd ever find anywhere else." He leaned on the podium and folded his hands. "You're tired of the bullshit, right? Tired of fluctuating prices and no guarantees. Tired of just making ends meet. Then let's change that. Let's make you all some money." His eyes moved across the room. "To be honest, I'm envious of you all, I really am. This is like finding oil in your backyard, or a certificate for Apple stock." He paused once more as he considered his final plea. "Would you have taken Apple stock twenty years ago? You're damn right, you would have." He watched as several members of the crowd nodded slightly. "Well, here's your opportunity. Apple stock in the form of modified corn." He allowed his words to hang in the air. "All you have to do is sign."

The room remained silent. Every eye was trained specifically on Ryan. For a moment, he wondered if his confidence was unwarranted, but after only a second, the man standing in the back of the room sheepishly turned away from the door. Every ear listened as he walked back to his original seat. Slowly, deliberately, Ryan allowed the scene to unfold. After a few seconds, the man sat back down in his chair.

Ryan nodded toward the crowd with a smile. Reveling in this newfound confidence, he turned to his right. "Steven," he said loudly with the same smile plastered on his face. "Take us home."

***

The airport terminal was a bustle of activity as Ryan walked down the long, wide hallway towards his gate. Overhead, the speaker relayed continuous messages about differing gates and airlines, though he paid attention to few.

To him, there was a magic in the airport, and it was one that crept across his body each time he entered. There was potential in every gate—a location yet to be discovered, or a locale waiting to be revisited. Here, among the countless persons walking across the tile flooring, he could become anyone doing anything. The possibilities were endless, and the serenity of opportunity was peaceful. He didn't have to be an ethanol presenter from Florida. He could be a spiritual advisor heading to the middle east, or a backpacker heading to Europe, or even a lover heading to Haw—

He stopped in his tracks as he heard a voice.

"*Ryan!*" the voice called from his left. It was a female voice, and one he barely discerned above the din of the terminal. Yet it was there. It was palpable. Even in the noise of his surroundings, he heard it. He heard *her*.

He turned toward the left side of the terminal and spied a restaurant. Eyes darting, he attempted to find her blonde hair somewhere among the crowd.

"Ryan!" the voice called, clearer this time.

Ryan blinked, and his pulse slowed. At the front row of tables, Maria sat alone.

Ryan took a deep breath. He picked up his bag from the ground and moved toward her.

"I thought that was you," Maria said as she moved her suitcase from the open seat.

"Thanks," Ryan replied as he moved his own bag from the aisle and took a seat. "Where's everyone else?"

"Steven is down at the gate," she replied. "Mike's taking a nap in another gate, and I haven't seen Donovan yet."

Ryan nodded. He noticed that she had an empty plate before her, though her glass of wine was still half full.

"Lunchtime wine," she said, sensing his gaze. "It's more of a celebration than anything."

"I don't judge," Ryan replied with a laugh.

She stared at him, and he felt almost uncomfortable under the gaze. He didn't know what to say.

"I owe you an apology," she said.

Ryan leaned back. "For?"

She smiled, as though he was being coy. "For yesterday. For my behavior. And for putting you in the back table initially."

"You don't have to apologize," Ryan replied.

"I do," she continued. "I was wrong. I underestimated you. You're a good guy."

Ryan laughed. "I think you properly estimated me."

She ignored this. "We got sixty-one sign-ups in the morning class," she said. "Forty-two in the afternoon. That's one hundred and three out of one hundred and thirty-five people."

"Seventy-six percent," Ryan added, having already done the math.

"Based on our first class, where we had what, one percent? Seventy-six is amazing. And it's all because of you and Steven. Your script changes, your free hats. Everything. You were good."

Ryan didn't meet her gaze.

"I can't believe I never saw that side of you before. I mean, granted, we really don't know much about each other, but you just stood up there and owned it. Confident, charismatic. You had them eating from your hand." She shook her head in admiration. "How'd you do it?"

"Do it?"

"Yeah," she replied. "How'd you present like that?

Ryan looked up to her. "I just told them all what they wanted to hear. They'll make money. They'll live the good life. I'm not even sure if it was all true, but oh well. I guess I just figured I had to step up since *we have a lot at stake.*"

His words triggered her memory, and he waited for her to acknowledge them. As she sat back in her chair, a waitress walked by and refilled her glass of water.

"You going to drink that?" Ryan asked as he indicated the water glass.

"How'd you figure it out?" Maria asked.

Ryan rolled his tongue against his teeth as he smiled. "Figure out what?"

"About Mike and me."

Ryan nodded. "Ah, about that."

"How'd you figure it out?"

"I'm going to assume you aren't drinking that," he replied as he reached for the glass. He unwrapped the straw that sat nearby.

"Did you like, spy, or something?"

Ryan put the straw into the water. "You give me too much credit."

"Then how?"

"I was in the vending room when he left your room the night before last," Ryan replied. He sipped the water. "I caught your goodbye."

"It was like 4:00 a.m."

"I don't sleep much…"

"And you just watched?"

Ryan sipped more on the straw. "I didn't want to interrupt."

Maria rolled her eyes with an embarrassed half smirk on her face.

"I assume it's a secret to the rest of the team then?" Ryan asked as he set the glass down.

"To Steven, yes. Donovan suspects, but he doesn't know."

"I feel privileged."

"And you can't tell."

"Of course."

"I'm serious."

"If I may," Ryan replied, slower in his diction. "Why the secret?"

"It's a secret to everyone," Maria answered. "It has been for over a year."

Ryan sat back. "Wait, what?"

Maria sighed. "Mike and I have been together for over a year. No one knows."

"No one knows?"

"Well, until you."

"How is that possible?"

"He lives in Clarinda, and I live in Omaha. It's easy."

"But…why?"

"Why?"

"Yeah. Why? Is he married? Are you?"

Maria took a deep breath. "Don't be ridiculous."

"Then what? Does mystery heighten the relationship?"

Maria grabbed her glass of wine. "No." She took a deep swig of the red liquid. "No, it's not that."

Ryan stared at her.

"His mother and father," she began. "They don't want their son to date someone like me."

"Like you?"

"Mexican."

Ryan felt his eyes grow wide. "Oh," he replied. "So…they're racist?"

"Prejudiced, according to Michael."

"What's the difference?"

"Nothing to the oppressed," Maria said as she took another drink. "Listen, they're a close family and he doesn't want to have that fight yet, so I respect that because I love him."

"And his parents?"

She sighed. "They're just ignorant. That's all. But he's not them, just the same as you aren't your parents." She paused as she considered her words. "That's why this job is so important. We get to be us, at least more than we would anywhere else. I can see him every day. I can spend nights with him. It's the first time I've felt like we're real."

Ryan considered her words. "But he'll have to tell them eventually…"

Maria nodded. "Eventually, yes. But not now." She looked out into the airport terminal. "Now we're just traveling together, hoping it doesn't end anytime soon." She returned her gaze to Ryan. "I guess I am more okay with lying."

Ryan chuckled as he reached for his glass of water and took a sip. "So you've got this, and Steven has his pride. What about Donovan?"

"Donovan?"

"Yeah," Ryan replied. "What's he got…*at stake?*"

"Oh." Maria studied the question. "Donovan is…out of his element living in Norfolk, Nebraska."

Ryan tried to follow. "How so?"

"There's not too many gay black guys out there."

"Oh," Ryan replied.

Maria smiled. "Everyone's got their secrets. Everyone lies to someone, I guess. At the end of the day, they're just small lies or big lies, I suppose."

Ryan nodded.

"So what's yours?"

Ryan leaned back as he adjusted his legs. "Mine?"

"Yeah, what's your secret? Why are you here?"

"Who says I have a secret?" Ryan inquired.

"Oh, that means you've got a big secret," Maria replied. She leaned onto the table.

"I have no secret." Ryan tried to brush off the comment.

"My God, it must be huge," she countered.

"I'm serious."

"Dear Lord!"

"I don't know what you want me to say."

"You've got to be hiding bodies," she replied. "Are you a serial killer? You are, aren't you? A good-looking Ted Bundy type?"

Ryan stared. "What? If…what?" He tried to reason. "If I was a serial killer, would it be wise to ask me that question?"

"If you were a serial killer, wouldn't you want to throw me off by asking that question?"

He considered her words.

"Besides," she replied, "serial killers have a distinct type, and young Mexican woman aren't the typical prey."

"You know this how?"

"I watch a lot of true crime docs," she countered.

He laughed as he sipped his water.

"I'm going out on a limb by saying that you aren't a serial killer, but you do have a secret," she said. "So what is it? Why is Ryan Collins out here with this ragtag group of lost souls?"

Ryan smiled as he contemplated the question. He took a deep breath as he stared at his water glass. "Well," he began before he trailed off.

She stared at him, as if encouraging the story.

Ryan nodded as he spoke. "Six years ago, I stole my dad's credit card and left behind my life in Florida for a cross-country trip." He considered his words. "That trip ended in South Dakota, where I fell in love with a truly remarkable girl." He paused, wondering if he had her attention. Carefully, he looked up to see her staring. He knew he had to continue.

"I was dumb and naïve, but she was far from any of that, and I made promises that I knew I couldn't keep. A few days and an assaulted cop later, I ended up in jail and then house arrest back in Florida. Fast forward through those dark times, I was free and, naturally, I returned back to that South Dakota town, only this time, she wasn't there."

His voice became softer. "She was gone. Her family was gone. No trace and no trail whatsoever." He paused for a moment before his tone returned to normal. "Now I didn't expect a happy ending, but it would have been nice to have some closure. Something more than how I left her. But closure wasn't for her." He took a deep breath. "So, I did what anyone would do. I moved on, found a job, and here I am." He smiled. "But to answer your second question," he said as leaned forward onto the table, "I guess I'm just out here hoping that if I travel this country enough, eventually I'll figure out where she went. And someday I'll see her sitting in a restaurant, just like this place, and I'll approach, and she'll see me, and it'll be like it was before. She'll see that I've changed, and everything will be good. Everything will be good." His voice trailed off before he straightened up. "So that's why I'm out here, I guess. That's what I'm looking for."

She stared at him as though his words held immeasurable weight. "What was her name?" Maria asked after a moment.

Ryan's mind answered.

Melanie Willis.

His mouth, however, couldn't form the words. He reached for his glass. Sipping the water, he allowed his own emotion to wash off him. As he set the glass down, he stared at his counterpart. He knew she was waiting for an answer that he was not going to give. Saying the name would make it all real. Saying the name would bring someone else in. After a long while, he leaned forward toward her.

"I'm just kidding," he said with a typical smile.

"W-what?" She blinked back to reality.

He began to chuckle. "I'm kidding. There's no girl. I'm just here to travel."

"Seriously?"

He stood up from the table. "Of course," he replied.

"You're such a—" she stammered, standing from the table as well.

"Great storyteller," he answered, moving ahead of her, and leaving the table. "I know." He attempted to conceal any further emotion, though the success was marginal. "Now, come on," he said, "we have a plane to catch."

Chapter 7
In Omaha

"Alright," Kim Anderson said as she stood at the head of a long table, "I know you all have a million other concerns outside of this meeting, including that storm that's coming in." She peered out the nearby window to see a heavy cloud deck. "I won't take up much of your time."

Around the table, the traveling core of Ryan, Maria, Donovan, Steven, and Mike sat alert. Clad in semiprofessional attire, each dared not move, lest they delay hearing their fates.

"Now, I know there's been rumors, especially with this midquarter call today," Kim continued. "But I want to assure you of your status." Her eyes moved to each of them. "Corporate has indicated that your jobs are still of significant importance. They're eager to see what you all can deliver." She reached into the folder in front of her and pulled out a piece of paper. "Your first two days in Chicago were tepid to say the least, but from day three on, and through Madison and Rochester, you all delivered better than we even expected." She set the paper down. "I have to ask, what changed?"

The group sat silent, as if unsure how to answer.

"I think," Maria said, "we just needed to get into our groove. The first two days weren't our best."

"Understandable," Kim replied. "I'm sure the whole presenting aspect, coupled with the travel, was a bit of a change for you all." She looked over the paper. "But with that said, now that you're settled into the job, and with your performance reports indicating that you're all satisfied in the duties, we want to ensure that we have no more wasted efforts."

The group continued to sit.

"I'm proud of you all," Kim continued. "But we will continue to be under intense scrutiny, so give it your best going forward." She set her paper back down and closed the file. "We've already got you booked for Sioux Falls tomorrow and Wednesday. Thursday and Friday will be in Sioux City, and next week, you'll head to Kansas City. How does that sound?"

The five presenters all smiled and nodded. No one spoke.

"Good," Kim continued. "Your email has your itineraries, and we also updated the PowerPoint a bit. Make sure you review."

Ryan's eyes went wide at the thought of having to update another PowerPoint. Next to him, he could almost feel Steven react the same.

"Good luck to you all," Kim replied as she stared out the nearby window to a darkened sky. "Now get out of here before the weather comes in."

***

Ryan stepped out of the bathroom some minutes later to find the corridor and conference room empty. Casually, he spied his watch to see it read 4 p.m. He moved toward the elevator and pushed the down button, waiting a moment for the doors to open. After a quick ride to the ground floor, he stepped off and moved through the large atrium toward the entrance vestibule. Peering inside, he could see through the outside doors that he had not outrun the weather.

A wild tempest of wind and water assaulted the outside concrete and roads of downtown Omaha.

Ryan stepped inside the vestibule to find that he was not the only one who had been forced to wait out the storm. A collection of about a dozen corporate workers were lounging along the walls and seated upon the marble floor. Small conversations were ongoing among some of the people, but for the most part, the vestibule was silent.

Ryan leaned against a nearby wall and attempted to stay as far from view as possible. Looking to his right, he spied his corporate support team sitting together, awaiting the rain, all looking rather irritated at the delay. Around the rest of the vestibule, he recognized no one.

"Ryan, come here," a voice sounded.

Ryan turned to see Kim Anderson beckoning him over.

"You didn't make it out either?" she said as he approached.

"Nope," Ryan replied. "I guess I should've hurried out with the rest of my team."

"No matter," Kim replied as she sat next to Allison and Mark, with Emma and her green headband sitting opposite. "We were just admiring the artwork here since we have nothing else to do."

Ryan chuckled as he saw the giant image of Mt. Everest adorning the wall above where they all sat. Beneath the image were the same words he had seen on his first visit:

Climb your toughest peak.

"Mark here was wondering if he could fit the picture in his truck bed," Kim said as Ryan continued to examine the work.

"Probably would need a bit bigger truck," Mark replied.

Ryan smiled.

"You seem enthralled by the image," Mark said after a moment.

Ryan turned to the group to see most of them looking back at him.

"More the saying than anything," Ryan replied as he met the gaze of the group. "'Climb your toughest peak' is a bit heavy handed next to a picture of Everest." He turned back to the large image. "Plus, Everest isn't even the toughest peak to climb. Sure, it's the highest, but toughest? K2 is tougher. Mt. Logan in Canada may be tougher. Heck, there are some mountains in China that haven't even been climbed yet."

"You know your mountains," Mark replied.

Ryan laughed. "I used to get *National Geographic* a year or so ago. I guess I had a lot of personal travel plans at one time."

"Not anymore?" Mark asked.

Ryan considered it, realizing he was delving further into himself than he wanted. "Maybe someday."

Mark nodded, and for a moment, Ryan wondered if he was out of the woods on questioning. Sensing further inquiries coming, he knew he had to change the subject. "So," he attempted. "How's everyone doing here?" He recognized the awkwardness of the question. "Emma, how's wedding planning going?"

Her eyes moved from the group and onto his. Instantly, a brief yet unmistakable silence hit the group like a freight train as Emma processed the question. Ryan's eyes grew wide with horror upon realizing that he had just placed her in a spotlight that she had no interest in being in.

"It's...good," she said.

Ryan swallowed the lump in his throat. "G-good," he replied before turning to Mark. "And Mark, been to any Husker games this year?"

He never heard Mark's answer. In his peripheral, he could see Emma's gaze turn to the ground, unnoticed by anyone else, as if attempting to register the interaction that had just occurred. He felt ashamed for singling her out. He felt mortified in her return gaze. But behind all that embarrassment, he felt a tinge of a different type, one that carved a small hollow into the furthest reaches of his brain and took up a residence so modest that it may have been ignored if not for how it had been placed. It was a feeling of, of all things, intrigue.

The rain ended after a few minutes, and Ryan found himself walking out the main door following his corporate counterparts. There was a mixture of goodbyes as the group parted toward their respective vehicles. Ryan loitered for a moment as the separation occurred, and then he turned in the direction Emma was headed.

"Hey," he called out some fifty feet behind her. "Hey, Emma."

She stopped ahead of him near an intersection and crosswalk. She half turned toward him as he sped up to meet her.

"Wait up," he said as he approached.

"Hey," she replied, masking what Ryan sensed as a lack of surprise at his following.

"Hey," he answered before straightening up. "Listen, I just wanted to apologize for earlier."

She turned her head, as if attempting to find a response.

"I…" He took a deep breath as he searched his vocabulary. "I shouldn't have put you on the spot like that. I was just—" He continued searching. "I-I don't know why I did it. But I'm sorry. It was none of my business."

"It's fine," she replied with a smile. "I should've given you a better answer."

"No, no," Ryan said. "You don't have anything to apologize for. I tend to say things that I shouldn't sometimes, and that was clearly one of them."

"It's fine," Emma smirked. "I get asked that question all the time, by almost everyone. You'd think I'd answer it better."

Ryan laughed. "It's alright. My mom asks me how I'm doing every time I talk to her, and I always screw that up."

Emma smiled. "To be honest, I typically answer the 'how's wedding planning' question with 'it's going great and it's so much fun. I'm currently perusing wedding dress magazines and putting together a Pinterest board of colors and schemes. I'm really happy.'"

Ryan shrugged. "That doesn't sound fun. That sounds awful."

She laughed.

"If you had told me that word-for-word, I might have called you a liar," he replied as they both began to laugh. "So good job not giving me that answer."

"You don't think wedding dress shopping is fun? I'm surprised." Emma continued to speak through her mirth.

"To be fair," Ryan answered, "I've never done it, but I'm just taking a wild guess."

"Maybe one day you'll get your chance for dress input," Emma responded. "Maybe a sister or your own girlfriend or fiancé."

Ryan laughed. "Well, considering the sister will be more likely at this point in time..."

"How old is she?"

"I don't have one," Ryan replied much to the humor of Emma. "But as of today, it's more likely."

"Stop it," Emma replied with a smile. "You know that isn't true."

Ryan shrugged. "You got a lot to learn about me then."

A silence grew between them, though Ryan could sense it was not due to awkwardness.

"Would you like to..." Emma spoke, though she seemed unsure of her words. "I don't know, grab a cup of coffee or something?"

Ryan felt his body tense up.

"Coffee?" he heard himself ask. "Now?"

He could see trepidation etched on her face. "Yeah?" she replied as though it were a question. "Is that alright?"

He had no idea if it was alright. "Sure," he replied.

"There's a shop on the next block," she said as she turned toward the intersection.

"Yeah," Ryan replied. "Okay. Coffee."

"You don't have anywhere else you need to be, do you?" she asked.

Ryan struggled to ascertain his situation. "No. No, I don't think so. Do you?"

He could see her deal with a similar struggle.

"Not that I can think of," she replied as they crossed the road.

"Good," Ryan replied, walking slightly behind her.

"Good," she responded.

His mind raced as he followed her past the storefronts to the coffee shop.

"Have you been here before?" she asked as they approached.

Ryan shook his head.

"It's good," she replied as they entered. "I end up coming here more often than I should. I even park my car in the garage next door just so I can pass by. That's weird, right?"

"If it's good, then it's not weird," he countered. "People do some crazy things for below average coffee."

"I guess you'll be the judge then," she said with a laugh. Turning to the counter, she rattled off a drink with a copious number of instructions. Ryan could barely follow. "You're judging me now, aren't you?" she said as she spied him staring at her.

He laughed. "I was already judging you when you said that car parking thing."

She shook her head as she swiped her credit card before moving to the pick-up counter.

"Sir?" the barista said from behind the pasty case.

"Iced tea," he replied.

"Black tea?"

Ryan shrugged. "Yeah. Whatever."

"$3.49."

Ryan pulled out his own card and swiped. Collecting his receipt, he moved to join Emma.

"You got tea?" she said with disgust.

"I like tea," he replied.

"Unsweet tea?"

He could almost hear an accent twang. "Iced tea," he answered.

"Tea is only tea if it has more sugar than tea," she corrected him.

"Is that so?"

"That's so."

"Well," he replied, "I'd agree with you normally, but considering we're in the wonderful Midwest, sweet tea is a little hard to come by."

"That's why you have coffee," she replied with a smirk.

Her drink arrived, followed by his. Allowing her to take the lead, he followed as she moved to a table near the corner of the café.

"So, you're a Midwest boy who knows about sweet tea?" Emma asked as he took a seat.

Ryan smiled. "Correction, I'm a Florida boy living in the Midwest."

"Florida?"

"Yes, and you're from…Tennessee?"

"You remembered."

"I got a thing about states."

"And mountains," she added.

He laughed, recalling the earlier conversations. "And mountains."

"Do you know state mountains? That's the real question."

"Hm…state mountains…"

"Yeah, like the highest mountain in Tennessee?"

Ryan racked his brain. "Mount…Nashville."

Her mouth dropped. "You *do* know your state mountains."

"That was right?"

"Not even close," she laughed as she sipped her coffee. "I don't think Mount Nashville even exists."

"Well darn," Ryan replied. "They'll need to name one that then."

She continued to laugh for a moment more.

"So what's the real answer then?" Ryan asked.

She smiled over her coffee before she leaned forward. "It's Clingman's Dome. It's in the Smokeys. Second highest point in the Appalachians if you believe that."

"I do," Ryan replied. "What's first?"

"No idea," she answered. "My high school project ended with Tennessee knowledge."

He laughed. "Well, I anticipate you giving me that answer someday. I need to look smart for my fellow mountain friends."

"You got a lot of those?"

"Tons," he replied. "We do annual mountain meetings and climbs." He leaned forward. "And I've got to say, it's impressive you know your state's highest mountain. I couldn't tell you what Florida's is."

"Does Florida have mountains?"

"No, no, I don't think so."

"It's probably like a sand dune or something," she thought aloud. "Or a tall palm tree."

He laughed. "You may be right."

There was a silence as they each sipped their drinks.

"So," Ryan said as he sat back. "How does a Tennessee girl end up way out here?"

"Here?"

"Yeah, here. Right here."

She laughed as she took another sip. "My life story is not very entertaining."

Ryan considered it. "Well, it's better than anyone else's here, so you've got that."

She looked around to see an empty café. "Fair enough."

"Let's not do life stories then," he said. "Let's just answer that question. What's a Tennessee girl doing in Omaha?"

"Well." She took a deep breath as she sat back. "I graduated college in 2014 with a marketing degree and I decided to take an internship at ConAgra."

"Interesting."

"My college roommate went to school for biology, and she landed an internship there, so I applied, just thinking, *Why not?* It was away from home. It put me on my own."

"Where'd you go to school?"

"Vandy."

Ryan's eyes grew wide. "Impressive."

"Is it?"

"It is. I'm a proud Tampa Bay alumnus."

"That's a school?"

"Believe it or not."

He smiled as she laughed.

"So you decided to just, on a whim, move to Omaha?"

She sipped her coffee again. "It wasn't permanent. I was barely dating my fiancé. I figured it would be cool to try it out."

"And?"

"I did two internships. Rented an apartment with my college roommate, and it was great, except for winters, but you know how that is."

"Yeah, they suck."

She smiled.

"So after the internships, you just decided to stay?"

"Not exactly," Emma replied. "I went back to Tennessee in 2016. Worked at a Macy's for six months and as a night clerk at the Four Seasons for a few weeks before I decided that neither of those were right for me."

He continued to let her talk, and he found that her voice provided more energy than the tea ever would.

"In the beginning of 2017, I almost took a job as a flight attendant before my old ConAgra boss called me and said that she'd moved to an ethanol company, and she had an actual position for me. Nothing glamorous, but it was closer to marketing than I had been, and that was all I wanted at the time." She paused as she chose her next words. "So I relocated once again to live with my old roommate, and that's where I've been for a little over a year now."

Ryan thought about her comments as he sipped his tea. "None of that sounds permanent."

"It doesn't, does it?" she replied with a laugh. "I haven't been in a permanent state of mind in quite a while. I guess I'm just winging it until…" Her voice trailed off as she looked at her cup before returning her gaze to Ryan. "Until the wedding."

"What's your fiancé do?" Ryan replied, more curious than ever before.

"Military," she replied. "Air Force. Or soon to be. We graduated together and he worked at an engineering firm for a year or so before he decided to go to grad school in Pennsylvania in 2015. He graduated last month and plans to join this fall, after we get married."

"Seems like a solid plan," Ryan responded.

"It does," she replied. Her tone didn't match the emotion Ryan saw on her face. "He wanted to get married right after graduation so he could enlist right away, but I wanted more time. It was a bit of a big deal."

He laughed. "Was it? I didn't hear about it in the papers."

"Not the print papers," she replied. "But if you Google me, you'll see the uproar I caused."

"Well, I'll certainly have to do that," Ryan said as he echoed her laugh. "I'm all for family drama."

"Well, my family is not short on it. You'll find it all right in that Google search."

They continued to laugh together until it subsided.

"So what about you?" Emma asked.

"Me?" Ryan asked.

"Yeah, you," she countered. "What are you doing here?"

Ryan smiled. "And here I thought you'd ask about what Google would show for me."

"I can ask that if you'd rather."

Ryan laughed. "I wouldn't."

She leaned forward. "Well now you've got me interested so I kind of have to."

"Be careful what you ask," Ryan teased.

"You must have a fascinating Google presence."

Ryan rubbed his tongue on his back teeth as he debated his next move. "Do it then," he said.

"Do it?"

"Yeah," he replied. "Google me. Ryan Collins."

"You're serious?"

"Yeah," he replied, serious but far from certain.

She stared at him for a moment. "Alright then."

He watched as she pulled her phone from her pocket. With elevated curiosity, he saw her type in his name. Instantly her face became illuminated with search results. He knew what she saw, as he had performed this exercise many times before. He continued to sit as she read any number of the results.

"This is…" She trailed off.

He sipped his almost-empty tea. "Heavy right?"

She looked up to him and then back to her phone. "Is it…true?"

The question was so simple, and he knew there was no way to ascertain a proper response.

No, he thought. *None of it. It was all false. He was wronged. He was made an example of. There was no way it was true.*

"Yeah," he said. "Yeah, it's all true."

She looked up at him as she set her phone down.

There was so much he wanted to say. He wanted to explain, to perhaps ease her mind. He wanted to tell her he was not the monster she read about. He wanted to tell her that all of it was his past self. There was so much he wanted to say, but his mouth never moved.

She looked down at her phone before returning the gaze to him. "Did you also sing a cover of Radiohead?"

Ryan swallowed. "What?"

She turned her phone and slid it to him. Looking down, he saw the articles indicating his crimes, but in the middle was a YouTube video titled "Creep—cover by Ryan Collins."

He smiled. "Nope," he said as she slid the phone back. "I'm pretty sure that's a different Ryan Collins."

She clicked play and let the sounds encapsulate their table for a few moments.

"That's a shame," she said after a few seconds. "This sounds good."

"It does," Ryan replied. He was content in letting the elephant in the room lie still.

She paused the video and removed the phone from the table.

"Well, I must say," she said, "your Google search is definitely more interesting than mine."

"Interesting is one way to put it," he replied. "You don't seem too fazed by it, if I may say."

She laughed. "Fazed? Should I be?"

Ryan shrugged. "I don't know. To be honest, I'm not sure how I'd take it."

She leaned back as she finished her coffee. "Well, you're not wearing an ankle bracelet now, and I also haven't seen anyone tailing you the entire time you've been here with me." She leaned forward as to whisper. "But to be honest, I don't read into the internet too much anyway. I much prefer making my own opinions."

"That's very open-minded of you," Ryan replied. He leaned forward to mimic her motions. "And to be honest, too, I kind of enjoy talking to you."

"Kind of?" she repeated as she leaned back. "Well, I suppose that's better than nothing. I guess I could say I *kind of* enjoy talking to you, too. We should make this a thing. Every time you manage your way back to Omaha. How about that?"

"I think that could work."

"Good," she replied as she pulled out her phone once again.

Ryan stared at her.

"Phone?" She looked up at him.

"Oh," Ryan replied, somewhat shocked. He read off his phone number, nonetheless.

"I just texted you," Emma replied. "Now we're phone friends."

"Phone friends indeed," Ryan replied, still surprised.

"So," Emma said as she once again put away her phone, "when will you be back in Omaha?"

Ryan laughed. "I imagine since you helped with our schedules that you'd know."

"Well, I know when your off days are," she replied. "But just because you're off doesn't mean you'll be here. You could be going home for a few days, or somewhere else." She turned her head with a wry smile. "I don't know what kind of life you lead, Mr. Collins."

"Well," Ryan replied, "I guess you should know that my off days are pretty dull, so I imagine I might be free during the next weekend."

"And you don't mind driving back here from Sioux City?"

Ryan looked upward as if to consider it further, but he knew the answer. "I think I can make it work."

She smiled as she leaned forward. "You must enjoy driving," she said.

He leaned toward her to mimic her movements again. As he did so, he took in her image, from her blue eyes and high cheekbones down to her rounded chin and then all the way up to her green headband that popped in the light of the café. It was an image he committed to memory.

"You have no idea," he responded.

***

It was after 10 p.m. before Ryan hauled his luggage into his room in Sioux Falls. Breathing deeply, he shut the door before he moved to his nightstand to empty his pocket of his phone and wallet. As he turned away, he heard his phone vibrate. He returned to the table and illuminated the screen. Much to his disappointment, it was only a text from Maria.

Meet at IHOP next door at 6:30 a.m. tomorrow.

Exhaling, he moved to his contacts to see the newest name that had been added.

Emma Kelle.

His finger hovered over the "text" icon. He clenched his teeth as he contemplated his options, knowing that there were risks with either path. Finally, he set the phone back down, angrily content in his decision.

"She's engaged, you idiot," he said to himself as he moved into the bathroom. He emptied his suitcase of his toiletries before he started the shower. As he awaited the warm water, he took yet another deep breath. His sturdiness was waning.

***

Several minutes later he exited the shower and, clad in a towel, returned to the nightstand. Sitting on the side of the bed, his mind continued to race as he considered everything before him. Over his shoulder, he spied the nightstand clock that read 10:45 p.m.

Too late, he told himself. *Too desperate,* he added.

Yet he continued to sit unmoved.

After a few seconds, he found his hand reaching for the phone. Bringing it close, he reasoned away excuse after excuse. His mind was made up. He illuminated his home screen and unlocked the phone. His finger moved to the contacts button.

New Facebook Message.

His finger froze. His eyes bolted to the icon that now displayed at the top of his phone. His pulse quickened. His hands grew sweaty.

His previous actions forgotten, he moved his hand to the top of the phone and opened the notification.

With bated breath, he read the message before him:

Hey Ryan, it's been a long time. I'm not sure if you remember me, but I'm pretty sure you remember my sister. I'm currently an ag student at the University of Sioux Falls and my department received an email about a seminar by Central Plains Ethanol being held here in town. I saw that you were one of the ones leading it and it was a blast from the past. Anyways, hope your doing well. Let's catch up sometime.

Max Willis

Chapter 8
181 Miles from Omaha

"You okay, Ryan?"

The voice broke him from his trance, and he turned to see Steven sitting across from him.

"Where'd everyone go?" Ryan asked, shaking himself into the present.

"They left about five minutes ago," Steven replied. "Maria and Mike went to go get the hats and pens. Donovan went to go get donuts."

Ryan nodded. Around him, the IHOP was quiet. He looked down to his watch to see it read 7:30 a.m. before he looked up to see Steven staring at him.

"What's up?" Ryan asked.

"Are you okay?" Steven repeated.

"Yeah," he lied. "Why do you ask?"

Steven sat back. "You sat there, unmoving, for over ten minutes." He considered his words. "And we didn't see you at dinner yesterday."

"I got in late," Ryan replied. "I got tied up in Omaha with the weather and everything else."

Steven seemed at first hesitant to accept the answer, but after a few moments, he smiled. "Fair enough," he replied as he attempted to get up from the table.

"What?" Ryan replied, sensing that he was not being bought.

"Excuse me?" Steven countered, sitting back down.

"What's with the look?"

"The look?"

"Yeah," Ryan replied. "You seem to have more to say."

Steven smiled. "It's not my place."

"Not your place?"

"No, I just wanted to make sure—"

"You don't believe me."

"What?"

Ryan sat back in his booth. "You don't believe me. You ask if I'm fine, I tell you I am, and you don't believe me."

"I didn't say that—"

"You didn't *not* say that."

"I just..." Steven's voice trailed off.

"What?" Ryan replied.

"I just want you to know," he stammered as he struggled with the words. "I just want you to know that if you need to talk to someone, I'm here."

Ryan's jaw lowered. "If I need to talk?"

"Yeah, if you need to talk."

"Why would I need to talk?"

"Ryan, I'm just saying."

"Just saying what?" Ryan continued. "Be honest."

Steven shook his head as though he regretted even starting the conversation. "It's just…"

Ryan remained still.

Steven gritted his teeth. "I'm not one to judge another man, but your lifestyle might be hindering your attitude."

Ryan laughed. "My *lifestyle?*"

"I don't want to get into this," Steven replied. "I just wanted to let you know that if you need an ear to talk to, I'm here."

"What's my lifestyle?"

Steven took a deep breath, and Ryan could sense an inevitability in his face.

"The girls," Steven began. "The drinking. The zoning out during conversations. The clear lack of sleep. The overall detachment you show towards pretty much everything." He leaned forward as he continued to speak. "I'm not here to judge, I just think it's taking a toll on you."

Ryan took a deep breath.

"I'm not sure what happened last night," Steven replied. "But you don't look like you just 'got in late.' Honestly, you don't even look like you're here at all. I mean, physically yes, but not mentally."

Ryan turned towards his counterpart. "Your honesty is refreshing, you know that?"

"I just—"

"You're fine," Ryan replied with a laugh. "You're good." He took another deep breath. "How do you know about my *lifestyle*, anyway? You spying on me?"

Steven sat back in his chair. "I mean, I don't *really*," he replied. "I just saw in Chicago when I came to your room."

Ryan nodded.

"And when we were sitting in the restaurant working on the presentation, a woman walked past you and…" He considered his words. "Well, she raised her middle finger at your back as she walked past."

Ryan laughed. "I see."

"I wanted to tell you then," Steven replied. "But I didn't know how."

"It's all good," Ryan replied. "I got her note back in my room. It pretty much summarized her feelings, and the finger."

"I'm sorry," Steven said.

"Don't be," Ryan replied. "It isn't worth your time to be sorry about me."

The pair sat in silence for a few moments.

"I got a message last night," Ryan said after the silence had drawn past the point of comfort. "A Facebook message."

Steven leaned towards the table with undivided attention.

"It was…" Ryan began. "It was from a past life. From someone I hadn't heard from in a while."

"Is this person close to you?"

"Not really," Ryan answered. "But his sister is a different story. *Was* a different story."

"I see," Steven replied.

"I just know that if I respond, we'll end up talking, and if we end up talking I'll end up turning the subject to his sister, and it won't be good."

"Why won't it be good?"

"Because I'll find out what she's been up to, or where she lives, which is what I've been trying to do for a long time now."

"I don't see a problem with that situation."

"You don't know her," Ryan said with a smile. "She's intoxicating. Only recently did I feel like I didn't need her in my life, and now the opportunity exists to let her back in."

"But you just said you don't need her," Steven replied. "Why even pursue it?"

Ryan considered the question for a long while. Just as he was about to answer, however, he jumped from the stupor he was falling into. "Why do you want to hear this? Why do you care?"

Steven jolted at the tone change. "Why wouldn't I?"

"Because," Ryan replied, "I'm a mess. You're a beacon of God. You've got your shit figured out. You don't need me bringing you down. My life would just depress you."

"No one is perfect," Steven countered.

"Well, some of us are a hell of a lot closer than others."

"We all sin," Steven replied. "It's a part of life."

"I find you sinning a bit hard to believe."

Steven laughed. "Well, I don't go about it quite like you."

"That sounds judge-y…"

"I promise it isn't."

"But seriously," Ryan replied, tone turning stoic. "Why do you care?"

"Because," Steven replied. "We're friends."

Ryan's eyes went wide.

"Aren't we?"

Ryan took another deep breath. "You think we're friends?"

Steven shrugged. "Why not?"

"I guess I just didn't think about it like that," Ryan replied.

"Well," Steven countered, "now you can."

Ryan returned to his normal tone. "Alright then. I guess we're friends."

"Good," Steven replied. "Then as your friend, I want you to know that if you need to talk, I'm here for you."

Ryan nodded.

"I'm serious," Steven said. "I'm here for you."

Ryan smiled. "I appreciate that."

Steven sat back from the table. "And I must say, being my friend does have its perks. Not only do you get my opinions on the most recent *Star Wars* novels, but you also get homemade Christmas cookies each year."

Ryan smiled. "Is that so?"

Steven shrugged. "I usually have to make a couple hundred for the place I volunteer at, so invariably I have leftovers."

Ryan shook his head. "Volunteer? God you really are a saint."

"And as to your situation with the message," Steven said as he received his receipt with a "thank you" to the waitress. "I'm reminded of a quote." He walked out the front door toward the waiting rental car as Ryan followed. "'For which of you, desiring to build a tower, does not first sit down and count the cost, whether he has enough to complete it?'"

Ryan moved to the passenger door. "Who said that? Orson Welles?"

Steven looked up from the driver's side. "Jesus Christ said that."

Ryan shrugged as he got inside the car. "Close enough."

***

The restaurant was darker than Ryan would have liked, and that made it especially difficult to maneuver through the throngs of people waiting for a table. Sidestepping each of them, he finally managed to spy the main dining room. Adorned in all manner of cowboy and ranch decorum, the room was louder than the foyer entrance, and alongside the vision difficulty, Ryan also now strained to hear.

Back corner, Max had messaged him five minutes ago. Instinctually, his feet carried his body toward the destination, and as he passed table upon table of patrons shouting above the din of the music and other patrons, he entertained the thought of turning and walking out.

An arm waved at a corner table, and Ryan felt his fear grow larger.

"Ryan! Over here."

The arm connected to the body and Ryan traced it to the young man's head and voice. It was unmistakable, even after all these years. Ryan clearly saw the boyish looks under a plastering of long brown hair, prominent dimples that were somehow less pronounced than in his memory, and the deep green eyes he had first spied alongside his sister in South Dakota.

"It's really you," Max said with an awkward smile as he stood from the table and stretched out a hand.

Ryan instinctively grasped it, seeing that the boy he once knew for all of two days was now a tall and lanky young man. "It's really *you*," Ryan replied with a laugh. "I can't believe it."

"Sit, sit," Max beckoned. "I was honestly surprised you agreed to meet."

The two sat facing one another. Ryan noticed that a drink was already in place for his counterpart, and he wondered how long he had been waiting.

"Same here," Ryan replied. "I was shocked to see your message."

"I figured you wouldn't respond, or you'd politely decline."

Ryan laughed. "Decline? Of course not. Why would I do that?"

It was Max's turn to laugh. "I mean, come on, I've read the stories and seen the news. I'm sure your time in Shannon wasn't one you wanted to revisit."

Ryan leaned back in his chair. "Good thing we're not in Shannon then, isn't it?"

Max sat back as well, with his mouth slightly ajar. "You look almost the same as I remember. Your clothes aren't as…disheveled and you look better kept, but still almost the same."

"Were my clothes really that bad?"

"They stood out…"

"Glad to know I made an impression, I guess."

Max laughed. "It's safe to say that you made an impression on most of the town."

Ryan smiled as a waitress brought by a water glass. He took a sip before setting the glass back down. "So *you* clearly aren't in Shannon anymore."

Max breathed out. "I haven't been for over five years."

"That long?"

"Yep," he replied. "Me and my dad moved here back in 2013. The summer between sixth and seventh grades."

Ryan caught a missing name in the description.

"You're in college now?" Ryan replied. "Did you graduate early?"

"Dual enrollment," Max replied. "High school isn't really my thing, so I decided to spend as little time there as possible."

"Any plans on what to study?" Ryan responded, knowing he was asking a question he hated to hear.

"Not really," Max replied. "Agriculture is huge around here, so a lot of the people I know are thinking that. I'm still exploring."

"Well, I seem to remember a theater interest," Ryan said.

Max laughed. "Yeah, that and Little League didn't pay off too much."

"You were pretty good, if I remember properly."

"You don't remember properly," Max quipped.

Ryan laughed and then took another sip of his drink.

"My sister loved those plays of mine," Max continued. "I think I did a lot of that crap for her."

Ryan froze as he heard the words, but he quickly attempted to maintain composure. "We do a lot for people we care about."

"That's for sure," Max replied, seemingly oblivious to Ryan's internal struggles.

The waitress came back around, and Ryan quickly scanned the menu in front of him as Max ordered his meal. Soon after, the waitress took his own order and stepped away from the table.

Silence took ahold of the table for a moment as Ryan considered his next words. "So, your sister," he began as nonchalantly as possible. "She here in Sioux Falls too?" He cringed as he heard his own words.

"Mel?" Max replied, still even in tone. "Oh, no. She left Shannon in 2012, I think. It wasn't long after you were there."

"Oh," Ryan replied. "Where—where'd she go?"

Max thought about the question. "A lot of places. I think she started in Texas and then was in California for a bit. Now she lives in Hawaii."

"Hawaii?"

"Yeah," Max replied. "Random, I know. She's a nurse or *was* a nurse. Now she's…" He struggled as he thought. "To be honest, I don't know *what* she is. Something medical. She travels a lot too; I do know that."

"Do you two talk often?"

Max sat back in his chair. "Once a month or so she'll call. Dad doesn't talk to her, but I do. He's a little bitter over her leaving."

"I see."

"What about you?" Max asked. "What have you done since Shannon?"

Dammit, Ryan thought. He knew getting the subject changed back would be a delicate effort.

"Well," he began as he sat back, "I spent some time in Florida before I decided to move back to the Midwest."

"Why's that?"

Ryan grated his teeth. "I just figured the area suited me, I guess. I lived in Iowa for a bit before I took my current job."

"And now you *teach*?"

"Something like that," Ryan replied with a laugh. "It's more like selling, honestly. My company makes ethanol, so I go around and get farmers to plant a specific corn that makes ethanol production easier and cheaper."

"That sounds…"

"Boring?"

Max laughed. "Not what I expected of you."

"Well, what did you expect?"

"I don't know," Max replied. "When we first met, you seemed so…"

"Disheveled?"

"Mysterious. Roaming. Like a truck driver or something."

Ryan laughed. "You thought I'd be a truck driver?"

"Or a backpacker? A guy who lives with grizzly bears?"

"I'm not sure that pays well…"

"I mean, I'm basing this off—what, two days? But still. You didn't seem to be the suit-and-jacket-type selling stuff."

"If I'm being honest," Ryan replied, "I typically just wear a button-down shirt."

Max chuckled as he took another drink. "You know what I mean."

"Of course," Ryan replied. "To be honest, backpacking sounds a whole lot more fun. Grizzly bears, not so much, but still." He paused as he considered his words. "I guess you never know where you're going to end up."

Max nodded, though Ryan sensed his words meant little.

"Did you ever get your friend home?" Max finally said.

Ryan felt his face turn to confusion.

"Back in Shannon," Max explained. "You said you were helping your friend get home to see his family for Christmas. Did he make it?"

"You remember that?"

"Surprisingly, yes," Max retorted. "Not sure why."

Ryan laughed. "Well yes, we did get him home. Though he was actually going through a loss, so I guess I kind of lied about the family part."

Max nodded. "But you came back?"

"Huh?"

Max shrugged. "You came back. You came to the restaurant."

"I did." Ryan felt his tone turn suspicious.

"I wasn't there," Max replied quickly. "I just heard about it."

"From?"

"My classmates. Teachers. Google. Honestly, everyone."

"Oh."

Max leaned forward sheepishly. "Can I ask what actually happened?"

"You honestly don't know?"

"No!" Max exclaimed. "Nothing other than what I heard and read. It's been on my mind ever since, and I just feel like I need to know."

Ryan's eyes grew wide as he concluded that his invitation was nothing more than a naïve inquisition.

"I mean, one minute, Mel and Dad are working at the restaurant and everything's normal, and the next minute, she's gone, the restaurant's sold, people are talking, and we move here. That's a lot to process."

"Yeah, it is."

"And the only commonality between those eras is that one ends with, and another starts with, your visit."

Ryan nodded, realizing the true reason for Max's request to meet.

"I feel like it's an important moment that I know nothing about."

Ryan smiled. "What does everyone say happened?"

Max sat back. "Oh, I've heard everything. You were one of the FBI's most wanted. You stole a million dollars from a casino. You were planning on blowing up the town. I heard it all."

"Those are quite elaborate."

"I heard that you almost killed the sheriff. One classmate said that you came back to finish the job and there was a shootout. I heard a lot."

"Do you believe any of it?"

"I know you went to prison, but that's just what the news says. Other than that, though, no, I don't."

"Why not?"

Max considered the question. "Because I think you'd be in prison a long time if you were a 'most wanted.'"

"True."

"And honestly, small town people like to make up stories when they don't know the answer, which means that the answer is probably a lot more...delicate...than blowing up a town."

"Delicate?"

"Yeah," Max replied. "More intimate. Something involving, maybe, my sister."

Ryan smiled nervously as he looked down at his water glass. "What does she say?"

Max took a deep breath. "Well, that's the other part. She doesn't say anything."

Ryan continued looking at his glass. "She hasn't mentioned me?"

"Not once," Max answered. "I've asked too. She just brushes it off, or says she has to go. It's like you don't exist. With any normal person, I'd think it just wasn't important, but with Mel…"

Ryan knew what it meant with Mel.

"What happened in Shannon?" Max finally said after a moment of silence.

Ryan looked upward, internally debating his next moves. Finally, he took another deep breath as he returned the gaze of the boy across from him.

"As I was driving my friend home, we ran into car trouble in Shannon, and over the next few days, the sheriff found out that we were 'wanted,' as you said." Ryan laughed as he contemplated it. "The crime, however, was going to be thrown out as soon as I got back to Florida. My parents just wanted me home more than anything. But unfortunately, we decided to make a run for it out of some stupid logic. And when we were caught, instead of finally surrendering, we made another brash decision to escape."

"You beat him up."

"Something like that, yeah," Ryan replied.

"And Mel?"

Ryan took another deep breath. "Before all that mess, I wanted to stay in Shannon. I didn't want to leave the town or her, but I did because I needed to get my friend home. And by making that decision, I broke some promises I made to her."

"But you came back…"

"I did," Ryan replied. "I came back by myself. I wanted her to know I was sorry. But in doing so, I got arrested anyway."

Max took another drink. "They should've let you go."

Ryan smiled. "It wasn't in the cards."

Max considered the words. "Dad always said that the sheriff was a hothead. Mel did too. She always talked about how much she hated him." He paused for a moment. "Good thing he moved north after you left."

Ryan nodded as he focused in on Max's words. "Does Mel talk about the past a lot?"

"All the time," Max replied. "Between that and things I used to do as a kid. It's annoying sometimes."

Ryan smiled. "How about her current life?"

Max shrugged. "Other than where she's traveling to, not much. She usually tells me where she's going in hopes that I can come visit, but I never can. It's not like I can go visit her in Florida over Memorial Day or in California this fall. Those places aren't close."

Ryan's ears perked up. "She's going to be in Florida over Memorial Day?"

Max obliviously continued. "Around then, yeah. West Palm, I think? Palm Beach maybe? Something Palm. Some conference that week."

"I see," Ryan replied.

"But yeah, between her merry travels and my childhood traumas, our chats are pretty much always the same."

"Maybe," Ryan thought as he spoke, "maybe she just likes remembering good times."

"Well," Max replied, "I've certainly learned not to bring up you anymore."

"That's probably smart."

"I'm glad you can talk about it though," Max concluded as the waitress appeared with their food.

"Yeah," Ryan replied. "I'm glad too."

As the waitress handed out the food, he couldn't help but think about the past. It was all he seemed to concern himself with. And yet with her? Did he even cross her mind? Was the silence she held onto merely a blanket of indifference, or was it a sweltering quilt of agony?

He stared at his food as his mind pondered all outcomes.

Regardless of the reasoning, one thing stood out for certain — silence had never screamed so loudly.

S.D. Goldman

Chapter 9
181 Miles from Omaha

Ryan's phone lit up early on the morning of May twelfth. Rubbing his eyes, he turned toward the hotel nightstand and reached for the device. He allowed his eyes to adjust before he brought the screen toward his nose.

It was a text message from Emma.

Hey—sorry, but I'm gonna need a rain check for today. Something came up. Maybe next time you're around.

Ryan blinked a few times as he stared at the screen. After a moment of contemplation, he hit "reply."

No worries, I understand. I'll let you know next time I'm in town.

Send.

He stared at the screen. He saw three dots indicating that she was responding. Seconds later, the icon disappeared with no new message.

Ryan continued to stare.

"Well," he muttered. "That's disappointing."

He opened Facebook. Rolling onto his back, he held the phone up over his head.

There were no new messages.

He pressed "search" before typing "Ma." Max Willis prepopulated. He reread some of the messages he had sent and received the night before after deciding to respond. After, he clicked on the young man's name before scrolling through his feed, as though his detective work would provide a lead not seen last night or the day before. Unfortunately for him, though, there were no new posts. No new images to link him to his true search. There was nothing on her.

Ryan clicked "search" again. Biting his tongue, he typed "Emm." Emma Kelle prepopulated, and he clicked. His eyes narrowed as he stared at her image.

Her profile picture showed her in a pure state of excitement as she stood some distance in front of a large stone wall, hands stretched high as though she herself was shocked to be in the locale. Ryan smiled at the jubilation in her face. It radiated from her denim capris to her green headband that glistened in the sun.

He clicked on more of her pictures. Most were older, either from college or perhaps high school. Few depicted any boys. Searching through albums, he spied an engagement photo accompanied by a few other date pictures. Ryan stared at them. He clicked on one of the photos to see the tagged.

Emma Kelle

Jay McKnight

He clicked on the latter's name.

Private.

Ryan tapped the back arrow and stared at the picture.

From the image, Ryan could sense that Jay was tall and muscular, with a solid head of dark black hair and high, prominent cheekbones. His smile was radiant, as though he made a life off his photogenic nature.

"Looks like goddamn Superman," Ryan muttered under his breath.

His eyes moved to Emma and back to Jay. They seemed happy. They seemed content.

He moved back to her main profile and to the photos that showed her alone.

Here, she seemed ecstatic, as though wonder and amazement poured from her being. Elation etched itself across her face as though she was a child. But more than anything, he noticed, she seemed fulfilled.

He closed the screen and set the phone on the nightstand. Raising upward, he allowed his feet to hit the ground.

He heard his phone vibrate.

Reaching for it, he opened the screen to see another text message.

On second thought, let's meet today, Emma texted.

Ryan stared at the screen.

You sure?

Seconds ticked onward as he awaited a response. Finally, he saw the typing icon, followed by a message.

Yes. Noon?

Sounds good.

Good. Meet you at the coffee shop.

Ryan continued to stare at his phone, even after the message was received. After a moment longer, he set the phone back on the nightstand, though he continued to stare in its direction.

"Well," he muttered. "That's surprising."

S.D. Goldman

***

It was past noon when Ryan stepped into the coffee shop in downtown Omaha. Removing his sunglasses, he peered around the small café until he spied the blonde girl with the headband sitting toward the back corner.

"Sorry I'm late," he breathed as he sat down.

She looked down to her phone. "Only a few minutes."

"It's a longer drive from Sioux City than I thought," Ryan answered.

"Did you hit traffic?" she asked before her lips turned up in a smile.

Ryan chuckled as he considered the desolate drive between the locales.

"I got you an iced tea," she said after a moment. "I hope that's alright."

Ryan noticed the drink in front of him. "You didn't have to."

"I didn't want to," she replied. "No one should ever have to order that, but I figured I'd be nice."

"Have you tried it?"

"Never."

"One day it may be the only option, who knows."

She sipped her coffee. "If that's the case, then I'll die of thirst."

Ryan shook his head as he sipped the bitter beverage. "Ah, refreshing."

"You can't hide that miserable face."

They laughed as she sat back from the table.

"So," Ryan said after the laughter had ceased. "You enjoyed our coffee shop talk so much you decided you wanted to recreate it?"

She stared at him over her cup. "Is that your way of asking what we're doing?"

Ryan sipped his tea again. "Clever."

"Well," she countered. "Now that you're here, I figured we'd go down to the park and just walk."

"I do enjoy walking."

"Good to hear," she replied. "Does that mean you're ready?"

He grabbed his drink and stood up. "I was born ready."

***

"I have a confession," Emma said as they strolled along the sidewalk down Douglas Street.

Ryan's ears perked.

"It's a pretty big one," she continued.

"What is it?"

She stopped on the sidewalk. "I never had something come up this morning."

Ryan turned toward her, confused.

"This morning I texted you to postpone. I said I had something come up, and that wasn't true."

"Oh."

"I just..." She stared at him. "Is this wrong?"

"Wrong?"

"Yeah," she replied. "Me and you. Meeting. Being friends."

Ryan shrugged. "I'm—"

"I mean, I'm engaged. You're single. This seems wrong to go out like this."

Ryan continued to stand there, unsure of the direction of the conversation.

"I've been thinking about it a lot," she continued. "And I canceled this morning because I thought that hanging out with you would send the wrong signals. I even thought about going home for the weekend. In fact, I walked to my car and got in."

"But you didn't..."

She looked up. "Yeah, I didn't."

"What changed your mind?"

Her face became a weak smile. "I felt bad about canceling on you. I felt like I'd have fun with you. I don't know. That's wrong, isn't it?"

"Well," Ryan said, "I'm not the best on moral decency."

"Just tell me I'm not crazy."

"You're not crazy."

"I'm serious," she replied, though the smile remained.

"I am," Ryan countered. "You're not crazy. We're friends. Friends hang out. You're showing me around Omaha. That's it."

She stood as though she had more to say, but after a moment, she began walking again. "You sure?"

"I promise," he replied, joining alongside her. "I'll even stand four feet away from you if you'd prefer. And no holding doors."

"That's mighty courteous of you," she said as she laughed.

"Hey, that's the situation we're in. You'll pay for your own stuff too."

"But I already bought your tea."

Ryan shook his head. "These mixed signals have to stop."

"Be quiet," she replied with more laughter.

They continued walking in the bright afternoon sun, down the concrete sidewalks towards the Missouri River. The city was quiet except for other families and couples enjoying the weekend air.

"I like how you immediately made your confession," Ryan said after a few moments.

"What do you mean?"

"I mean you didn't wait. You said it right away."

"Well, it was bothering me."

"I know, I usually bottle up stuff like that," Ryan explained. "It's pretty open of you to say that."

She shrugged. "I don't like secrets. They don't do anyone a lot of good. It's just better to be honest, like you were with your...past."

Ryan laughed.

"Were you disappointed when I canceled?" she asked after his laughter subsided.

"Was I disappointed?"

"Yeah," she explained. "Upset. Miffed."

Ryan looked over to her as they walked. "Honestly?"

She returned his gaze. "Yeah."

"Yeah," Ryan replied. "I was. I Facebook stalked you for a good ten minutes afterwards."

"Did you?"

Ryan nodded. "I did. I'm that guy."

"Had you not stalked me before?"

"Maybe..."

"What'd you find?"

He shrugged. "Not much. I loved your profile picture in front of that wall though."

"Ah, the Great Wall."

"Great Wall?"

"Yeah," she replied.

"Of China?"

"Is there another?"

"You were in China?"

She laughed. "Yeah, I was in China. That's an older picture though."

"When?"

She looked skyward as she recalled the date. "Senior year? Seven years ago?"

"For what?"

"We went to teach English. It was a summer thing. A lot of fun though."

"That's awesome," Ryan replied. "I don't think I've known anyone who's been there."

"Really?"

"Yeah," he replied. "Where'd you go?"

"A lot of places. Beijing, Tianjin. We went to the Great Wall for a few days."

"And you taught English?"

"I mean *taught* is a loose word," she said with a laugh. "But I tried to."

"That's so cool," Ryan added. "Have you been to any other exotic travel locales?"

She turned to him as they continued walking. "Well, you'd know that if you were a better Facebook stalker."

"Fair enough."

"Let me see." She scrunched her brow as she thought. "I've been to Paris, Switzerland, Italy…"

Ryan's jaw dropped.

"…Belize, and Mexico on a cruise with family," she replied. "Still fun though."

"You're a worldly traveler."

She laughed. "I didn't plan any of them," she explained. "Most were family trips. Belize was for church work. I'm not nearly the backpacker that you think I am."

"But still," Ryan countered, "that's a whole lot more than me."

"You've never traveled?"

"Well sure," he answered. "But usually just in the U.S. I've been to quite a few different states."

"Well, there you go," she countered. "I haven't been to many states."

"Really?"

"Pretty much everything between here and Tennessee," she answered, "and I've been to Disney World a few times, but that's about it."

"What a sheltered life," Ryan mused.

"It's been tough," she pined.

"Well, there we go," Ryan summarized. "You can be the worldly travel expert for me, and I'll be your stateside guide."

They continued walking, though now they were beyond the concrete buildings and into the heart of the riverside park. Slowly, they strolled onward, as though the day extended into eternity.

"So," he said after a moment of reflecting on his previous statement, "I should think before I speak from now on."

She laughed. "You're fine. I just—"

"I know," Ryan replied, though he was unsure if he did.

She smiled at him, and he looked back at her. Their eyes met for only a second, but it was long enough.

She replied, "Any more discoveries from my Facebook?"

Ryan bit his lip. "Well," he replied, "I think I'd rather know if you learned anything from mine."

"From *your* Facebook?"

"Yeah."

"You think I've stalked you?"

Ryan shrugged. "Maybe?"

She strolled in silence for a moment. "Well, I have," she replied with another chuckle. "But I didn't need to."

"Didn't need to?"

"No," she answered. "Ryan Collins is well known around Omaha."

"Around Omaha?"

"In our work office," she clarified.

"In the work office?"

"Yeah." She shrugged. "There's a lot of post-college girls who work there, and a lot of them vacation in Spirit Lake."

Ryan felt the lump grow in his throat. "Is that so?"

"It is," she replied, and he could sense her sensing his nervousness. "It seems that when you came in to apply, some of them might have remembered you."

"Some of them?"

She laughed. "One or two."

"Oh God."

"You didn't know?"

"Know what?" He could feel sweat bead on his brow. "That some girls I may have met in Spirit Lake were from Omaha?"

"Or worked for your company?"

He laughed. "No, I didn't. To be honest, I don't usually talk work. Who were they?"

"Just some girls," Emma replied. "Nobody important. Did I strike a nerve?"

Ryan nodded. "A little, yes."

"I'm sorry."

"No," he replied. "You don't need to be sorry. *I'm* sorry. I didn't realize my…" He thought about his words. "I didn't realize my reputation was so tanked."

"I didn't say that."

"It was more or less implied."

"Well, I didn't imply it."

Ryan smiled.

"I'm sorry if I upset you," she said after a moment.

Ryan sighed. "No, you're fine. I just…"

"Don't like people talking about you."

Ryan considered it. "Kind of, yeah. I mean, even if it's true."

Emma nodded. "I understand. True stuff is the worst. People talk about me all the time. Especially with this engagement."

"Yeah?"

"It's as though every day I'm not announcing a date, they think something's up, and to be honest, them being right is what hurts the most. I don't like it when they're right."

Ryan debated furthering the comment, but considered against it.

"Well," he said after a moment, "I won't judge you. I mean, I'll judge you, but only based on what we talk about, not what someone else says."

She turned and looked at him. "I appreciate that," she replied. "And likewise, to you."

Ryan smiled.

Soon they were to the river and walking alongside it. The Missouri flowed fast in the opposite direction, and Ryan admired its tenacity as they strolled. Occasionally, a tree trunk or large log would float downriver past them, and it proved quite a sight to see such force. It was as though the river provided the only turbulence on an otherwise bright and beautiful day.

"Have you ever been there?" Emma pointed after a few moments of bliss.

Ryan spied the large building on the left of the river walk. "I haven't been anywhere down here."

"Well," she replied, "you're in for a real treat. Do you like museums?"

Ryan couldn't remember the last time he was in one. "I do."

"You do?"

Ryan sensed that his tone had indicated a falsity. "I really do. I just haven't been to one in a while."

She approached the building and increased her pace toward the door. "Well, this is a neat one. Mostly history."

Ryan looked at the door as they entered: *Lewis and Clark National Historic Trail Visitor Center.*

"Everyone always talks about the zoo here," Emma continued as they entered the large building, "but I think Omaha has some good museums too."

Ryan found himself immersed in the nineteenth century, as exhibits full of animals and recreated settings surrounded the space.

"What do you think?" she asked as she watched his reaction upon entering.

"This is pretty cool," Ryan replied as he stared at an old rowboat surrounded by thick faux trees.

"Right?"

"Do you come here often?" He moved to a glass case full of tools and other devices.

"Here? No," she answered. "I mean, I've been by myself a couple times, but you kind of look weird when you do that."

"No one else finds this interesting?" Ryan replied, knowing full well that his question was much denser than it appeared.

She seemed to catch on. "Not really, I guess."

Ryan moved on to a map that showed the entire westward expansion. "St. Petersburg has a history museum. We went once, but it was pretty small," he said as he stared at the map.

"Is Florida's history very interesting?" she asked as she stared at the map alongside him.

"No," he replied with a laugh. "Not like this." He motioned to the large map complete with trails and battle sites. "Florida pretty much goes from Spanish settlement to Seminole Wars to retirement communities."

She laughed next to him.

"And honestly, we typically skip everything pre-Walt Disney and Tony Montana."

"Who's Tony Montana?"

Ryan turned. "Tony Montana? *Scarface?*"

Her face remained blank. "Is that a movie?"

He nodded. "It is a movie."

"Oh," she replied. "I'm not a huge movie person."

Ryan considered the thought as she moved on to a new map, this one of the Plains Indian Wars.

"So St. Petersburg doesn't have any other museums?"

Ryan appreciated her ability to change subjects. "Well, they're famous for the Dalí Museum, and Tampa has an aquarium."

"I like aquariums," she replied as she stared at the map. "Art is alright."

"But you prefer history museums?"

She shrugged. "I just like learning things. I hated history growing up, so now I'm trying to learn how to love it."

"Fair enough," Ryan replied.

The remainder of the museum passed by in a blur as Emma and Ryan moved throughout the rooms before exiting and returning to the main walkway along the river.

"For what it's worth," Emma said after some moments, "the girls at work never pegged you as a museum guy, so you've already exceeded expectations."

Ryan smiled. "I guess that begs the question—what did they peg me as?"

She lifted her eyes upward, as though thinking of the answer. "Oh, I don't know. I think the word 'playboy' was thrown around. Maybe 'Lothario' is another."

"That's a fancy one."

"It's from a book, I believe."

Ryan smiled.

"But yeah," she concluded, "that was pretty much their summarization."

"Do you believe it?"

"Well," Emma answered, "as I know nothing about your love life, I'd say I haven't enough information."

"Well, you can ask me," Ryan replied.

"I suppose I can. Though you could lie…"

"I won't," Ryan responded.

"You won't? That sounds like what someone who lies would say."

"True, but I doubt I'll lie."

"How will I know?"

Ryan thought about the question. "Well, you won't like the answer, so that's how you'll know it's the truth."

"Fine," Emma replied as they walked even slower now. "Mr. Ryan, are you a playboy?"

Ryan smiled. "I…" He trailed off as he thought. "I have earned my dubious reputation."

"Alright," she replied. "And that reputation is clearly not something you take pride in."

"More or less."

"So you maintain it, why exactly?"

Ryan shrugged. It was an answer that eluded him.

"Have you ever been in love?"

Ryan considered it. "Yeah," he replied.

"Yeah?" She stared at him.

"Yeah, I have been in love."

"When?"

"I guess a few years ago."

"That's a long time to be between loves."

Ryan rubbed his hair as they continued onward. "Yeah, well, some of us may not know how to move on so well."

"Oh," Emma replied. "This sounds like a deep story."

Ryan laughed. "Not really, I just recently realized that maybe I haven't moved on from her as well as I thought."

"Did she move on from you?"

"No idea," Ryan replied. "We haven't spoken since."

"And social media?"

"She isn't on it. She's like a ghost."

Emma laughed. "Were you together long?"

Ryan contemplated it. "Three days."

"Oh."

Ryan turned to her. "Crazy, right?"

Emma glanced at him before looking back ahead. "I don't think so."

Ryan nodded. "I appreciate that, but I'm pretty sure it is."

"Why'd you recently realize you aren't over her?"

Ryan considered the question. "Well, her brother randomly messaged me, and just talking to him about her made me think more about it."

"Did he tell you where she was?"

"Not really," Ryan answered. "But he gave me some idea."

"Are you going to go find her?"

Ryan laughed as he looked over at her.

"What? I'm speaking as a friend!"

"Are you?"

It was her turn to chuckle. "I mean, it only makes sense that you can't move on until you get some closure."

"I've heard that somewhere before…"

"Do you think there's a future with her?"

He could barely comprehend the question. "I'm not sure."

"Well, it sounds like it's worth finding out."

Silence overcame them as they walked toward a long bridge that spanned the river.

"What about you?" Ryan asked after a moment.

"What about me?"

"Have you ever been in love?"

Emma considered it. "Odd question to ask an engaged woman."

"Odder still that she hasn't answered instantly."

She laughed. "Yes. I have been."

The silence that lingered begged for interruption.

"You want to ask if I still am, don't you?" she said.

"Kind of, yeah," Ryan replied.

"Well," she stammered for a moment. "I suppose I'm not sure."

"I see."

"I guess I need to figure that out, don't I?"

Ryan contemplated the response. "It can wait."

"Can it?"

Ryan laughed. "Yeah, let that be future Emma's problem."

"Future Emma? She's got a lot of problems."

"Maybe," Ryan replied. "But current Emma doesn't."

They exchanged glances as the sidewalk curved toward the bridge. Ryan attempted to further unlock the girl in the green headband, but it seemed as though she had played all the needed cards already, and any others would be kept close to the vest. He could feel her pain in the idleness of her love situation, though he knew best not to dwell too much on it. It was indeed a future problem. The present was perfect as is.

"Where on earth are we headed?" Ryan said after some uphill walking.

"The Bob Bridge, clearly," Emma responded as she pointed ahead.

"What's the Bob Bridge?"

"You don't know about the Bob Bridge?"

Ryan shook his head.

"The Bob Bridge is the only pedestrian river bridge that connects two states."

"Really?"

"Yeah, and it's super cool."

Ryan laughed. "Is it?"

"Yeah."

"You sure it's the only one?"

"No," she replied, voice now giddy with anticipation. "But that sounds really awesome."

Ryan followed her lead as they stepped onto the bridge that was moderately busy with other patrons.

"This," Emma continued. "This, to me, is the coolest Omaha site."

"A bridge?"

"That connects two states," she corrected.

"Excuse me," he said with a laugh.

"You'll see," she replied, leading him onward.

They passed person upon person as they walked onward over the Missouri River. Ryan happened to catch a glimpse into the raging waters to see that their intensity had not diminished.

"Don't fall in," Emma called out some steps ahead.

"I don't think I will," Ryan replied. He jogged to catch up to her.

"I wish more people would come see things like this," Emma said as they continued their stroll. "It's such a neat idea."

"Where does the bridge go?" Ryan asked as they reached the main span.

"Just across the river to Iowa," she replied. "I haven't walked past the end to see. I assume a casino or something."

"Sounds like Iowa," Ryan replied.

They approached the middle section and Ryan saw a delineation in the concrete showing Nebraska from Iowa. Down the middle was a border indicating the state line.

"Cool, right?" Emma asked.

Ryan stared at it for a few seconds. It was quirky and unique, but also interesting in a way he had not expected.

"Stand in each," she said, prodding him onward.

Ryan smiled as he stepped into Iowa while keeping his back foot in place.

"What a traveler!" Emma cried.

He stepped fully into Iowa and watched as she recreated his movements. Smiling, she stared at him as she stood in two places, and he couldn't help but recall her earlier image, plastered against the Great Wall. Her face here was similar, almost directly the same. She was unrestrained and relaxed. She was fulfilled in a way he could never describe. Standing in such a unique place gave her all the freedom in the world.

The moment lasted only a second before she stepped into Iowa.

"Cool, right?" she asked, breaking him from his memory etching.

"It actually is," he replied.

"And not in any way a rip off from *A Walk to Remember*," she said with a laugh.

Another man mirrored their movements with his family close behind. As he stepped into Iowa, he looked at Emma and Ryan.

"You all want a picture together?" he asked as he laughed at the absurdness of his actions. "I can take your picture."

Ryan turned to Emma, who stammered a response.

"Oh, no," she replied. "We're good. Thank you though."

"Sure," the man replied.

"Do you want me to take one of you and your family?" Emma asked once she regained her composure.

The man turned to his wife and children as each bridged the state line.

"Sure," he said after a moment. He pulled his phone from his pocket and handed it over. Slowly, the family each got into position on the divider mark. Each of the children posed in a way to mirror their parents.

Ryan leaned against the railing of the bridge on the Iowa side. He was only steps from the divide and from the raging waters that flowed beneath his feet, but he cared little about any of that. He watched as Emma steadied the camera on the family with the same blissful smile still etched on her face as before. She slightly turned toward him and smiled even bigger, as if realizing that he was watching her every move.

It lasted a second, but in that moment, Ryan needed no picture. The image of her smile and that camera would forever remain engrained in his brain.

The present was indeed perfect.

Chapter 10
192 Miles from Omaha

"How about you, Ryan?"

The group grew quiet as they all turned to him, and he realized that he had been called on.

"How—" he stammered. "How about what?"

"You alright, Ryan?" Mike asked from his spot next to Donovan.

"Yeah," Ryan replied. "Just daydreaming, I guess. Or tired."

"I hear you," Donovan replied. "It's been a long week."

"What was the question?" Ryan repeated.

"Plans for Memorial Day?" Maria answered.

"Oh," Ryan replied.

"I booked my flight back to D.C. from Wichita," Donovan said. "Not that I'm necessarily looking forward to going home, but a long weekend there is better than Nebraska."

Ryan looked at Mike. "What about you?"

There was a quick glance from Mike to Maria. "I was thinking of taking a nice weekend trip. Maybe head to the Ozarks."

Ryan almost asked Maria her plans, but then thought better of it.

"And you?" Ryan asked Steven.

"Just heading home," Steven replied.

"He already said that while you were dozed off," Donovan said with a laugh.

Ryan chuckled as he turned to Steven. "Sorry, man."

"So, Ryan, any plans?" Donovan said after a moment.

Ryan shrugged. "None yet, but we'll see. I need to make it through Wichita first."

"I know, right?" Mike replied. "This week has been brutal. And I'm not a fan of these Saturday classes."

Ryan nodded as the conversation continued onward without him. He was not a fan of the Saturday classes either, especially since they prevented him from heading back to Omaha.

It had been a long week in Kansas City.

He pulled out his phone and looked at the clock. 8:15 p.m. Tomorrow they would be departing for Kansas for another five days of classes, and the thought of another week was exhausting to say the least. He would rather be anywhere else. He *needed* to be somewhere else.

"You all ready?" Donovan said after the conversation subsided.

"Where you all heading?" Ryan asked as he zoned back in.

"Downtown," Donovan answered. "Power and Light District. Maria says there's some good clubs down there."

"That so?" Ryan asked as she and Mike stood up.

"Something to do," Maria replied. "You coming?"

Ryan looked at his phone.

"Plenty of drinks and KC chicks out there," Donovan said with a smile.

Ryan laughed but remained seated. "No, I'm good tonight."

"What?" the trio said almost in unison.

"Yeah," Ryan said. "I'm good. I might just watch some TV and relax."

"You sure?" Mike replied. "It's Saturday night."

"Yeah, I'm good," Ryan responded.

"Steven?" Maria turned to the man seated next to Ryan.

"Thanks," Steven replied as he got up. "Thanks, but I'm going to head back too. Call the wife and kids, all that."

"At least you got an excuse," Mike replied with a friendly glare towards Ryan.

"Relaxing is a great excuse," Ryan said with a laugh.

"Whatever, old man."

"Have a drink for me," Ryan called out as the trio left the table.

"Come have one yourself," Donovan called back.

Ryan ran his fingers through his hair as he leaned back in the booth. Steven still stood nearby.

"You aren't going?" Steven asked.

Ryan laughed. "No, I'm really not."

Steven stared at Ryan for a moment before he turned away. "Well, I guess I'll go call the wife."

"Good luck," Ryan replied. He thought he almost saw a smile on Steven's face. Soon enough, however, he was gone and Ryan was alone.

Shaking his head, he continued to sit at the table. He allowed his eyes to drift around the restaurant from the half-filled tables to the bar, where a variety of patrons sat in mostly silence.

Ryan scanned the back of their heads instinctually, one after another. Finally, he settled on the back of a younger blonde woman in a rather sleek blue dress. Staring, he could almost imagine her face, from the blue deep-set eyes to her vibrant pink lips and her soft, pale skin that radiated in the bar light. He could see it all, from the way she looked to the way she felt. She was right there, sitting twenty feet away.

The woman at the bar turned and met Ryan's eyes. He looked away, yet after a moment, he found himself looking back, and to his surprise, he found her still staring at him.

Smiling, he stood from the table and grabbed his nearby jacket. She watched him all the way.

He exhaled. He could pretend. He could imagine she was *her.* He could believe it all again.

He began walking, slowly at first, but then much brisker. In seconds, he was to the bar, and a moment later he was past it.

He saw her face turn upon realization. He continued walking. Down the hallway. To the elevator. As the doors opened and then closed, he took another deep breath.

He was done with bars. He was done with pretending. He was done with agonizing over things that were and weren't. He was done with it all.

He was done chasing ghosts.

***

What are you up to on this fine Saturday night?

Ryan lay back on his hotel room bed as he stared at his phone screen, awaiting a reply he hoped would come soon. Finally, he saw three dots of typing.

A thrilling night of reading and rom-coms.

Ryan smiled. *That sounds absolutely thrilling.*

Emma's response was quick in return. *Well, when your roommates are out on dates and you feel like the old hen of the group, this is what you do.*

Ryan turned to his side. *My friends are out clubbing somewhere in KC.*

Sounds exciting. More typing. *You didn't want to go?*

Ryan considered it. *No.* He knew he needed a better answer. *Just wanted to relax tonight.*

There was a small lapse, and Ryan wondered what she was thinking. Then, more typing.

Well, Titanic *is on TBS if you want some real fun.*

Ryan laughed. *I honestly don't know if I've seen it all the way through.*

I've seen a movie you haven't? Whhaaaattt?

Ryan smiled as he turned on his TV. *I know, shocker.*

Well, it's an amazing movie.

Ryan turned the channel to TBS. *Considering you've seen five movies in your life, that's high praise.*

Hey, you. I've seen at least seven.

My apologies.

Ryan alternated between his phone screen and the television. He needed something more to say. *Whatever happened to Billy Zane?*

Immediately he saw her typing. *Who?*

Ryan laughed audibly. *LOL. Her fiancé.*

Oh. I never knew his name.

He was in a few things.

Hold on, I'm IMDB'ing him. Ryan awaited further response. *Nope, haven't heard of him.*

Ryan laughed again. His fingers moved quickly. *He was in* Back to the Future.

Never seen it.

Ryan's mouth went wide. *We'll have to change that.*

Soon, another text from Emma. *His post-*Titanic *roles were a TV Batman show and* Pocahontas 2, *so I'm not sure* Titanic *did much for his success.*

Ryan pulled up the actor's IMDB page as another message from her came in.

He was also in The Silence of the Hams. *Not sure what that is.*

Ryan laughed. *Me either, though I feel like I should.*

Ooh my favorite part is coming up.

Ryan looked up to the television as her messages continued to scroll in.

Here it is.

Ryan watched as DiCaprio stepped through the windowed door and into the main atrium, looking as apprehensive as ever.

He is so young.

Ryan continued to watch him attempt to mimic the other boat patrons as the scene played on. Then Billy Zane walked past.

There's the star of Pocahontas 2.

Ryan laughed as he returned to the screen. In seconds, Kate Winslet appeared, complete with another text.

OMG. That double take when she appears.

Ryan watched her proceed down the stairs. Leonardo took her arm.

I saw that on Nickelodeon once and always wanted to do that.

Ryan laughed again as he read the text. *You really know this movie. I'm shocked you've never seen this.*

Ryan sat further back onto the bed as the movie played on. *I mean, I've seen parts. Like the boat sinking and him not getting on the door.*

So sad!

Ryan considered it. *I just don't think I've watched it start to finish.*

Add another item to the list then.

Ryan smiled. *Fair enough.*

There was a pause as the movie continued.

Another text came in. *What did you all talk about at dinner? Anything good?*

Ryan thought on the question as he typed his response. *Memorial Day plans. Nothing much.*

Her response was quick. *What are your Memorial Day plans?*

Ryan quickly typed out his answer. *Hopefully hanging out with yo—.* He stopped typing and stared at the draft. Quickly, he deleted the response and typed a different message. *Not sure yet. You?*

He held his breath as he saw her typing.

Tennessee.

Ryan exhaled. Of course that was the answer. How could it not be? He stared at her words and sensed that her direct response showed reluctance on her part.

Oh. Well, that's logical. It was the only thing he could think of.

Yeah.

Ryan struggled to find other words to say. His charm was coming up short. *Maybe next time I'm back, we can hang out again.*

He saw her immediately typing. *I'd like that.*

So would I, he typed out. He stared at it intently, judging how it would be received. In seconds, however, he deleted the message. He looked to the television and back to his phone. *This dinner scene is intense*, he typed.

***

It was well after 10:00 p.m. when his phone began vibrating.

Ryan awoke from his brief nap and bolted upright. Instinctively, he reached for his phone and found it near his thigh.

"Hello?" he breathed into the phone.

"Are you still watching?" he heard Emma say.

"What?" Ryan shook his head. "Oh yeah, the movie, yeah."

"Liar," she said softly.

"Alright, I fell asleep maybe ten minutes ago," Ryan explained.

"Well, you have to stay awake for this ending," she said softly. "I wanted to make sure you did."

Ryan turned and saw the TV was still displaying the movie.

"Best ending of a movie," he heard her breathe into the phone.

"You're talking so softly," Ryan breathed back.

"Roommates are home so I have to be quiet," she replied.

Ryan watched as the movie began its ending scenes, with the camera moving back under the water to rediscover the mighty ship.

He heard her begin the iconic melody of the song through the line, and he smiled.

"Your singing voice is impeccable."

"Be quiet," she replied. "Doesn't this just hit you in the feels?"

The ship began to return to its heyday, and the water faded away. Ryan watched as the doors reappeared and then opened to the main atrium in a clear cut to the scene he had first stumbled upon.

"This is my second favorite scene," Emma said through the phone, and Ryan heard a sniffle.

"Are you crying?"

"No," she hurriedly said, though he distinctly heard tissues. "No."

He laughed as Kate and Leo appeared again on-screen before the image faded to white.

"What a movie," she replied innocently through the phone. "Aren't you glad you saw that?"

"It was quite something," Ryan replied honestly.

"You can go back to sleep now, I just wanted to share that," she said quickly. "Sorry for waking you."

"You can wake me anytime," Ryan replied. He rolled his eyes at his own words. "I'm glad you called."

"It's nice to hear your voice," Emma said.

"Same," Ryan replied.

Silence.

"Well," she said. "Good night. Sleep tight."

"You too," Ryan responded. He wondered if he could find any more words to say.

Click.

Ryan pulled the phone from his ear and stared at the home screen. In the background, the *Titanic* credits played on, oblivious to him. He set the phone back on his nightstand and lay back upon his pillow, slowly allowing his eyes to close. Then, in a quick fluid motion, he reached back for the phone and pushed the ringer volume to its highest tone.

Setting the phone back down, he closed his eyes and went to sleep.

***

"Have you ever volunteered anywhere?" Steven asked as he sat across the table from Ryan the next morning. "You don't have to answer, I was just curious."

Ryan sat horizontally on the booth as he sipped his orange juice. "That's a random question to ask."

Steven laughed into his coffee mug. Around him, the restaurant was bustling. "I'm sorry if I offended."

"You didn't offend. To be honest I use to go help with my grandparents at a soup kitchen, but that was a long time ago." Ryan sipped his orange juice as he stared at his counterpart, and he considered how weird it was that he was awake so early on a Sunday while the rest of his group was sleeping off their hangovers. "I assume you have many places that you volunteer?"

Steven shrugged. "Just one." He paused for a moment, as if thinking about how to explain his next words. "It's a men's group where I help with arts and that sort of thing."

Ryan stared at his counterpart. "Men's group?"

Steven nodded. "Yeah," he replied. "So what made you stop volunteering?"

Ryan shrugged. "I'm not sure. I just stopped. Life got in the way."

"And your grandparents?"

"Still do it, I think. I haven't talked to them in a while though." He considered his words. "I guess that sounds pretty selfish now, doesn't it?"

"Not necessarily," Steven replied. "Things happen, even with me."

"You?"

Steven chuckled. "Yes, me."

Ryan leaned forward. "So you haven't been the church-going-master-volunteer your whole life?"

Steven leaned back from his coffee mug as though apprehensive. "Let's just say I didn't handle high school too well. Bad influences. Tough crowds. And my... personality... didn't help."

"Personality?"

Steven raised his eyebrows. "Believe it or not, I used to be a lot chattier and more unable to read a room."

Ryan nodded, though he was not quite sure if he believed it.

"I had some *friends*," Steven said as he air-quoted the last word. "They were a lot like me at first, but as they got older, they matured more towards drinking and drugs. If you think I talk a lot now, imagine me on alcohol."

"How long were you like that?"

"Just a few times," Steven replied. "Then I went to college and the issue stopped being alcohol and started being..." He trailed off as he considered his words. "Adult entertainment."

Ryan felt his jaw drop. "You watched porn?"

Steven shrugged, and for the first time, he seemed in discomfort. "While I was lost yes, yes, I did. But luckily, I had a roommate who attended church groups and did lots of volunteering and I saw him as someone to emulate. One day, I cleared my search history and followed him. Best decision ever."

"What kind of porn?"

"Ryan..."

Ryan shrugged with a smile. "Just asking. Seeing if you got any deep fetishes or not."

"I won't be disclosing that."

Ryan laughed, though his tone turned to ambivalence. "So church groups saved you?"

"That and the men's group," Steven added leaned forward in his booth. "It helps my soul if that means anything. Makes me feel less alone. I bonded more with my wife. I found friends. I discovered a community that accepted me, and in the end, that's what I needed more than anything."

Ryan nodded and said nothing more as he looked off at people in the diner.

"What?" Steven asked after a moment.

Ryan stared at him wide-eyed. "I didn't say anything."

"I know," Steven replied. "But you look like you've got something to say."

"I do?"

"Yeah."

"Well," Ryan said as he sat upright in the booth. "I don't."

"Nothing at all?"

Ryan gnashed his teeth. "You think I'm really fucked up, don't you?"

Steven reeled back from the table. "I never said that."

"Yeah, but you think it, right?"

"Not at all."

"That's why you're sharing your past and all that."

"No, I'm just—"

"You think I'm a train wreck?"

"No, I don't."

"Then why do it?" Ryan's voice balanced between annoyed and accusatory.

"Because..."

"Because why?"

"Because you asked!" Steven replied. "Stop trying to rile me up to say something I'll regret."

Ryan immediately backed away from the table.

Steven took a deep breath and leaned forward. "You asked me so I told you. No ulterior motives." He took another breath. "And no, I don't think you're...effed up. But I do think you think you are—and if I'm being honest..." He looked around the table before dropping his voice to a whisper. "I think you should maybe care less about what I think of you and more about what *you* think of you."

Ryan stared at him, expressionless. His blank face turned slowly to a smile, and then to laughter.

"What?" Steven asked.

Ryan began to cackle hysterically.

"What?" Steven asked, slightly more annoyed.

"You," Ryan howled between laughs. "Your seriousness! Your...intensity!"

Steven sat back. "Oh, I get it," he replied. "I understand." His expression turned from annoyed to irritated.

"I'm sorry," Ryan replied. "I just...forget...that you can have such intensity!"

"Maybe you *are*...messed up," Steven countered. "Maybe you are."

"*'Less about what I think of you and more about what you think of you,'*" Ryan mocked as his mirth continued.

"Alright, alright," Steven replied as he stood up. "I see."

"I'm sorry," Ryan countered. "I'm sorry. Sit. Sit, please," he repeated as his laughter died down. "I promise I'm sorry."

"I bet," Steven countered.

"Alright," Ryan said as he dotted his eyes with his napkin. "Let me make it up to you. Ask me anything."

"What?"

"Ask me anything," Ryan repeated. "You shared your vices; you can ask me anything and I'll answer. Embarrassing or not."

"How is this the same?"

"Just do it," Ryan replied. "Whatever you want. Any of my demons or past transgressions. Do it."

Steven sighed. "I don't think—"

"Do it," Ryan repeated as he sat upright at the table. "You shared, and so will I."

Steven clenched his teeth. "Fine," he said after a moment. "What happened with the Facebook message?"

"The what?"

"The Facebook message," Steven replied. "The one you were debating on responding to. What happened?"

"Oh," Ryan replied. "Well, I responded."

"And?"

"And it went exactly like I thought it would."

Steven nodded. "So you learned about his sister?"

"Apparently they don't talk very much, and when they do, it's safe to say I'm not a discussion topic." Ryan stared out the window nearby, thinking as he spoke. "I'm not really sure what that means." He took a deep breath. "She lives in Hawaii, works in the medical field and attends conferences across the country."

"She travels like you."

"She does," Ryan replied. "All over, apparently. I'm sure California, Texas..." His voice grew softer. "West Palm..."

"Florida?"

Ryan continued to stare outside as he recalled an interesting message received a few nights back. "Yeah, he said she'd be there over Memorial Day. Some conference around then."

"You going?"

Ryan turned his head. "What?"

"Aren't you from Florida?"

"Yeah, and?"

Steven stared. "Well, are you going to see her?"

"I'm from Clearwater...across the state."

"Oh," Steven replied. "So you're not going?"

"Why would I go?" Ryan snapped.

"I don't know," Steven answered. "She seems like someone you want to get ahold of, so I just figured."

"That's the past," Ryan replied. "And it belongs there. Plus, West Palm is a big place. How do I find her in a city of hundreds of thousands?"

"You said she was at a conference. Google medical conferences during that time."

Ryan stared at Steven.

"What if she doesn't want to see me?"

"I'm not telling you to go," Steven replied. "I just asked."

"But you're insinuating."

"I just asked," Steven repeated. "She seems like someone special. I just figured that if you had the opportunity, you'd go, especially with nothing else to do over the weekend."

Ryan's mind immediately went to his initial plans for the weekend. He thought of how one text had completely changed his outlook.

Tennessee.

It hit like a gut punch, the overlooked aspect of a growing passion. She was engaged, and there was nothing he could do.

"If I went," Ryan replied, "what would I say?"

"How do I know?" Steven replied. "I don't even know what she is to you."

Ryan ignored the comment. "How would she respond? Punch me in the face? Hug me? Would she hate me? Does she?" He clicked out of his stream of consciousness and found Steven staring at him.

"Only one way to find out," Steven replied.

Ryan bit his tongue as he took a breath. "You're telling me to go."

"No," Steven replied. "I'm saying that if these questions bother you, then maybe answers are what you need."

"That sounds like you're telling me to go."

"Again," Steven replied, "I know nothing about this situation. I'm not telling you to do anything."

Ryan shook his head. "Well, I could really use some advice one way or another."

Steven stared at him in silence for a moment. "Fine," he said. "Here's another good nugget: 'Therefore do not worry about tomorrow, for tomorrow will worry about itself. Each day has enough trouble of its own.'"

Ryan considered it. "That doesn't help much."

Steven smiled. "Well, I thought it might."

Ryan stared out the window. His mind and his soul were tired—tired of thinking and worrying, and tired of wanting. He wanted things he couldn't have. He wanted a life he didn't lead. Perhaps this was a chance. Perhaps this was his moment of decision. All his struggles and pains, perhaps they had paved the way for this outcome, a chance to reclaim what was lost. A chance to ignore his indiscretions and truly seek what he longed for more than anything else. Perhaps this would lead to peace and a fulfilled life. Perhaps this is what he was meant to do.

"So?" Steven asked as the silence grew on.

"That quote," Ryan replied, turning from the window at long last. "It was Orson, right? Welles?"

"No," Steven said as he shook his head in disdain. "It was Jesus again."

"Damn," Ryan replied with his first true smile in some time. "One day I'll get that right."

Chapter 11
1,764 Miles from Omaha

Ryan exhaled as he sat in the middle seat toward the back of the plane. His hands sat crossed against his chest, and further down, his legs stretched as far into the cramped space as possible. To his left, a woman continued to snore, much as she had done for the entirety of the three-plus hour flight. To his right, a man in a polished suit sat watching a movie Ryan didn't recognize.

Ryan unlocked his arms and rubbed one hand with the other. He looked down at his fingers and saw them shake slightly. He closed his eyes and returned his arms to their crossed position.

It took an eternity for the plane to unload, but once Ryan was able to stand in the aisle, he grabbed his duffle bag from the overhead compartment. Following the man he'd been seated next to, he deplaned swiftly.

Seconds later, he was standing in the terminal surrounded by a variety of people. Through the large airport windows, he saw a mix of palm trees and bright, radiant sunshine. His left hand gripped his bag as he stared out into the Floridian setting, and almost immediately, he felt his right hand begin to tremble. Taking a deep breath, he looked down at his hand and casually slipped it into his pocket.

He was here, for better or worse. He had made it intact.

He had made it to West Palm Beach.

***

"How may I help you, sir?" said a younger woman behind the counter at Enterprise.

"Hi," Ryan replied. "I need a car."

"Certainly," she replied. "Do you have a reservation?"

"No, I don't," Ryan said.

"OK," she responded. "Let's see what we have available. Unfortunately, I know we don't have any compact or economy cars, being that it's a holiday."

"I figured," Ryan replied.

She continued to type into the computer.

Ryan felt his pocket vibrate at his side. Instinctively, he pulled it out and saw a text from Maria.

Are you OK? Steven said you took a personal day today?

Ryan quickly typed his response: *I'm good. Just needed to head out a day early.*

"I only have full-size SUVs," the woman at the desk said. "Will that work?"

"Sure," Ryan replied.

"For how long?"

"Just the weekend," he answered. "Returning on Sunday."

She resumed typing into her computer. Ryan pulled out his license and credit card and set them on the counter.

He felt his phone vibrate again.

That sounds sketchy as hell. Are you ok? Will you be in Kansas on Monday?

Ryan gritted his teeth as he typed a hastened response. *Yes. I promise I'm fine.*

He waited a moment for a reply. *Ok. Whatever you say.*

"Prepay gas or insurance?"

Ryan looked up from his phone and shook his head.

"Alright," the woman replied as she handed over some paperwork. "Out the door behind you and down the stairs to the garage. Give this form to the employee out there and he'll show you to your car."

"Thank you," Ryan replied.

Ryan turned from the desk and began to walk through the automatic doors. His phone vibrated again.

Stopping, he reached for the phone and saw what he had been looking for: a Facebook message from Max Willis.

Seriously? You're in West Palm? Dude, that's awesome. What a coincidence. Last I knew, she was still there, though I think her conference ends today. I'm not sure exactly which one, but the one at the Palm Beach County Convention Center sounds right. I can always reach out to her and ask if you want. Let me know! —Max

Ryan stared at the link below the message to see a convention regarding travel nurses. Gritting his teeth, he hastily typed back. *No need, this is more than enough info. Thanks so much!*

Pocketing his phone, he walked out to the attendant on duty.

"SUV?" the man said as Ryan handed over the slip.

"Yep," Ryan replied.

The man nodded and led Ryan to a row half filled with full-sized vehicles.

"Any in this row," the man said. "Keys are in the cup holder."

"Thanks," Ryan replied as he began briskly walking the row. Instinctively, he reached for the first vehicle he came to, but as he gripped the door handle, his eyes caught a glimpse of a different option across the row. He let go of the truck's handle before walking around it towards the vehicle that had caught his attention. As he approached, he stared at it from front bumper to back, wholly pleased with his find.

"I think this will do," he said confidently.

Seconds later, the truck was in gear and peeling out of the lot.

***

"Hello," Ryan said into his phone as he drove one-handed down the highway. "I was just trying to meet a friend who attended your medical conference. Do you know which hotels were offering discounted rates?"

"Oh sure," the voice on the other end said. "Let me see. There were a few."

Ryan exhaled.

"Looks like the Marriotts of West Palm and Palm Beach Gardens. Then there was also the Westin here in Palm Beach, and the Hyatt as well."

"Thank you," Ryan replied.

"You'll probably want to hurry though," the voice said. "I assume most people are flying back this afternoon."

Ryan nodded, though he knew he couldn't be seen. "Thank you again."

Quickly, Ryan found himself pulling off the highway and onto a shoulder. Staring at his phone, he pulled up one of the hotels in question. Seconds later, he had the phone number and was dialing away.

"Hello," he said after a moment. "Yes, hi, I'm wondering if you have an airport shuttle?" He waited a moment. "No? OK, thank you."

Taking a deep breath, he pulled up the next one.

"Hello, do you have an airport shuttle? Yes? And what is your checkout time? Noon? You wouldn't be able to tell me if a guest was still checked in there, would you? You don't give that information? Understood. Thank you."

He dialed two more numbers, each with a split answer on the questions asked.

"Marriott, Palm Beach Gardens," Ryan said to himself after a moment. "Or Westin, Palm Beach."

He held his thumbnail in his teeth as he considered the options, knowing that any further delay could be detrimental.

"Fifty-fifty…" he said as he thought aloud. Quickly, he pulled his phone up.

"Hello," he said into the device. "I just called about the shuttle. Let me ask one more thing—do you have an on-site restaurant? No? Not on-site? OK, thanks."

Ryan threw the phone into the passenger seat and jammed the car back into drive and returned to the highway. He had a destination. He had an idea. It was now fate's turn.

***

It was just past 11:30 a.m. when Ryan arrived at the Marriott in Palm Beach Gardens. Running his fingers through his hair as he shut the vehicle door, he quickly looked at himself in the side mirror before proceeding across the lot towards the main entrance of the large high-rise hotel.

He approached the automatic doors, and seconds later, he was stepping inside. As he found his feet crossing the barrier, a new feeling plunged itself into his being. He stopped between the sets of doors.

The feeling was deep and overwhelming. It gripped his soul, and it tightened around his mind until nothing was left but a fog. It was a feeling he had not felt in some time, yet one he knew perfectly.

Doubt.

What was he doing? What on earth was going on? *This is crazy*, he thought. *This is completely incredulous.* How could he simply show up, unannounced? How could any of this make sense to her? How did it make sense to him?

It didn't, he knew. There was no sense. There was no logic.

He shouldn't be here. He should be back in Kansas City. He should be with his team. He should be in Omaha. He should be anywhere but here. It wasn't right. Maybe she didn't want…

He blinked wildly as he thought onward. It had been so long. What if she was just inside these doors? What if she was waiting? What if this was exactly what was meant to happen? Maybe Max and the message and the perfectly timed flight and the rental car and the hotel questions, maybe they were all driving him here, to this moment. Maybe the rest of his life awaited on the other side of those automatic doors.

"You alright?" a voice asked from behind him.

Ryan half turned to see a valet staring at him.

"Yeah," Ryan replied unconvincingly. "I'm good. I just…needed a moment."

He turned back to the doors.

"I get it," the valet said from behind. "It's a big hotel."

Ryan closed his eyes and ignored the world beyond him. He took a deep breath. It was now or never. Maybe it was crazy. Maybe it wasn't right. Or maybe it was. He had to know. He had to find out.

He stepped forward. The door opened.

Ryan opened his eyes to see a large lobby that grew skyward as he entered.

Stepping further in, he saw a full set of desks to his left, where a variety of people stood being attended to by the agents. Directing his eyes to the middle of the spacious lobby, he saw a large sign on a decorative easel.

Airport shuttles leave every hour on the hour.

Ryan looked at his watch. 11:42 a.m. He took another deep breath. His eyes darted around the couches in the lobby, but he saw nothing that resembled what he was looking for. For all the commotion in the space, he found himself focused and calm.

He looked to his right to find a large restaurant that opened into the main lobby. Swallowing a now-growing lump in his throat, he moved toward the restaurant, spying on the tables as he approached.

He looked at the bar and found it half full of mostly men. His gaze turned to the outer tables, and still nothing.

What if she's not here?

His eyes continued to move over tables, but still nothing.

She has to be here.

His pulse increased. His brow began to perspire.

She has to be here.

He took a deep breath. His eyes closed.

She has to be here…

He opened his eyes.

His breath caught in his throat.

The first thing he saw was the blonde hair. It was darker than he expected, but he knew it perfectly. Bound into a high ponytail, she sat with her back to him at a table just off the side of the bar. She was clad in a dark blue blazer, and she appeared to be staring at her phone, which lay in front of her on the table. Nearby, a brown roller suitcase sat untouched, as though perpetually awaiting motion that had not yet come.

Ryan began to move. As he drew close, he could see the fair skin just above the blazer edge that made up her perfectly straightened neck. He could see her feet from under her chair, out of their flats, curled upward and resting as though the shoes were nothing more than an inconvenience.

He took one more deep breath as he drew even closer, and in that step, his confidence grew exponentially. He could smell her perfume. He could feel her presence. There was now no doubt in his mind.

"Waiting for someone?" he asked as he approached her side.

There was no startled response. There was no sudden surprise. With a half-smile on her face, Mel looked up from her table.

"Not really," she said, her smile growing in its fullness. "But you showed up anyway."

Chapter 12
1769 Miles from Omaha

Mel watched as Ryan took a seat directly across from her. Steadily, he placed both his hands on the table.

"I'm going to take a guess," Mel said after a moment, "that this *encounter* we're having isn't nearly as random as you're going to make it out to be, is it?"

Ryan felt a smile inch onto his face. He expected nothing less. "What makes you say that?"

She cocked her head to the side.

"What?" Ryan replied. "You don't think this is random?"

"Six years," she countered. "I've avoided Florida for six years, and the first time I'm here, in your home state, you just happen to show up."

"Magic, isn't it?"

"Bullshit is more likely."

"I'm a little offended you avoided Florida for so long."

"Well, someone once told me it was hot, humid, and full of terrible drivers."

"All true," Ryan said as he nodded.

"And that it's a lot of people confined to—and I think this is a direct quote— 'very confined spaces.'"

"The person who told you that sounds pretty smart."

"Words can be deceiving."

"Ouch."

"You earned that."

"True," Ryan replied. "Did you make it to Disney World?"

"My view on happy people hasn't changed much," Mel answered.

Ryan smiled. "If I'm not mistaken, you weren't a fan."

Mel smiled through a side-eye glance. "But seriously," she continued. "Did you stalk me? Did you hack into my work calendar? Social media?"

"We both know you cover your social media tracks well," Ryan replied.

"Not well enough."

Ryan leaned back in his chair. "Why is coincidence so hard to believe?"

"It's not the coincidence that's hard to believe."

"It's a holiday weekend," Ryan attempted to reason. "And the odds of someone spending a holiday weekend in Florida are quite high because everyone in this country loves Florida."

"Specifically West Palm?"

"Well, neither of us are rednecks, so that leaves out the panhandle. And last I knew, we were both relatively poor, so that leaves out Miami. You wouldn't touch the west coast, and because I live there, I wouldn't either, and no one is going to Jacksonville unless they're abducted. So that leaves West Palm, the Keys, and Orlando. One out of three."

"Do you actually believe this?"

Ryan heard the comment but continued in his thought. "Now hotel-wise, you're a smart person, and everyone with a hint of sense knows that the Marriott benefit program is the best of all of them, so it's logical you'd be at a Marriott property." He leaned forward again. "So, factoring in our three locations and the number of Marriott properties in each, our odds are about one in one hundred. Furthermore, factor in the fact that your brother told me you were here, and it made it much easier."

"There it is," Mel replied.

Ryan laughed. "He reached out to me if I'm being honest. And no, it wasn't to talk about you."

"You think I'll believe that?"

"Not at all," Ryan replied. "But it's the truth."

Mel bit her bottom lip as she leaned back from the table.

"Don't be mad at him," Ryan replied.

She turned her head. "Who said I was mad?"

Ryan shrugged. "Well, *mad* is the most unreasonable response to have, and unreasonable generally describes your MO."

She smiled as she continued to stare at him.

"I'll leave," Ryan said in all seriousness. "If you don't want to see me or talk to me, just say the word. I'll be gone."

She took a deep breath. "Last time, it took two cops and a standoff to get you to leave."

Ryan stared across the table. "Maybe I've matured."

She chuckled.

"And for the record," Ryan added, "the standoff and cops leading me away were not a part of my plan."

"Really?" she asked after a moment. "Having a gun pointed at me wasn't what you expected?"

"Technically, it was pointed at me," Ryan said.

She glared at him.

"But no, I don't think I expected to make it to the diner counter where you were, if I'm being honest."

Her face added confusion to her initial glare.

"I thought he would shoot me straight up," Ryan replied. "I didn't expect such resolve on his part. I would have shot me."

"So what?" Mel replied. "You were going to martyr yourself? That was the plan?"

Ryan considered the absurdity of the statement. "It was more of an *oh well* type situation."

"*Oh well?*"

"Yeah," Ryan replied. "Whatever happens, *oh well*. It wasn't well thought out."

"Clearly."

"In all honesty, I just wanted to see you," he said. "I wanted to tell you what I thought and all that. That was my focus."

"And you'd do all that while being shot?" she replied.

"I guess," Ryan replied. "Listen, it wasn't the best plan."

"Clearly," she replied, voice growing in intensity. "And after you've bled out all over the diner floor, did you think about who'd clean it up? Or if anyone else would be innocently shot in the crossfire? And did you think that maybe that place was my family's livelihood, and having a guy get lit up at the diner counter wouldn't be great for future marketing? Did you happen to think about those things while you planned your noble sacrifice?"

Ryan's voice became quite small. "No, I didn't."

He heard her take a deep breath, as though reining in her control. He couldn't recall a time when she had lessened her edge. The silence that grew around them became deafening. He looked down.

"What was prison like?" she asked after a moment.

He looked up to see her in a much calmer state than before. He became unnerved at the sudden change.

"Did they send you to *Papillon* or something?"

Ryan felt a smile cross his face, though his uneasiness continued. "Most people usually go with a *Shawshank* reference. I think you're the first to use *Papillon*."

"I'm nothing if not unexpected," Mel replied, wide-eyed.

"I get some *Green Mile* too," Ryan said. "But honestly, people's prison movie knowledge is generally quite limited."

"It's a shame," Mel replied. "There are so many good ones. Why do they ignore *American History X*? Or *Midnight Express*?"

"Probably because of the prison rape."

Mel sighed. "Fine. What about *Escape from Alcatraz* or *Cool Hand Luke*?"

"Better examples."

"Speaking of that," Mel replied, "I've been watching *Orange is the New Black*, mostly on my plane trips, but it's nice to see female prison representation."

"I'm sure you make a great travel companion for any parents with kids."

"Nosey people shouldn't snoop," Mel replied. "Not my fault."

Ryan laughed, and another silence fell upon them. He quickly found himself lulled back into a state of comfort as he sat across from her.

"Did anyone actually figure out what you went to prison for?" Mel asked.

"The real reason?" Ryan replied. "That someone's cop ex-boyfriend didn't like me talking to his ex and found any reason he could to arrest me?"

"Theft is a pretty good reason."

"To beat the shit out of me?"

"I think *that* was more for the ex-boyfriend part."

Ryan shook his head. "If Bo hadn't hit him, he probably would have killed me."

Mel nodded. "Probably."

Ryan considered her words but remained quiet for a moment. This was not the conversation he had been wanting to have with her. "Where are you living now?" he asked as he smiled.

"You're asking as though you don't already know," she replied.

Ryan chuckled. "Max really didn't tell me much."

"I'm sure he told you enough," she responded.

"You live in Hawaii," Ryan said as he leaned back forward. "And you work traveling in some medical field."

"There you go," she summarized.

"You really don't tell your brother much, do you?"

"He knows what he needs to."

"I think he wants to know more."

"More?"

"Yeah. It seems like you keep him at a distance, that's all."

"Are you an expert on sibling communication?"

Ryan bit his bottom lip. "I've been here maybe ten minutes, and we've already argued at least twice."

"It kind of fits our MO, doesn't it?" Her tone was borderline mocking, and Ryan could sense danger.

"You know I hate the personal questions," she said. "I hate the *past* questions and the *how are you doing* questions. You know that."

"I asked where you were living…"

"And?" she replied. "I don't know where you live. I don't know anything about you or what your past six years were like."

"Then ask."

"And what? Get to know each other again? Is that the plan?"

"I can always leave if you'd prefer."

"I just hate feeling cornered. You had this encounter planned. I didn't. It's a lot. Especially when you ask your prodding questions and I know nothing."

"I live in Iowa," Ryan interjected. "Not Florida, if you believe that."

Her head snapped back from the table.

Ryan considered his previous statement. "Well, I *did* live in Iowa. Now I just have a post office box and an empty apartment that someone else is probably squatting in."

She mulled his words over. "Where in Iowa?"

"Spirit Lake," he replied.

"Where's that?" she asked.

Ryan thought about it. "It's nowhere, really."

"Why there?"

Ryan laughed. "Who the hell knows." He took a deep breath. "Once I was out of the wonderful Florida penal system, I did some traveling and wound up taking a job at an ethanol plant there."

"Where'd you travel?"

Ryan hesitated. "Florida to Shannon. Then I headed back east."

"Not much of a vacation."

"Not really," Ryan replied.

"So you've been working at an ethanol plant?"

"A month ago, I took a new job in the same company. Travel based. Essentially selling our product to prospective farmers. That's where I'm at now. I travel around with a team of people and give PowerPoint presentations on the thrilling subject of fermenting corn."

"Good money?"

"Enough to randomly book a flight from Kansas City to West Palm."

"The American Dream," she replied. "Look at you."

"It could be worse," Ryan responded. "Get to see new places. Try new things."

"Bang random chicks and leave," Mel added.

Ryan felt the breath catch in his throat.

"I'm sorry," Mel replied. "Do you prefer 'meet-up' or 'romance' instead?"

Ryan bit his lip again. "I think 'hook up' is a more proper term."

Mel laughed. "I think you're right."

"Is that enough information for now?" Ryan asked in a desperate attempt to change the subject.

"Does that mean you want to know about me?"

"No pressure," Ryan answered. "We can talk prison rape or any other subject if you'd prefer."

"Travel nurse is the proper term for my job," she replied. "Though I feel like the travel is sometimes negligible."

"You don't travel?"

"I expected a lot of international work," she replied. "War torn nations and all that. That's what I prepared for."

"But you don't go there?"

"No," she replied. "Though I do spend a lot of time in Texas, if that counts."

Ryan smiled.

"Fucking Texas," she said as she exhaled. "Overall, I mostly do a lot of domestic work."

"What made you go into nursing?"

She shrugged. "In-demand job. I can be anywhere. It just made sense."

"And the writing?"

She didn't respond, and he could sense he had struck a desolate nerve.

"Of course you'd remember that," she said.

"How could I forget?" Ryan found himself lost in admiration. "Your poetry was quite good. Plus, your thesis on classic novels? It was good. Really good." He paused. "Hell, I expected you to be a published philosopher or novelist by now."

"A victim of necessity," she replied after a moment.

Ryan considered her words and knew just how true they were. "Well hey, at least you're in Hawaii."

She nodded slowly. "Yeah. Yeah, I am."

"What?"

"What?" she repeated.

"You don't like Hawaii now?"

"I never said that."

"You implied it."

"I didn't."

"Okay fine, you implied you aren't happy."

"Did I?"

Ryan smiled. "Yeah, you did."

Now it was her turn to smile. She stared off towards the bar and the silence grew around them. He watched her intently and studied her face. There was so much he remembered—the deep, oceanic eyes that were both calming and entirely alert, the skin that shown naturally beautiful despite being hidden behind clothing or makeup, the way single strands of hair fell around her ears as though escaping the ponytail they were confined to. It was as though her whole being was conflicted with itself.

"Where did six years go?" she said in a voice that Ryan had not yet heard. It was anguished. It was labored. It was honest.

"I don't know," Ryan replied.

She turned to him but said nothing.

Ryan leaned forward, and for once, he knew exactly what to say. "How about no personal questions?"

He watched as she swallowed the lump in her throat.

"Just the here and now," he added.

She nodded, and her eyes lit up. "I can work with that."

"Good," Ryan said. "The past doesn't matter. We are where we are."

She leaned back in her chair. "I couldn't have said it better myself."

"So what are you doing now?"

"Now?"

"Yep," Ryan replied. "Now. Today. Tomorrow. This weekend."

She laughed as she looked down to her bag. "Well, I'm pretty sure I'm going to board a flight to L.A. before a nice two-hour layover, and then another flight to Honolulu."

"Why?" Ryan asked directly.

"*Why?*" she asked incredulously. "Because I'm going home, Ryan."

"Why?" Ryan repeated.

"Because home is where people go when they're done working."

"But it's a holiday weekend."

She glared at him. "You don't strike me as a Memorial Day celebrator."

"Don't go home," he said, ignoring the comment. "Stay here."

"Stay here?"

"Yeah," he answered. "Stay with me."

She scoffed. "Why is that a good idea?"

"I'm not sure it is," Ryan replied. "But if history is any indication, we'll have a good time together."

"You must remember history differently than I do."

"Then let me make it up to you," Ryan countered. "No stress. No personal questions. Just me and you and a good time. When you're done, I'll personally drive you to the airport."

"I assume you have something planned for this good time?"

Ryan shrugged. "Not really, honestly," he said. "But we'll get out of this hotel for sure. Maybe drive south."

"South?"

"Yeah, south," Ryan said. "We'll drive down past Miami and get out in the Keys. Just drive. Unless you're already tired of islands…"

She smirked.

"There's no reason not to," Ryan argued. "Worst thing that happens is we part ways, and six years from now, you'll avoid Florida."

"Something tells me that will only work for so long," she countered.

Ryan laughed. "What do you say?"

Mel looked down at her luggage, and Ryan could tell the decision weighed heavily. He wanted to say more, he wanted to do anything to make her agree, yet he remained silent.

"You still got that charm about you," she said.

Ryan chuckled. "Is that so?"

"Yeah," she replied. "It almost makes up for the whiney, self-loathing other parts of you."

"Suddenly that doesn't feel much like a compliment."

"Do you have a car?" she asked.

"No, I walked here from the airport," Ryan mocked.

She glared daggers at him.

"Yes," he replied, internally chastising himself for joking at such a critical moment. "I have a car."

"Alright," she replied, though her voice still didn't exude confidence. "Let's see it."

***

"You're shitting me," Mel said as they strolled through the parking lot.

"What?" Ryan replied as he moved to the tailgate.

"Of course you'd rent a Jeep," she said.

"It's what they had available," Ryan said as he stood waiting for her luggage.

She shook her head as she moved her luggage back to him. He loaded it up next to his own bag.

"I'm sure it is," she replied as she opened the passenger side door.

"It is," Ryan pleaded as he shut the tailgate. He moved to the driver's door and opened it before climbing inside.

"And it just so happens to be the car you had the first time I saw you."

"That one was a bit older," Ryan replied. "But it is quite a coincidence, isn't it?"

"Is anything you say true?" she asked as she buckled her seat belt.

Ryan considered the statement. "Yeah," he answered. "It's true when I say I'm really happy to see you." He turned to look at her, and for a moment, their eyes met.

She smirked as she turned back to the window. "There's that charm again."

"Call it what you want, but you're in the car," Ryan replied with a laugh. He quickly started the engine.

"I'm already regretting it," she countered sarcastically.

"Come on," he argued. "There's so much time ahead of us to regret. Don't worry about doing it now."

He heard her audibly laugh. "Just drive," she concluded.

Ryan shifted the Jeep confidently into gear with one more glance to his passenger. "With pleasure," he replied.

Chapter 13
1,903 Miles from Omaha

The late May sun beat down on the Jeep as it careened down Highway 1 from the mainland of Florida and into Key Largo.

Ryan kept one hand on the wheel and another down at his side as he drove onward, occasionally glancing to see what his counterpart was doing. Most of the time, he found her staring off into the mangroves with no expression on her face. She said little, and deep down, he found it harder than normal to decipher her mood. Perhaps she was quiet out of discomfort, or perhaps it was out of agitation. Perhaps this was all a mistake after all.

Regardless of her reasoning, he felt his confidence waning. Instinctually, he pressed the gas petal slightly harder than before, hoping that the destination would improve the morale.

"Do you have any friends?" Mel finally asked.

Ryan considered the question for a long while.

"Is it a confusing question?" she asked.

"Kind of," Ryan replied. "I'm just curious how this doesn't fit into a personal question."

He turned to see her smile next to him.

"You don't have to answer," she replied. "I just figured I'd ask."

"What do you define as *friends*?" Ryan asked.

"I have to define it?"

"Yeah."

"You know that by asking that question, you're essentially answering mine."

"Maybe we have different definitions of the word," Ryan replied.

"Okay." She breathed deeply. "What's your definition?"

"My definition?"

"Yeah, how do you define a *friend*?"

Ryan considered the question. "Well, I figure a friend is someone who you have commonalities with," he reasoned. "Someone who you enjoy being around."

"That's a vague answer," she replied.

"Do you have a better one?"

"You can have commonalities with any number of people, that doesn't make them friends," she argued. "Plus, just being around someone doesn't make you friends. It means you tolerate them."

Ryan gritted his teeth as he kept his eyes ahead.

"Try again," she concluded with a smile.

"I feel as though anything I say will be below your standards," Ryan replied.

She smirked. "Then up your standards."

"Fine," Ryan said. "A friend is…" He trailed off as he thought. "A friend is someone whose funeral you'd go to without being required."

"Wow," Mel replied. "That's dark."

Ryan didn't respond.

"And still incorrect."

Ryan scoffed. "Of course it is."

"People go to other people's funerals just to make sure they're dead," she said. "That doesn't sound like a friend."

"Have you ever gone to a funeral to make sure someone's dead?"

"No," Mel replied. "But I also don't go to funerals."

"That's a very Mel thing to say," Ryan countered.

"Funerals are depressing as hell," Mel argued. "They're full of crying people and other people trying to look good just by attending, when the person they're actually *remembering* couldn't give a rat's ass about what goes on."

"Dissing funerals and religion all at once," Ryan mocked.

"It's true," Mel replied. "Tell me it's not."

"I haven't been to a funeral in a long time," Ryan said.

"Funerals are dumb, take my word for it," she replied. "Who are they for anyway? Not the dead person."

"I think they're more for the family," Ryan countered. "For closure."

She turned and glared at him.

"What?" Ryan could see her gaze over his arm.

"Closure?"

"I mean, it makes sense."

"There's no such thing as closure, especially in death," Mel replied. "I'm a little alarmed you'd even suggest it."

"I didn't say I *believe* in it," Ryan said unconvincingly.

"Closure is a made-up term for people who can't accept what is and what isn't. Something happens and then we try to make it reasonable, and if it isn't reasonable to us, then we search for closure, especially in death. We say, 'she lived a good life,' or 'she's in a better place,' or some bullshit like that. We seek closure for actions of other people, when in reality, we'll never understand why others do what they do, just like they'll never understand how their actions make us feel."

Ryan bit his tongue. "That feels directed towards me."

Mel's eyes narrowed. "Or my dead mom, but yeah, make it about you."

Ryan felt the air deflate from the car as he continued to drive on.

"Closure," she breathed out as she spoke. "Closure isn't for funerals. Closure is for weddings."

Ryan chose his words carefully. "To be honest, I was going to say that friends come to your wedding," he said slowly. "But I figured that wouldn't go over well either."

She smiled and he did as well.

"I take it that if I died, you wouldn't be coming to my funeral." Ryan bit his lip as he awaited the answer.

She turned to him and stared for a moment. "You'd be correct," she replied. "I will come to your wedding though."

Ryan laughed nervously. "Oh, you would?"

"Yeah," she replied. "Hell, I'd even bring a gift."

"Ah," Ryan said.

"I'd make sure to offer the bride my condolences," she mocked. "And then tell you that she's completely out of your league."

"You say that now?"

"Yep," she replied. "Doesn't matter who she is. That's what I'd say, and that'd be the truth."

"That's very generous of you."

"What are friends for?" Mel replied with a laugh.

Ryan felt a pain in his chest as he continued with his foot on the gas.

"So are you going to answer the question?" Mel said.

"The question?"

"Do you have any friends?"

Ryan shook his head. "I have some friends."

"Like?"

"A couple in Iowa."

"Names?"

"Why?" Ryan replied. "You plan on doing some stalking?"

"Maybe," she countered as she stared at him. "Hey, I'd learn from the best."

"I didn't stalk you," Ryan argued softly.

"Okay," she mocked. "Names?"

"Stein," he replied. "Aaron."

"You good friends with him?"

Ryan shrugged. "We're friends."

"Have you talked to him recently?

"What's recent?" Ryan replied.

"That's a no," she inferred. "Who else?"

Ryan nodded, knowing he was getting nowhere.

"Come on," she replied. "Who else?"

"I don't know," he said. "I guess I work with a couple people who may consider me a friend."

"Do they?"

"Yeah." He contemplated his words. "One particularly, but I think I'm a bit too perverse for him."

"You sure he's a friend then?"

Ryan's initial laugh turned into a wry chuckle.

Mel leaned her head on her arm. "So who else is your friend?" She waited as he thought. "Come on, you have to have some."

Ryan exhaled. "I think this is pointless."

"Any childhood friends? Any people from Florida?"

Ryan considered it.

"Who were your school friends? Who did you associate with?"

Ryan adjusted his hands on the wheel. "I didn't really associate with anyone. I had people I'd talk to and maybe hang out with."

"Names?"

Ryan grated his teeth. "I guess there was Al and Kenny. More when I started working."

"Where'd you work? First job?" She turned to sit, facing him.

"Chuck's Chicken."

"What the fuck is that?"

Ryan laughed. "It's a chicken restaurant." He could almost feel her glare.

"I get that," she replied. "But like, fried chicken?"

"No," he said. "It's more sandwiches and that. You've never had one?"

"No," she answered. "And based on the name, I hope to never have it."

He chuckled.

"So, who were your friends at Mr. Chuck's?"

Ryan bit the inside of his cheek. "My best friend there was Michael."

"Michael?"

"Yeah."

"Al and Kenny and Michael?"

"Yep."

"What happened with them?"

Ryan shrugged. "I don't know. Al and I went to elementary school together, but we ended up going to different high schools. Kenny and I went to different colleges."

"And Michael? When did you stop being friends?"

Ryan thought about the question. "I don't know if we ever *stopped* being friends."

"When did you last see him?"

"Do you have a point with this?"

"Eventually," she replied.

Ryan smiled at her brashness. "It's probably been many years."

"Many years?"

"Yeah," Ryan replied. "At least since I graduated college."

"Did you work at Chuck's Chicken throughout college?"

"On and off," Ryan replied. "Then after college, I began a wildly successful career at a department store that ended with me fleeing the state."

"And Michael?"

"We just didn't talk again."

"That's your answer?"

"It's the truth."

"Didn't you go back to Florida after Shannon?"

"Yes."

"For years?"

"A couple."

"And all that time? You didn't once reach out?"

"I couldn't exactly leave the house."

"Probation? No phone calls? Nothing? Hell, you didn't even talk on Facebook?"

"I hope you're getting to a point here."

"When did friends stop being important?"

It was a question so honest and raw, yet full of the same kind of brazen force that he had, for so long, remembered in her. What was left of the pain in his chest subsided completely.

"When did we get to the point where we just didn't care anymore?" She shook her head. "The people that we worked so hard to manage throughout those formative stages, we just now don't need? It's weird. Why do we let them go?"

"Some people can do it," she continued. "Some people can keep their friends, but you and I, we're just not made like that. I wonder why that is."

He stared off ahead of the car.

"Friends are people we use," she concluded. "We use them to learn from or grow from, and in turn, they do the same to us. They're people we have connections with for a period lasting minutes or decades. They're who have our backs so we're not all alone in this hellhole of a world."

Ryan smiled. "That's both poetic and amazingly cynical."

"I think that defines me well," Mel replied. She turned away from him and returned to the window as she peered out across the turquoise waters they drove along. "You didn't mention that guy you were with in Shannon. The guy who *saved your life*."

Ryan thought about her words. "Bo?"

"Yeah," she countered. "He not your friend anymore?"

Ryan shrugged as he continued driving onward. "No, he is."

Mel let the answer linger. "You sure?"

"Yeah," Ryan replied. "He is. We just haven't seen each other in a while."

"How long?"

He smirked. "Six years."

"You see," she replied. "I'm going to guess that you probably won't even keep up your with the *friends* you have now, especially since the one already finds you too *perverse*."

Ryan considered it as he turned to her. "I guess we'll just have to wait to find out."

He could see her smirk in the reflection of the window. "There's that witty charm," she said faintly.

"What was that?" he asked.

Her smile grew in the reflection as he stared at it, unbeknownst to her. Somehow, despite the topics of the conversation at hand, he had felt as though maybe, just maybe, he had begun to chisel down her defenses.

"Nothing," she said aloud as she continued her ocean stare smile.

Ryan smiled as he turned back to the road. If there had ever been pain in his chest before, it was all but forgotten now.

He lifted his foot off the gas ever so slightly. Despite his early premonitions and fears, this was now a drive he didn't mind taking slow.

***

"I honestly don't recall ever seeing you wear a purse," Ryan said as he wiped his face across the table from Mel.

She looked up from her plate before looking over to her right to see her bag in question. "What?"

"Your purse," Ryan explained. "I don't remember you ever wearing one. Or having one. All that time in Shannon."

"Three days?"

Ryan laughed. "I don't know why I don't remember it."

"Well, considering you visited in December, maybe it was cold and I was hiding it. Or maybe I didn't need one, considering I didn't really need car keys or money."

"Maybe," Ryan replied.

"Are you insulting my womanhood?"

"No!" Ryan replied quickly. "I just don't remember it, that's all. I mean, I never saw you in business attire either."

She looked down to see that she still wore the same white button-down blouse she had been in since first seeing Ryan. "Well, professional attire wasn't necessarily required at the truck stop diner."

Ryan laughed.

"Same with you," Mel countered after a moment. "Khaki pants and a plaid button-down are a long way from the Busch Gardens sweatshirt."

"I'm sure that left quite an impression," Ryan replied.

"That you were either twelve or extremely poor."

"Both were indeed possible."

"I figured as much."

"Attire was not very high on my list during that journey."

"Clearly," Mel replied. "But it's nice to see some things change. You look decent all polished up."

"Decent?"

"Yeah," she answered. "Decent. It's a good change."

Ryan smiled and took a sip of his drink, noticing that his previous highball glass was still on the table.

It was early evening in Key West as they sat at the outdoor patio of the seaside restaurant. The air was warm with a light breeze rustling through the filled tables, and Ryan felt at home in the setting. His sleeves rolled upward, he sat comfortably across the table from Mel, who continued to nibble at the food on her plate.

"Speaking of change," Ryan said after a few moments. "You really don't write anymore?"

Mel emptied her margarita glass and stared upward at him.

"You don't have to answer," Ryan replied, "but I did answer your friend question."

She looked off to the side and bit her lip.

"Another round?" the waiter asked as he approached and removed their plates.

"Yeah," Mel replied without looking to Ryan. "That'd be good."

The waiter moved away, but Mel's glance didn't return. Finally, after a long deliberation, she looked back to Ryan. "No," she answered. "I pretty much stopped writing once I left Shannon."

Ryan nodded. "Any reason?" He could tell he was pushing the subject into dangerous territory. "You were seriously good at it."

She took a deep breath and another drink. "I told you," she replied. "Life. Life happened. Writing... there just was no longer time for it."

Ryan stared at her. After several moments of silence, he could see her grow more and more uncomfortable.

"Fine," she said as she took another drink of her now-empty glass. "When I left Shannon shortly after your self-martyrdom, I didn't really plan much. I just left. I had a friend out in California, and I showed up at her door, and then I took it one step at a time. I worked, I went to the local community college for a bit, and after four years or so, I was able to make it out from under all my debt."

"How'd Hawaii come up?" Ryan asked as the waiter brought another round by.

She smirked. "LinkedIn."

"You're shitting me. Someone actually got a job from LinkedIn?"

"I know." She laughed. "I'm one of the few who kept mine updated."

"Of all the socials I could have stalked you on," Ryan replied.

"You missed that one."

"Damn," Ryan followed. "So you just took an offer to nurse out there?"

"Yeah," she replied. "Went out all on my own. I got off the plane and had the whole world in front of me. It was surreal."

Ryan smiled. "That's wild."

"Yeah," Mel concluded. "Once there, I really found my own. Moved a few times. Eventually landed my current job."

"And no writing."

"And no writing." She contemplated her response. "I think about it from time to time, but between the twelve-hour days and the travel, I just don't have time."

"What do you think of?"

"What?"

"Writing. You said you think about it from time to time. What do you think of?"

"Nothing. Just ideas, I guess."

"Like?"c

She smiled. "Like ideas," she replied. "And they're only for me to hear for now."

He nodded as he ran his fingers across his glass. Her mystery was always most appealing.

"Ready to get out of here?" he asked after a moment.

"And go…?"

"Walk?" Ryan offered.

She considered the request before finishing her drink.

"Does that mean yes?" Ryan inquired.

"Sure," she replied with a smile. "Why not?"

***

Duval Street was littered in patrons and vibrant buzzing lights as Ryan and Mel stumbled out of one of the numerous bars, each holding a beer in their hands. While still coherent and accessing most of his senses, Ryan could distinctly feel a tipsy nature to his movements. His words, however, didn't seem to stumble.

Mel, on the other hand, didn't seem much fazed by the wave of rounds. In fact, Ryan found her distinctly upbeat and in full control of her movements. He was a little surprised, given how the evening had progressed.

"What about you?" she asked as they strolled.

"What about what?" Ryan replied.

"Well writing has been a casualty of my life, so what has been a casualty of yours?"

"Casualty?"

"Yeah," she repeated. "Your cost." She took another drink. "What costs have you had to make in becoming," she stared up and down at him. "You."

"Who said I had any costs?" Ryan replied with a laugh. He could feel his vision blur slightly.

"I did," Mel replied. "I said you did."

"Why?"

"Come on, Ryan," she replied. "In all your years to get here, you haven't made any sacrifices?"

"I don't think so," Ryan replied.

"Friends?" Mel countered. "I know that's at least one."

Ryan took another swig. "What about it? It is what it is."

"Family?"

"Just fine."

"So you still talk to your parents every week?"

Ryan laughed. "I talk to them enough."

"You're just...perfect?"

"I didn't say that," he answered. "But everything I've done has gotten me here, so I can't complain."

"You can still be remorseful for the things you've lost along the way."

"What good is that?" Ryan replied. "It doesn't change anything."

Mel laughed.

"Listen," Ryan said as they reached a large open square. "I've had regrets, sure, but lately, they do nothing for me. I am who I am, and I'm doing just fine with that."

"Confidence," Mel summarized with a weak smile. "Unbridled confidence."

"Oh, come on," Ryan replied. "Are you going to tell me you, Queen of all the Cynics, sit in your Hawaiian home and contemplate your regrets?"

Mel began to walk further into the square as Ryan followed. "I didn't say that," she answered.

"That's what I thought," Ryan replied.

"But I at least know I have them," she countered.

"I have them too," Ryan replied. "I just don't feel like dwelling on them. I like who I am."

He could see her smile weakly alongside him.

"You going to tell me your other regrets now?" he asked as their slow walk finally found the edge of the island. Beneath their feet, the calm gulf waters lapped at the rocks as the streetlights illuminated the scene. Around them, all matter of activity was ongoing, from people strolling along to street performers surrounded by crowds of people.

"That seems quite personal," Mel replied as they both stood and surveyed the scene.

"I won't tell," Ryan said with a smile. His vision blurred, and he could feel the alcohol taking over.

Mel considered it. "I'll tell you what," she replied. "I'll answer one question honestly. Anything you ask. But that's it. You get one."

"One?"

"I'm feeling generous," she replied as she leaned against the railing. "And tipsy."

"Well, let me think," Ryan said.

"While you think, I'll walk," she replied as she tossed her beer bottle into a nearby trash can. He watched as she began walking onward, past a musician with a guitar in hand who sat strumming with eyes closed. Slowly, she stopped as though admiring the music he played.

Ryan felt the breath catch in his throat as he stared at her before him. Suddenly, he felt removed from the setting entirely. He was no longer in Mallory Square. He was no longer in Key West. He was no longer in Florida.

It was snowing. He was sitting in the driver's seat of a Jeep he owned six years ago. Through the windshield, he saw her, just as she was now, just as she'd been then.

She looked upward, as though a thousand stars held her attention. The smile on her face was pure, blissful. She looked down at the snow with her back still half turned, and he watched as she bit her lip, as though she had never been more content.

He knew this memory; he had dreamt it a thousand times. He, in his car; she, just beyond his reach in front of him. He, wondering what the next move would be, knowing that it just might change everything. This moment was all he had wanted. It was all he had dreamt of. It was all right here before him, as it had been six years ago.

"I thought of my question," Ryan said as he walked up to where she stood.

She turned fully as the guitar sounded around them. "And?"

"Will you dance with me?"

He watched as she swallowed the lump in her throat. "Dance?"

"Yeah," Ryan replied, holding out his hand.

"That's your question?"

He nodded.

She looked around, as though unsure of the situation.

"You can say no," Ryan replied, though he hoped she would not.

Wordlessly, she took his hands and slowly pressed herself to him. For a moment, awkwardness ensued as their drunken steps attempted to mirror one another. Before long though, they were perfectly synchronized, dancing beautifully to the musician's chords.

After a moment, she leaned her head against his chest, and he inhaled deeply as he caught the scent of her hair, of her. He closed his eyes as he both recalled and once again memorized how she felt as she lay against him. It was just as it was in his memory, except now her scent had matured. He even caught a faint smell of smoke from her, and he wondered if it was new or just never noticed.

Together, they rocked back and forth, as the dance continued onward.

He wanted to say more. He wanted to tell her things he had never said before, things about *love* and how she made him feel. He wanted to say all these things, yet somehow, the words would not come.

"Are you okay?" he said.

She pulled back slightly as her eyes met his, and in that moment, he saw an openness that he had missed before. He saw her fragile, vulnerable. He saw a wistfulness in her eyes, as though there were words she wanted to speak as well. Perhaps she wanted to say what he did. Perhaps they were perfectly in sync. Perhaps he even saw a tear in her eye.

She pressed her head back into his chest as they continued dancing.

It was a wonderous setting in a flawless locale. The music played onward, combined with the slight breeze that rattled the palm trees and the streetlight glow, adding to the ambience around them. He couldn't have pictured a better setting. It was almost perfect.

He allowed the alcohol to take full effect as he became indifferent to the world around him. There was no more scents. There was no more tears. All that mattered was her. All that mattered was this moment. He wanted it to continue into eternity.

It was perfect. It was almost perfect.

Chapter 14
2,000 Miles from Omaha

Sunlight cascaded in through the curtains as Ryan stirred. He moved his hands to his closed eyes and rubbed them.

His head burned while his eyelids remained closed. As he attempted to open them, he found the light from the window exacerbated his pain. He returned his hand to his side as he continued to lay still.

The sheets he laid upon were cool and comfortable. Even with his eyes closed, he could feel the peace and solace in the space. His ears detected little in the way of noise other than the hum of the air conditioner. It was almost as though he were alone.

Did he remember where he was? Did he remember anything? What had happened last night? Had he said something stupid? Had he done something stupid? He could barely recall anything.

He tried once more to open his eyes as he turned onto his side. The pain was blinding, but somehow, he managed to get them focused.

The first thing he saw was the nightstand, which was adorned with a lamp and a clock reading 8:00 a.m. Next to the clock, he saw his wallet and watch, though there was no organization in their placement.

Looking past the stand, he spied the large window behind airy, white curtains. Sunlight illuminated the entire space, and as his eyes focused further, he saw his clothes on the floor.

He raised slightly and waited for the world to stop spinning. In that moment, he heard a rustle to his left. Turning, he saw Mel standing between the bed and the door, fully dressed, bag in hand.

"Shit," she muttered.

Ryan sat up and shook his head as he attempted to focus on her. "What's going on?" he asked through blinking eyes.

She said nothing and continued to stand.

"What...happened last night?" Ryan asked as he rubbed his brow. He swallowed several times as the risk of vomiting grew with each motion.

Mel continued to be silent. Ryan turned his eyes back to her and saw a similar hungover look on her face. Her hair was tied back into a disheveled ponytail and her blouse was wrinkled in multiple places.

"Apparently," she said, "we got a hotel room."

Ryan breathed as he continued to compose himself. "Apparently." He moved his legs toward the edge of the bed. "Do you remember anything?"

"Dancing," Mel replied curtly. "And then walking back up the street. It gets a little hazy after that."

"How did we get a room?" Ryan questioned.

Mel shrugged. "It seems we used my credit card," she answered as she pulled it from her pocket. "It was sitting on the nightstand."

"Oh," Ryan replied. He smiled as he put his feet on the ground. Slowly, he closed and opened his eyes again before turning to look at the bedsheets. "Did we...?"

She remained stoic. "Don't..." she said.

Ryan took a deep breath as he turned back to look at the giant window. "Where, uh..." He attempted to speak, but his stomach made it tough. "Where are you off to?"

Mel looked down to her clothes, and then to the bag in her hand. "I'm—" she said. "I'm leaving."

"Leaving?"

"Yeah."

Ryan rubbed his fingers through his hair. "Oh." He tried to stand but found it difficult. "Well, hang on," he said. "I'll be ready in a few."

"No," Mel replied. "I'm leaving alone."

Ryan heard the comment, but it made no sense. "Alone?"

"Yeah, alone."

"Where are you going?" Ryan said as he turned back to her.

She gritted her teeth. "I'm going home, Ryan."

"Hawaii?"

"Yes."

"Oh," Ryan replied. "Why?"

"Why?"

"You don't want...breakfast? Or I can drive you..."

"No." She turned toward the door.

"Wait a minute," Ryan said in a tone louder than his previous words. "Just wait a minute."

"Ryan," Mel replied as she half turned back. "I'm leaving *now*."

"Wait though," he said as he reached for his pants on the ground. "Just wait."

"I don't want to wait—"

"Why?" he said as he grabbed the waistband of his khakis and pulled one leg through. "Why are you leaving?"

"Please," Mel replied. "Please don't do this."

"Don't do what?"

"This," she replied. "Just let me leave."

"I deserve an explanation," he said as he slipped another leg through slowly.

Her voice raised in tone. "I don't owe you anything."

Ryan slid on the pants. "I know," he said as he shook his head. "I didn't mean that. I meant...I just don't understand."

"I'm not asking you to understand," she replied. "I'm just asking you to let me leave and not make a big deal of it."

He scrunched his brow. "How can I do that? What...what about yesterday?"

"It was a mistake."

Ryan reached for his shirt. "Whoa, what?"

"It was a mistake."

"A mistake? Slow down..."

"I'm leaving," she replied before taking a step toward the door.

"How do I get ahold of you?" Ryan asked. His voice squeaked as he spoke.

She stopped feet from the door, back turned to him. "You don't."

"I don't?"

"No."

He attempted to stand, but the dizziness overcame him. He tried again, this time gripping the nightstand as he did. He turned toward her. "What do you mean?"

"I mean you don't get ahold of me. Not anymore."

"I don't get it," Ryan repeated. "Last night...it seemed so...what happened?"

"You should've just stayed asleep," she muttered under her breath. It was still loud enough for him to hear. She turned to him. "I told you not to do this."

"We're perfect though," he countered. "Help me understand."

"Perfect," she scoffed.

"We are," he replied, voice tinged with pain. He began walking slowly around the bed before sitting on the edge, facing her. "That's why I came here, to find you. It's because we're perfect. We're both cynical and passionate. We love the same things. We both... We're both..." He trailed off as he settled his stomach. "We're the same person. We get along so well."

"And?" she answered.

"And we should be together. There's nothing stopping us now."

"No, Ryan," she replied.

"Why?"

"*Why?*"

"Tell me why."

"I don't have to."

"Give me one reason then," he replied. "Give me one good reason." He rubbed his throbbing head. "Tell me why we shouldn't be together, because all I see are reasons why we should."

"Don't do this…"

"Tell me," Ryan replied. "Tell me why."

"Please, Ryan."

"Tell me," he repeated in a voice just under a yell. "You've got to give me something."

Silence filled the space between them. It was a void he knew he couldn't eclipse. He sat upright as his pulse increased. "Tell me," he pleaded.

She took one more deep breath. "Because I'm married."

The words came out, but Ryan didn't hear. "You're what?"

"I'm married," she repeated.

He stared at her as she kept his gaze.

"Bullshit," he replied with a laugh.

"I'm serious."

"And I'm saying bullshit," he replied. "You aren't married." He could feel his palms grow sweaty.

She shook her head.

"Prove it," he replied, using the only words he could muster.

He could see her bottom lip drop in condemnation. Her eyes grew smaller as she glared at him.

She moved to the dresser of the room as she let go of her suitcase. Setting her purse on top, she rummaged inside before producing two rings, one encased in diamonds, that she confidently slid onto her left ring finger.

"Happy now?" she asked boldly.

Ryan continued to sit on the bed as the walls began to crumble around him.

"I took them off when I saw you approach," she explained. "I didn't want to have this discussion."

"How—" Ryan said as he looked to the floor, attempting to make sense of it all. "How long?"

"Long enough to make this a mistake," she replied as she looked around the hotel room.

"Why did you—"

"Stop it," she replied as she shouldered her purse. "Stop it."

"You got into the car," he replied. The painful tone now dominated his voice. "Why did you get into the car?"

"Don't even," she countered. "Don't you *even* try to blame me."

He swallowed a growing lump in his throat. "What about…us?"

"Us?" she replied coldly. "It's been six years, Ryan."

Ryan stared down at the bed he sat on.

In the ensuing silence, he could hear her phone vibrate in her purse. He watched as she pulled it from the bag and put it up to her ear.

"Hello?" She spoke calmly. "Yeah, I'll be down in just a second."

"Don't go," Ryan said as she put the phone back into her purse.

"Goodbye," she replied before turning and grabbing ahold of the doorknob.

"Mel, wait," Ryan pleaded, to no avail. "Mel, wait. Mel." He stood from the bed as she stepped out into the hall. He moved forward to grasp the closing door but fell into the wall. "*Mel*"

He picked himself upward with much effort and moved back to the bed to his shoes. Standing again laboriously, he blinked as he turned to the window. Looking downward, he saw a waiting taxi.

"*Mel!*" he screamed as he saw her exit the building underneath and enter the cab.

He attempted to control his breathing.

It had all changed so quickly. He had just woken up. *What happened?* How had it all gone so wrong? How could he have let her leave like that? *And she had even called a taxi…*

Ryan's eyes went wide.

A car. He had a car. He could drive to the airport. He could still find her. Surely the plane wasn't leaving right this second. He still had time. *He could do it.*

He flailed across the room toward his suitcase and threw it onto the floor. He had no idea where his keys were, but he knew they couldn't be far.

Rummaging like a madman, he threw shirts and socks over his shoulder as he dug further and further. Emptying it, he moved to the nightstand, where he shuffled through watch and wallet in an attempt to locate the keys.

"Where are they?" he said as he scoured the room, next moving to the dresser, and then her nightstand. "Where are they?"

He felt emotion rolling through his veins. He was so close. Find the keys and everything would be fine. Find the keys.

"Where are they?" he growled. He moved into the bathroom and as he flipped on the light, his faded headache came back to full force, and he stumbled as he reached for the toilet. *"Where…are…they?"*

His voice broke as he turned to the counter and threw item after item onto the floor in a desperate attempt to locate the keys. His knees hit the floor as another wave of nausea hit with full force and rendered him immobile. He once again grasped the toilet.

Stomach heaving, he allowed spit and sweat to fall into the toilet bowl. He closed his eyes as his heaving intensified.

Seconds later, he fell back onto the floor and crawled out into the room, now roaring in a voice full of anguish and pain.

"Where are they?" he repeated over and over as he spied under the bed and under the dresser. *"Where are—"*

He coughed, and saliva drooled from his mouth. Clutching his aching stomach and his jarring head, he rolled over onto his back as his world began to spin.

"Where…" he said, now motionless on the floor. His eyes focused on the ceiling above, as if an answer would somehow be found there. Then, moments later, his pupils rolled back, and his eyelids shut.

He was silent once more.

***

He stirred some five hours later.

Groaning in agony, he pulled his disheveled and sweat-covered body upward as he stared at the clock.

His head ached even worse than his muscles. He could barely recall his previous actions, but he knew what they had entailed. Looking around the floor, he saw bedsheets and personal items together in a catastrophe of rubble on the floor. It looked as though a bomb had gone off.

He stood upright and moved into the bathroom to find a mix of liquid on the floor at the base of the toilet. He didn't know if it was spit or vomit.

Biting his tongue, he turned the faucet on and reached his head underneath, allowing a slow and steady stream of the liquid into his mouth. He drank for several minutes.

Painstakingly, he removed his shirt and then his pants. He needed a shower. He needed to clean up. He needed to leave this place.

Taking a deep breath, he pulled the shower curtain to the side. An object caught his gaze.

Lying in the tub of the shower were his car keys, placed as though they had been deliberately laid. On top of them was a small, scribbled note comprised of only one word.

Don't.

***

It was past two when Ryan stepped into the lobby, bag in hand.

Wearing a button-down tucked haphazardly into his shorts, he approached the counter, still wearing his sunglasses.

"Can I help you, sir?" the agent said from behind the desk.

Ryan produced his key and set it on the counter. "Checking out."

"Certainly," the woman replied. "Thank you for staying."

Ryan turned from the desk. "Do you know…" he said after a moment, turning back. "Do you know where the Salty Crow is?"

"Sure," the woman answered. "But it doesn't open until five."

Ryan took a deep breath. "My car," he said. "I think my car is there."

"Oh," she replied. "It's two blocks down to Caroline Street, and then take a left. You'll find it about three blocks down on your left."

"Thank you," Ryan replied, turning.

"Do you want your room receipt?" she asked.

Ryan grated his teeth. "Fine."

She handed over the piece of paper and he took it before stuffing it in the front of his bag.

"Thanks for staying," she replied.

"Yep," he replied before slinging his bag over his shoulder. Seconds later, he was out in the warm Key West air, and he took another deep breath as he closed his eyes. He attempted to clear his mind, to think of anything other than the situation at hand, yet he knew it was no use. Not even the bright sunshine and tropical air could ease his mood. He opened his eyes.

"Fuck this place," he muttered.

Without another word, he proceeded down the road toward Caroline Street.

***

"Jesus," Ryan mumbled as he leaned forward across the hotel bar counter. "It costs a lot to get drunk in Miami." His eyes were fixated on the tab in front of him.

The bartender laughed as she wiped down a glass. "That's why when you get drunk here, you should just stay drunk. Cheaper that way."

Ryan smiled as he fumbled for his wallet. "Apparently."

He pulled out a credit card and threw it onto the bill as he leaned back in his chair. Blinking, he continued his smile as his previous libations washed over him. There was no pain anymore. There were no memories of the morning. There were no memories of the solo drive. It was just the smoothness of now. It was just the oblivion of the liquor.

The bartender approached. "This one's from the end of the bar," she said as she pushed another glass in front of him.

Ryan opened his eyes and saw the beautiful liquid. Nodding, he reached for the glass and turned to look down the bar top.

Watching him intently was a younger woman in dark jeans and a bright, flowery blouse. She was bathed in the darkness of the setting, but Ryan could see her smile as their gaze found each other.

Slowly, he rose and moved down to her end.

"Getting free drinks," he began in his most normal voice possible. "That's not something I'm used to."

"You looked like you could use one more," she replied as she held her own glass.

"Ryan," he said as he stuck out his hand.

"Krista," she replied in return.

"What brings you to Miami?" Ryan said effortlessly as he sat next to her.

"Bachelorette party," she said.

"For you?" Ryan joked.

She snickered.

"Where are the other members?" he asked, fully aware of his tipsiness.

"Asleep," she replied as she sipped her drink. "As are most people at 1:00 a.m."

"Not you and I," Ryan countered as he held his drink in his right hand. "We must be the true party animals."

"I guess we'll see about that," she said with a smile as she set her drink back down.

Ryan stared as she looked from him to the drink in her hand. There was no blonde hair on her head, instead replaced by the darkest brown. Her eyes were not blue, but instead a deep hazel. Ryan took a deep breath as his gaze moved to the top of her head, looking to see a green headband that never showed.

He hated Mel. He longed for Emma. But tonight, he had neither. Instead, he had a drink in his hand and a different woman on his arm, a woman whose name he would never remember.

He reached for his drink and sipped it before setting the glass back down.

"I guess we will," he said.

Chapter 15
455 Miles from Omaha

The slide changed as Ryan stood at the front of the large, windowless conference room. It was not unexpected. Ryan had been anticipating the change as he held the clicker in his hand, however the slide that appeared felt new to him, as though he had not thoroughly examined it before.

He stared at it over his shoulder, reading as the bullet points outlined a conclusion of reasons why PX1 corn was the true way to go. Next to each line was an image, from a stack of cash to a full, vibrant corn plant. Yet there was one that stood out more than anything else: an image of a happy couple next to a bottom-line point that read "less time worrying—more time for life."

Ryan stared at the line and image as the crowd of over a hundred prospective patrons watched him intently. He had the crowd eating from his hands, and he knew it. The momentary pause now only added to the effect as he considered his words.

"It's kind of bullshit, don't you think?" he said as he turned back to the crowd. He could see a sense of shock in their faces. "I mean it is, isn't it?" he asked as he stepped to the side of the podium and leaned upon it. "This notion that some corn can remove the worry in your life? I mean, come on, that's a bit pretentious."

His eyes moved toward the back of the room, where Steven and Maria sat slack-jawed as they stared at him. Even to the side, Donovan took a step forward, but Ryan's quick glance cut him off.

"I know," he continued. "This isn't in the script, but let's be real, this corn isn't going to remove your worry. At least not fully." He paused as he surveyed the room. "It isn't going to make the credit card bills stop coming. It isn't going to make your nagging family members stop calling. And your wives?" He chuckled as he hung his head. "It sure as hell isn't going to stop them bitching."

The crowd laughed nervously, while in the back, Ryan could sense his team's eyes grow wide.

"I've spent almost three hours telling you what this shit can do," Ryan said. "Excuse my French, by the way." He pushed up off the podium with the clicker in hand. "But let me tell you what it isn't going to do. It isn't going to buy you a boat in Panama City. It's not going to make your land more fertile than your neighbor's. It isn't going to right the wrongs that people have done to you." He paused as he considered his words. "So when I see shit like that last line—*less time worrying*—I'll be honest, it kind of pisses me off." He reached one end and turned to move to the other.

"Two weeks ago, I was in Miami getting as hammered as physically possible." He paused as the crowd laughed together. "I'm serious. I was wronged and I just wanted to drink until oblivion. And I did too. And you know what? At no time did the bartender or the housekeeper or any of the random women I met tell me, 'You'll spend less time worrying if you do this.' Why didn't they tell me that?" He looked around the room. "Because if they had, they'd be bullshitting me." He took another deep breath.

"I didn't drink and pass out and all that to stop worrying. I did it so I'd forget what to worry about. And boy, did I forget it. God, it was glorious. But of course, nothing lasts forever, and here we are. I traded

Miami for Oklahoma City, and those women for you sorry-looking lot."
The crowd laughed.

"Listen," Ryan concluded. "Everyone here is looking for the 'next big thing,' and the truth is that this corn—it isn't that. Sorry to tell you, but there is no magic product to make you stop worrying or to make your life exponentially better. But I can tell you, that like my friends Jack and Jim, this corn, and this yield, can make you forget your problems, at least temporarily, as you hold that nice check from a yield that the grain companies would struggle to match even ninety percent." He took one more deep breath as he reached back to the podium. "A little more money, and a lot less work; they won't solve your problems, but they may help you forget some of them. And for the ones you just can't quite forget wholly…" He paused as he leaned forward. "That's what Miami is for."

***

"What the hell was that?" Maria asked as the last patron exited the conference room and the doors closed.

Ryan set his clicker onto the podium and began assembling his notes. The rest of the room was quiet.

"Ryan? You going to tell us what that was?"

Ryan looked up from the counter. "What *what* was?"

"Oh, I don't know," Maria replied. "Your little sexist and degrading tirade?"

In the back of the room, the door opened as Mike entered and stood near the table.

"Sexist?" Ryan questioned.

"*Wives bitching?*"

Ryan ran his tongue along his back teeth.

Maria stood from the table. "Especially when your audience had some females in it?"

"It was a term of endearment," Ryan replied.

"Oh, was it?" she continued her assault. "And just telling everyone about how drunk you were two weeks ago? Were you endearing yourself there too?

"I was…" Ryan measured his words. "Pontificating."

"You were being an asshole."

"I was trying something new."

"I don't think being an asshole is new for you," she replied.

"I was leveling with the audience," Ryan explained. "I saw a crack to invoke a statement, and I did it."

"A statement not even closely related to the product at hand."

Ryan shook his head as he removed his suit jacket. "You had no problem when we made jokes about how the government sucks and all that."

"No, I had problems," she replied. "But those generally come off harmless. These ones today, they're offensive."

"Other than you, who's offended?"

There was silence before Donovan spoke. "She's kind of right," he said after a moment. "You did cross a line."

"*I* crossed a line," Ryan repeated as he rolled his tongue over his teeth. He turned back to the table. "Tell me, how many sign-ups did we get today?"

Steven took a deep breath as he looked to his form. "Ninety-four percent."

Ryan's face contorted into a controlled shock. "Ninety-fucking-four? That sounds almost like the best of the year, doesn't it?"

Steven nodded reluctantly.

"You should all be thanking me," Ryan replied.

"Success is no reason to be offensive."

"Fine," Ryan countered. "You want to go back to the old ways then? Before Steven and I saved your asses?"

"Why are you being like this?" Maria pleaded.

Ryan leaned onto the podium. "I'm tired of not getting respect. Okay, so what, I made some off-color jokes. It worked. That's the take home. That's our best class yet."

"At what cost?" Donovan interjected.

"The cost? You tell me, boss. You're the ones who desperately don't want to go home." He looked around to each of them to see their faces all shy away. "Yeah, that's right. I don't give a shit if this ends today. But you all, you're the ones with skin in the game. And without me, you're sitting at forty percent at best. Who changed up those videos? Who added personal touches and hats?"

"We're a team, Ryan," Maria said. "We're a *goddamn team.*"

"And we still are," Ryan replied coldly. "But if you think for a second that we'd be here without my decisions, you're sadly mistaken."

She shook her head. "I lied," she said as she looked down at the table. "You aren't just an asshole. You're the worst kind of asshole—one who thinks he's important."

She turned and walked out of the conference room without another word.

"Jesus, man," Donovan said as the door closed. "What's the matter with you?"

Ryan shook his head and moved to the back table.

Donovan scoffed as he looked to Mike. Both turned and exited the room.

In the silence, Ryan continued to pack up the materials around him. Steven stood nearby.

"You got something to say?" Ryan said as he turned to the silent team member.

Steven considered his words. "Sunday we're having my daughter's birthday party at our house," he said. "You should come."

Ryan stared at him with materials still in his hands. "Seriously?"

"There'll be cake and all that." He picked up the boxes of leftover hats and flyers from the back table.

"I was referring to this discussion," Ryan replied. "Do you have anything to say about that?"

Steven sighed as he moved to the exit with his hands full. Turning, he shook his head. "No, Ryan. I don't. I don't need to tell you what you already know." Without another word, he left the room.

***

Ryan stayed in the room until well into the evening. After he had cleaned up the space, folded the tables, and restacked the chairs, he found himself sitting in the last remaining seat as he collected his breath and stared throughout the now-empty room. His chair was the only island left behind.

He knew he was in the wrong. He had been in the wrong for the last two weeks. It was a level he was on, however, and he no longer cared to leave it. If he had learned anything over the last twelve-plus days, it was how effortless it was to be spiteful and desolate. It came naturally, as though it had always been within. He had no need for work, no need for friends. He found what he needed in the hotels and bars, and that was adequate. It was easier this way.

And yet as he sat in the vacant conference room, he couldn't help but feel the nagging presence of ignominy that extended beyond his being. Even if he didn't feel it entirely within, he knew that others did. They saw his actions and his disengagement. They saw his carelessness. They saw his resolution.

"*Being an asshole isn't new for you...*" he repeated aloud.

He closed his eyes and then reopened them. The room still sat cold and empty, with no sound other than his deep breaths. If he had ever been alone before, it paled in comparison to now.

Getting up, he moved his chair to the other stacks along the wall. Rubbing his head, he grabbed the last remaining binders left on the floor and stepped into the hallway, taking care to shut the door behind him.

Just then, his phone in his pocket began to vibrate.

Exhaling, he pulled it from its location. He stood in place as he looked at the screen.

Mom.

His finger hovered over "accept." He wanted more than anything to drop his finger down, yet it remained in place. Finally, after much deliberation, his finger fell to the red circle.

He continued walking towards the stairwell leading to his room.

Another vibration. This time a voicemail. Ryan stopped as he stepped onto the first stair. He closed his eyes as he pulled the phone to his ear and pressed "play".

"I figured you wouldn't answer." His mother's voice seemed both distant and disheartened. "You never do. Your cousin Brandon is proposing to his partner down here over Labor Day weekend and he wants the family there. That includes you. He knows you won't come, but I said I'd ask you anyway. It'd be nice to see you. Or hear from you. But you don't need to make an excuse. I just figured I'd let you know. Love you."

It was minutes later before Ryan opened his eyes. Phone still to his ear, he allowed it to drop slightly. He swallowed as he looked up and then down in the open stairwell, finding it empty as it had always been. It was just like the conference room before. It was just like the hotel room in Key West. He was alone. He was always alone.

He couldn't stop disappointing those around him. He couldn't right the wrongs he had committed. He couldn't change levels even if he had wanted to. And now? Perhaps he no longer wanted to. Perhaps this life was just too hard. Perhaps he was bound to always be this way.

Binders in hand, he continued his climb up the stairs without another word.

He could do nothing else.

Chapter 16
In Omaha

Ryan stared at the text on his phone as he sat at the coffee shop on Douglas.

Meet at four.

He was unprepared for such a request after a day spent sitting through more presentation changes and status updates, yet upon seeing Emma briefly as she sat in an adjacent conference room, he felt his phone light up.

Moments later, he watched as she strolled in through the front door. Standing from his seat, she spied him over the commotion throughout the location.

"I just ordered this," he said as she approached. He motioned to the cup on her side of the table. "I didn't want you to think it's been sitting here for forty-five minutes."

She smiled as she took a seat. "I'm impressed you ordered at all."

Ryan shrugged as he sat. "Full disclosure, I stumbled a bit." He motioned to the counter. "I'm pretty sure they'll be happy if I never come back in again."

She laughed. "I doubt that's true." She picked up the cup and gave a sip. Her mood was more subdued than usual, and Ryan detected a remoteness as she sat almost sideways on her chair, as though ready to stand even though she had just sat down.

As she sipped, he noticed the engagement band on her ring finger which gripped her coffee cup. She ran her thumb over the bright diamond in the centerpiece. He had never seen her wear it before, and he wondered if he had simply overlooked it altogether.

"How have you been?" she asked as she set the cup down. "I was thinking you might have forgotten about me since I haven't heard from you."

He considered her words. "I assumed…" He trailed off. "I figured you didn't want random men texting you over the holiday weekend."

"Or the two weeks since then?"

Ryan's eyes broke her gaze as he looked towards the floor. "I guess I just didn't know when it was best to text you." After a moment he looked back up.

"Probably for the best," she replied as she held her cup. "How was the status meeting today?"

He exhaled. "Same as usual. Don't worry about the company projections. We're doing great."

"And are you?" she asked. "The team, I mean."

"We've had some stumbles personally and professionally," Ryan replied. "But we're hanging in there."

"Personally?"

Ryan nodded, "It's delicate. I guess I've just been in a weird place recently."

"Any reason?"

He scoffed. "A lot of them," he answered. "But I'm sure you don't want to hear my problems."

"Honestly?" She thought on the question. "It'd be nice to hear anyone's problems but my own."

"I don't know," Ryan replied. "I've just been going through a few things. Mentally. Emotionally. It's nothing, really." He paused for a long while, sensing that his answer was not working as well as he had hoped. "To be honest I haven't really talked about it with anyone."

"You can talk to me about it if you'd like." Emma said.

Ryan smiled weakly. "I guess I just figured out that there isn't anything there with that woman I told you about previously."

Emma nodded.

"So that's pretty much over."

"Did you get closure?"

Ryan scoffed. "Not really to be honest. But that's not unexpected given our relationship," he said with a laugh. "To be honest I'm kind of wondering why I even tried. Like what was my actual goal?"

Emma shrugged.

"Sorry," Ryan said sheepishly. "I didn't mean to unload my problems."

"No I'm sorry," Emma replied sincerely. "I'm sorry that happened. But on the bright side, now you know."

Ryan nodded. "I guess so," he replied. "How about you though? How've you been?"

She considered the question. "About the same, I suppose."

"You seem…" He attempted to find a word that was easier to hear. "Distant."

She smiled as she picked her cup up. "Do I?"

"A little," he replied. "Not that it's any of my business."

She sipped her coffee and set the cup back down. "I'm sorry for that."

"No need to apologize," he replied. "Did you at least have a good time back home?"

Her gaze moved back to her cup and she didn't immediately reply. He watched as she contemplated her thoughts, and he found himself drawn into her deep blue eyes above her high and eminent cheeks. Above all this, however, was the perfectly parted blonde hair complete with the token he most recalled.

"It was nice to be home," she said.

He returned his gaze back to her eyes to see them well with water.

"Are you okay?" Ryan said cautiously as he leaned forward.

Immediately on his deduction, a tear rolled from her eye and down her cheek. She quickly grabbed the napkin under her cup and dotted her eye. "I'm fine," she said. "I'm fine, I promise."

"You're crying," he replied obviously.

"I'm fine," she repeated, turning from him as she continued wiping her eyes.

"Did I say something?"

"No, no," she answered. "I promise, I'm fine." He could see her attempt a few quick deep breaths. "It's just been a long couple weeks."

"I can go get more napkins," Ryan replied as he rose slightly.

"No, please no," she said as she wiped. It appeared the tears had stopped. "I'm sorry. God, I'm sorry for this. It's so embarrassing."

He could see her face was red from first emotion and now shame.

"It's OK," Ryan replied as he returned to his seat. "I just…" He attempted to find words. "Crying isn't a sentiment I'm really used to."

She muttered a quick chuckle.

"I feel like I need to do something," Ryan said. "You sure you don't need tissues or water or something?"

"No, I promise," she replied as she turned fully to the table. "Thank you though."

Ryan sat rigid in his seat as she set the napkin back on the table and took another deep breath.

"You don't deal with crying women, I take it?" she said after a moment.

He realized his face likely appeared pale. "No, not really," he replied. "Angry and bitter, yes. Crying? Not really."

She laughed, and he was happy to see her grow more comfortable.

"Well, I'm sure they just don't do the crying in front of you."

"Likely yes," he replied. "And given how I just responded here, that's probably for the better."

She laughed again. "Well, I'm sorry again," she said. "I tend to cry more than the usual person."

"That's…okay," Ryan replied. "It's a pretty normal emotion."

"You look terrified."

"Well, it matches how I feel then," he said with a smile.

She returned the smile. "You aren't a crier then?"

"Are you asking if I'm a small child?" he replied. "That's a no."

She scoffed. "Children aren't the only ones allowed to cry."

"For men, they are!"

"You haven't cried since you were a child?"

Ryan considered it. "I broke my arm a few years back, and I'm pretty sure I cried then."

"Okay, well, pain is different."

"Still crying."

"How about an emotional cry? Any time?"

"No."

"Movies? Music?"

"Who cries during music?"

"I do!" she replied confidently. "A good heartbreaking ballad?"

"Sorry," he replied.

"Adele, Taylor, nothing?"

"Taylor Swift?"

"Is there another?"

"Can't say I've listened to much, let alone cried from it."

She stared across the table from him. He immediately detected condemnation. "Are you judging me for not listening to Taylor Swift?"

"One hundred percent," she replied. "Just like you judge me for movies."

Ryan contemplated the statement. "Fine," he responded. "We'll work on movies for you, and you can help educate me on the musical musings of Ms. Swift."

"Deal," she quickly replied. "And maybe then you'll tap into your emotional side."

"I have a perfectly good emotional side."

"Not if you don't have a good cry every now and again," she countered.

"Is that so?"

"Crying is cathartic!" She opened her hands and looked skyward. "It just feels good."

"You didn't look good when you were doing it."

"Well, of course not when it happens," she explained. "But afterward, it makes you feel alive. Like everything makes more sense. It's a few moments of pure self-realization and deep inward reflection."

"Inward reflection?"

"When I cry," she continued, "it's like a reset. It's like me saying, 'I'm going to self-reboot.' And after the tears, I feel stronger. I feel more understanding, like I *get* my life better. I feel renewed."

"Is this crying or throwing up?"

She glared at him.

He laughed. "I guess I've just never needed that."

"You will," she replied. "It's human to cry. It's in our DNA."

"Maybe one day then," he replied.

"You'll tell me when it happens, right?"

He smiled.

"I'm serious. Your big emotional cry. I want to know."

"When it happens," he responded, "you'll be the first to know."

"Good," she said. She picked up her coffee cup and took a sip.

"Can I ask you something?" he asked after a long pause.

"Why did I cry?" she replied.

His words caught in his throat. He contemplated changing his question. Biting his lip, however, he thought better. "What are you doing tomorrow?"

"Why do you ask?"

Ryan shrugged. "Well," he attempted to explain. "I kind of got roped into attending a birthday party for a guy's daughter..."

"You're friends with someone's daughter?"

"It's Steven," he explained.

"You're friends with Steven?"

Ryan contemplated the question. "Yes? I mean, he's a good coworker."

"If you're going to his daughter's party, then I think you're friends," Emma reasoned.

"Well, I was trying to come up with excuses not to go, if that means anything."

She laughed.

"But after I thought more on it, it might be fun to go...with you."

"With me?"

"If you want."

"I mean, it sounds fun."

"It sounds awful," Ryan replied much to her amusement. "I'm seriously even wondering why I'm going."

"And yet you want me to tag along."

"Misery loves company. Plus, it might be less awful if you join."

She smiled as she looked down at her coffee cup.

"Of course, it may still be awful, in which case I'll bolt immediately and leave you there."

"What a gentleman."

Ryan shrugged with a smile. "What can I say?"

He watched as she rubbed her ring.

"I understand if it's a little weird," Ryan attempted to say. "With the...engagement and everything."

"I'll go," she interjected.

"You'll what?"

"I'll go," she replied as she looked up. "Yeah, I'll go."

Ryan stared at her, relieved. "You sure?"

She nodded as she smiled over her cup. "Yeah," she replied. "I'm sure."

Ryan leaned back from the table and nodded. "Good," he said, unsure of what to say next. His mind was more focused on the shock of her answer than anything else.

"We can listen to Taylor on the way," Emma finally said as she sipped from her cup.

Ryan chuckled as he looked across the table to meet her deep blue eyes. There was a perfection there he couldn't quite explain, and yet it captivated him still.

"Great," he replied as he broke the gaze. "I'll bring the Kleenex."

Chapter 17
20 Miles from Omaha

Ryan stood bent at the waist as he washed his hands in the small guest bathroom. Looking up, he spied his reflection in the mirror.

His boyish face appeared older in this light. Perhaps it was the added stress of the past months, or perhaps something more maturing. Regardless, he appeared calm and content as he stared at his own figure staring back.

He shut off the faucet and dried his hands on the nearby towel. Taking a deep breath, he moved toward the door, opened it, and stepped back into the hallway. Moving down the corridor, he entered a large and empty living room, and took a moment to admire the space as he stood at its edge.

The house itself was older, yet the openness and vaulted ceilings aspired to a much later timeframe. Dual wood beams traversed the open headspace, and large radiating windows graced the far wall peering out into the backyard. It was an admirable place, and Ryan felt small as he stood alone in the room.

Moving toward the window, he peered outside to see a variety of colors, complete with a bounce house and several skirted tables full of gifts and food. Around these were a variety of people, young and old, all having what appeared to be a desirable time in the beautiful summer air.

Ryan turned slightly to see a wall of images bordering a staircase to the second floor. Walking directly to the first stair, he saw a collage of family gatherings from graduations to weddings, each with a distinct frame and each with a distinct image within.

Ryan reached out and picked up the frontmost image of Steven and his wife holding a baby in the hospital bed. Both adults looked exhausted beyond comprehension, yet there was joy in their eyes as they stared down at the swaddled infant in her arms.

Setting the image down, Ryan moved on to the next, from the same couple at a baseball game to another image of them slicing a wedding cake. The next was a full family photo with grandmothers and grandfathers and a whole host of people Ryan would never know. It all seemed picturesque. It all seemed happy.

"Find anything exciting?"

Emma's voice caused him to turn quickly with the picture frame still in hand.

He allowed his heart rate to return to normal as he saw it was just her. "They have a big family," he finally said as he turned to the wall of photos.

She moved toward him until she was alongside. "I feel most of them are at this party too," she replied. "There's a ton of people here."

"More than ever came to any of my birthdays," Ryan said with a laugh.

"Same," Emma chimed in. "I also never had a bouncy house."

"Yeah," Ryan followed. "My best was a McDonald's play place."

"County fair for me," she responded.

"Really?"

"September birthday," she answered as she too stared at the photo. "They rented a pavilion and gave us all wristbands."

"That's pretty awesome."

"It was a lot of drama," she replied. "But we were thirteen, so I guess that's to be expected."

He chuckled as they continued standing side by side.

"What do you think about this?" she finally asked as she motioned to the wall.

"What do you mean?"

"This," she answered. "This wall. Something you ever wanted?"

Ryan thought about his answer. "I can't say I've ever wanted a wall of someone else's pictures."

She laughed.

"My own family," Ryan continued. "Maybe."

"Oh? Maybe?"

"Why not?" he answered. "Someday down the line. I'm open to it."

"Down the line?"

He shrugged as he provided his most honest answer. "I don't know what tomorrow looks like, let alone what's even further past that."

He could sense her nodding alongside him.

"But if my wife and I decide that this is where our life is going to go, then why not?" he finally added. "No rush though. At least not on my end."

Her silence continued, and he grew quite uncomfortable having his thoughts linger so long.

"You?"

"Me?"

"Yeah," Ryan replied. "You want this?"

He watched as she glossed over the images intently. He could see the bright green reflection of her headband in the glass frames.

"Someday, yeah," she finally said. "Yeah, I think so. I'm open to it too." She moved to the far side as she continued looking at the images. "Doesn't have to be pictures though. Maybe tokens to remember places."

"You're going to have a wall of key chains?"

She turned and glared at him. "I didn't say key chains."

"Fine," he replied. "Magnets then?"

"Something like that, sure," she replied. "Something you can build on."

The back door opened abruptly and both Ryan and Emma jumped. An older gentleman appeared and immediately walked past the living room toward the bathroom. As he disappeared, Ryan turned to see Emma staring at him.

"Probably should go outside," she said with a laugh.

"Yeah, we've done enough Jimmy Stewart work here."

She stared at him as he moved toward the door. Turning back, he could see her still attempting to understand. "*Rear Window*," he said as he held the door open. "Add it to your list."

***

"I was wondering if you all had left us," Steven said loudly as Emma and Ryan approached the main table, where a variety of adults sat.

"Just admiring your pictures," Ryan said coolly as they took a seat in the folded chairs nearby.

"Ah, Steven's collage map," his wife said from his right.

Ryan smiled as Steven gave a look of defiance.

"Yeah," Steven said with a chuckle. "Because Julie never helped me hang a picture."

"Did you notice," Julie said, leaning forward to drown out her husband. "Did you notice how they're arranged?"

Ryan turned to Emma and shrugged. "No, I don't think so."

"Tell them." Julie motioned to her husband jovially.

Steven smiled. "My idea was to arrange the images into their geographic location in the U.S."

Ryan smirked as Steven continued speaking.

"I know," the quick-talking man continued. "It sounds crazy."

"It *is* crazy," Julie added.

"But photos are photos," Steven continued. "Arranging them with location-specific designations gives more context. Plus, I think it helps the kids with their geography."

"Do you really have images from all across the country?" Emma interjected.

Ryan half turned, almost surprised to see her find interest in the discussion.

"Not exactly," Steven explained. "We have a lot of Omaha in there, and a couple from Minnesota and a few Florida and other spots, but yeah, we've pretty much extended Nebraska to the Pacific Northwest until we make a trip up there."

"That's really cool," Emma replied with a genuine smile. "I would have never thought of that."

"That's Steven for you," Julie replied. "You never know what he'll come up with next."

Ryan remembered the first time Steven had brought up his wife, and how his eyebrows had risen. Now, however, his reaction was opposite. Julie was every bit his match, from his excitement to his optimistic attitude. With her short red hair, numerous facial freckles, and a cross around her neck, she was pretty by any standard, and Ryan could tell just how much she meant to her husband, and how much she had affected him as well.

As their discussions continued, Ryan quietly spied the birthday girl approach the table from behind her parents. With bright red hair under a flowered beret, she was the spitting image of both mother and father, and although she was only celebrating her fifth birthday, her attitude alone could have passed for much older.

"What's wrong, Liv?" Julie said as she sensed the child behind her. "What's all over your face?"

Clear enough, Ryan could see the mud splashed in her hair and across her brow. He watched as the little girl whispered into her mom's ear.

Julie turned back toward where her daughter had come from.

"What is it?" Steven asked.

"She said that she fell leaving the bouncy house, and that Mr. Ted got left behind."

Steven smiled as he turned toward Ryan and Emma. "Mr. Ted is her bear."

"Let's get you washed up," Julie said as she picked up her daughter. She turned to Steven. "You OK to watch Daniel and Tucker?"

Steven continued sitting, and Ryan turned behind him to see a group of boys between eight and fourteen splashing around in an above-ground pool.

"Yeah, I got them," Steven replied.

"I'll get her bear," Emma said matter-of-factly as she arose.

"That's alright," Julie said hastily. "It'll be fine."

"It's fine," Emma replied with a smile. "I don't mind."

"That's sweet of you," Julie replied. She looked at her daughter, who clung to her shirt. "Alright, let's get you cleaned up before cake."

In seconds, Ryan and Steven were left alone at the large table.

The silence settled in as Ryan surveyed the party around him. He was enamored with how content everyone seemed to be.

"I really do want to thank you for coming," Steven finally said after the moment of silence. "It means a lot."

"Of course," Ryan replied. "Happy to be invited."

Steven continued to peruse the scene. "And thanks for bringing Emma. She's wonderful."

"Yeah," Ryan replied as he spied her clambering through the bouncy house for the teddy bear in question. He smiled as he watched her attempt to dodge child after child. "Yeah, she is."

"I didn't even realize you were friends," Steven responded in an even tone.

Ryan nodded. "She said the same about you and me."

Steven laughed as he continued surveying the scene before them. "I guess you surprise us all from time to time."

Ryan continued to watch Emma, oblivious to the world around him. "I guess so," he finally said. "I guess I do."

***

"I think I'm good on kids for a little while," Ryan said as he buckled his seat belt.

Next to him, Emma laughed as she did the same. "It is nice to be able to drive away from them."

Ryan chuckled as he shifted the car into drive and proceeded down the city street. "Best kind of kids are the ones you get to leave," he replied with a smile.

She laughed.

Silence reigned. He turned from one road to the next as they proceeded towards a main highway.

"How old is Steven?" Emma finally asked. "Or Julie?"

Ryan shrugged. "Not sure, maybe thirtyish? Twenty-eight?"

He could see her shake her head. "Three kids so young."

"Yeah," Ryan replied. "Daniel had to be born when they were about twenty."

"Could you imagine taking care of a kid that young?"

Ryan considered it. "Well, I can't, but based on my Facebook, a lot of my old high school friends can."

He heard her chuckle alongside him.

"I wonder if they decided on the three," Emma continued. "Or if it just happened. Did they consciously decide for that level of stress?"

"Crazy part is," Ryan replied, "they seem happy."

"Right?" Emma exclaimed. "Like actually happy."

"Maybe some people like that structure," Ryan reasoned. "Marry early. Kids early. Adapt to the stresses early on."

"Maybe so," Emma said.

"But full disclosure," Ryan added, "I'm definitely not that kind of person."

She laughed.

"In case you didn't get that by, you know, me being single at thirty without kids."

Emma nodded. "No kids, huh?"

Ryan detected her sarcasm. "Oh, you didn't get that already?"

"I mean, you never expressly said that you didn't, so I didn't want to assume."

"Ah," he replied. "Well no, no kids. No dogs either."

"No dogs?" she replied. "What kind of psycho are you?"

"Do you have a dog?"

"My family does back home."

"But you, here in Omaha?"

She laughed. "Heck no. Do you think based on this conversation that I'd be ready to even take on a dog?"

Ryan laughed.

"My roommate has a hamster though. That's pretty cute."

"Hamsters are good," Ryan replied. "I mean, a pet is a pet."

"His name is Hammy, and I do absolutely nothing to take care of it."

Ryan smiled. "Probably for the best, from the sounds of it."

"You know," she said after a moment, "I genuinely wonder some days how I survive on my own especially considering all the chores and having to work and everything? Life is tough."

"It's amazing any of us make it, honestly."

"I think that's why I'm so amazed by Steven and Julie," Emma continued. "I'm the type of person who loves to sleep, and yet they're younger than me and raising kids and pets and a house. It makes me look lazy."

Ryan shrugged. "At least you have a place to rent," he responded. "My apartment was probably re-rented to some random dude."

"Really?"

"Probably," Ryan replied.

"What about your things?"

"I didn't have that much," he replied. "But he'll move them to a storage unit. Or sell them, who knows."

She didn't immediately reply.

"I didn't mean to one-up your story," Ryan replied after considering his words. "I think I did though."

"Oh, you totally did," she replied. "But it's alright. At least we have solidarity in being the type of people who don't have it together."

Ryan laughed. "Yes, we do," he replied.

Wordlessly, Ryan merged the rental car onto the highway as he increased his speed. Occasionally, he glanced over to Emma to see her with feet folded on the seat as she monitored the passing scenery.

"Jay has it together," Emma said quietly after some time.

Ryan heard the words but didn't know what to say. "What was that?"

She didn't immediately respond. Finally, she turned from the side windows. "My fiancé. He's got it together." Her voice didn't match her words and instead was tinged with contempt.

"Does he?"

"I'm sorry," she replied hurriedly. "I shouldn't mention—"

"It's fine," Ryan replied.

She shook her head. "It's just…he really has it figured out."

Ryan continued to sit quiet.

"He was ready for a family when we first met, I think." She continued. "And his life? I mean, from high school to college to the Air Force, he followed his plan to a tee." She paused as she considered her words. "Even now, he's got our next ten years planned out."

Ryan's eyes grew wide. "What's the plan?"

"Marriage this year," she recited. "First kid by middle of next year when we're thirty-one."

"First?" Ryan said.

"First of four."

"Oh," Ryan replied, mouth now ajar.

"We'll adopt, if necessary," she continued in words she knew by heart. "We'll also move at least two to three times as we transfer Air Force bases, but that's fine, as I'll be busy with the kids. And then after the service is up, we'll return to Franklin to build our dream house."

"Franklin?"

"It's a town near Nashville."

"I thought it was a turtle," Ryan said.

"It's where his family is from," she replied.

Ryan considered her statement. "Then what?"

"Then I can pursue my career if I want, I guess," she replied. "We really haven't thought much past Franklin. I assume we'll have to take care of his parents or something."

"You're really selling your enthusiasm for this ten-year plan."

"Am I?" she asked genuinely.

Ryan smiled. "No."

"Oh."

"But to be honest," Ryan countered, "it really doesn't sound much like *your* ten-year plan."

"Glad you caught that."

"Have you told him how you feel about this?"

"How I feel about the plan?"

"Yeah."

"No," she said as she shook her head.

"Why?"

"Why would I?"

"Because it doesn't seem like you're on board."

She considered the words as she returned to looking out the side window. "I don't know *what* I am."

Ryan wanted to say something, anything, yet his words would not form. He could only allow the silence to fill the car as he proceeded onward down the highway.

"Do you ever feel like you have no idea what's going on in life?" she finally said after a moment. "Like you have no idea what you're supposed to do or be?"

Ryan heard the comments and immediately smirked. "Every day."

"Really?"

"Yeah, every day," Ryan replied. "Every day, I feel like I'm just floating on aimlessly."

"Well, Jay doesn't ever feel that," Emma replied. "And part of me wonders if I'm just crazy or overthinking everything because I can't seem to get to his level of confidence. I often can't shake the fact that maybe I don't know if I *want* a ten-year plan."

"But you haven't told him this?"

She turned from the window. "No, I haven't."

Ryan shrugged. "Why not?"

She thought about it for a moment. "Because what if I'm just being dramatic? What if I'm just scared about being a wife?"

"*Are* you scared?"

"Terrified!" she exclaimed. "The thought of marriage is completely overwhelming, especially with the expectations of kids and all that so soon after. I can't take care of a *hamster* yet!"

Ryan smiled as he kept one hand on the wheel. He could hear her take a deep breath next to him.

"I know everyone has doubts though," she finally said. "I just don't know if mine will pass once I say 'I do' or if they'll still be there after that. That terrifies me too. And it has nothing to do with Jay or anyone else. It's all me. That's what he doesn't understand."

"So he knows you're feeling *something*?"

"Of course," she answered. "He just doesn't know what. Everyone knows something is up. We've been engaged for a long time and still haven't set a date. They just don't know why. He wanted to talk about it all weekend when I was back home, and I just couldn't put into words what I wanted to."

"But you just did," Ryan said.

"Well, yeah," she replied as she shrugged. "There's no pressure talking to you."

More silence.

"So now you know why my time back in Tennessee wasn't very good," she summarized with a smile. "Not that I really meant to just lay it all out."

Ryan returned the smile. "It's all good," he replied. "I can see how that'd be upsetting."

"Any advice?"

Ryan felt his eyes go wide. Advice?

Dump him.

Ryan tapped on the steering wheel as he attempted to hide his initial reactions. There was no game to play here. He had been honest up until now. There was no reason not to continue.

"Honestly?" He attempted to buy more time as he thought longer. "I don't know if I can give great advice without knowing your whole relationship. I mean, you've been together for a while, so this pressure hasn't been there the entire time, has it?"

"Not entirely," she replied.

Ryan formulated his thoughts. "I think it's okay to be nervous about marriage and all that comes after it," he finally said. "But as far as not having the same plan regarding your lives, that's a bit different, in my opinion." He thought more on it. "Your goals and career and wants should be just as important as his."

She remained silent.

"If you don't know what those goals or wants are, well then, that's okay too," he added as he moved the car toward an exit lane.

"Is it?" she asked honestly. "Because I feel pretty lonely not knowing what I want."

"You're right there with me then," Ryan replied. "And *not* knowing is a perfectly acceptable place to be, because one day, you *will* know, and when that day comes, I think you'll know the difference." He took a deep breath as he continued. "Until then, though, I'd embrace *not* knowing and enjoy the ride."

She half turned to him. "Sounds like you're telling me to make it a future Emma problem."

He laughed, understanding her recollection. "Exactly," he replied with a smile. "Or if you prefer, I can try to one-up your current situation so you don't feel as bad."

She fully turned back from the window and laughed. "You can one-up marriage insecurities?"

Ryan shrugged. "Prison was a cold, dark place."

He could see her roll her eyes as he began to laugh.

"No fair using that," she replied. "Everything looks decent compared to prison."

"I could go back to talking about how my belongings are probably scattered throughout eBay at the moment."

She laughed. "OK, you win, your life is much worse."

"Ah, it's not that bad," he replied. "Today was fun."

"Yeah," she replied as she turned to him. "Yeah, it was."

"Just two lost souls at a five-year-old's birthday party," Ryan responded with a laugh.

He could hear her laugh alongside.

"We're a mess," she replied in between her giggles.

"Yeah," he finally said as his laughter calmed. "But it's better than being alone."

"Yeah, it is," she replied evenly.

He spied her staring at him from the corner of his eye. Further words caught in his throat as he continued driving onward. He didn't know what else to say.

"You…hungry?" he finally asked after a long moment.

He could sense her debating the question, and he knew that she understood the question had nothing to do with food.

"Yeah," she replied. "I can eat."

"Good," he replied. "Me too."

He adjusted his hands on the steering wheel as he looked over to her. Her gaze had returned to her passenger window, but he could sense that she could see him in the faded reflection.

Eyes returning to the road ahead, he felt a smile crease his lips. Deep inside, he knew that something about the moment felt natural and pure. It felt effortless. It felt like this was the perfect place to be: him driving with her alongside. She was no longer engaged, and he was no longer a calamity. They were merely two people content in a rental as it moved onward down the road. Neither knew what lay ahead, and neither knew what to expect, but somehow, despite everything around them, not knowing was better than perfect could ever be.

Chapter 18
315 Miles from Omaha

"Not too bad," Maria said loudly as she gazed over the clipboard of presentation results as Ryan and Mike began taking down the tables in the large conference room. "You know, for some lacky who did nothing to help the team."

Ryan's ears perked as he heard the comment and both Donovan and Mike laughed softly.

"Two months," Ryan responded calmly. "For two months, I've heard that joke now."

"Eh, you've heard it only when I've felt like saying it," Maria replied coolly as she began folding chairs with Donovan. "Which hasn't been the *entire* two months."

Ryan bit his tongue as he accepted the barbs.

"And you'll probably continue to hear it for a while longer," Mike chimed in. "If I know Maria."

"Deservedly so," Ryan responded.

"Glad we agree on that," Maria replied with a smile. "You do deserve that."

"I was a little hot that day, I admit," Ryan added. "Probably said a lot I didn't mean."

"Most of it, I'd imagine," she replied.

Ryan shrugged. "I mean, I *did* work my magic in changing the presentation. I might have been bold in my comments, but still." He moved to a new row of chairs and began assisting in the breakdown of the room.

Steven entered the room with his own materials. Oblivious to the situation, he held up his phone before the entire room.

"Did you all see our change in plans?"

Ryan's laughter subsided first. "Our what?"

"Yeah," Steven replied. "Back to Omaha for Monday."

"That's sudden," Mike replied, laughter ceasing as well. "I was just beginning to enjoy Minnesota."

"Probably because we haven't been back since June," Donovan replied. "We've gone a long while without a status meeting."

"Yeah, I wouldn't worry," Maria continued. "We only had a schedule for another week or so anyway."

Mike pulled a piece of paper from his pocket. "I'll miss seeing…" He stared at it for a moment. "Marshall and Albert Lea."

"I doubt you'll miss them that much," Maria replied with a chuckle.

"Yeah," he said. "You're right."

Donovan stood from his mostly finished row of chairs. "So, we celebrating tonight?"

"Celebrating what?" Mike asked.

"Who the hell cares?" Donovan replied. "Let's go into the city and have some fun."

"You can't pass up a good time, can you?" Maria responded.

"Not when I'm near the city that molded Prince," Donovan replied. "I'll take any reason I can to live it up."

Ryan turned to Steven. "You interested?"

He knew that the idea was furthest from Steven's mind, yet the crowd's influence was too strong.

"Sure," he said. "Have to get to the airport there anyway for tomorrow."

"That's the spirit," Donovan replied. "Nothing like being hungover on a plane."

"That sounds miserable," Mike responded.

"Eh, it's a short flight," Donovan countered. "You'll be alright."

***

"That's the shit I'm talking about," Donovan exclaimed as Ryan approached from the bar. The remaining three members of the group sat in a circle of armchairs, while Donovan sat perched on a stool.

"What's he talking about?" Ryan asked as he joined the circle. He reached across and handed Donovan a drink before he sat down on another stool with his own drink.

"He claims he saw one of those guys over there in Oklahoma City," Mike explained through his unexcited disposition. "So now he's telling us how he was right back in Chicago when he went on and on about that coincidence stuff."

"I talked to the man," Donovan replied. "I talked to him at the bar while we were waiting for our drinks. And he's here tonight. Right here."

"Which guy?" Ryan inquired.

"The dude with the braids," Donovan replied as he pointed to a guy's back some distance off. "He had 'em different in OKC, but still."

"So go talk to him," Maria said. "See if he remembers you."

"It ain't about that," Donovan replied. "I remember *him*. That's the point. Just like I explained earlier. You all find that coincidence shit crazy."

"I don't think any of us believe you," Mike responded with a smile.

"Whatever, man," Donovan replied. "But it's true. That's the same dude."

"I'll go ask him," Ryan said. As he spoke, Steven got up next to him.

"I'm offended that you don't already believe me," Donovan replied.

"Fine." Ryan watched Steven approach the group in question. "I won't ask."

"Thank you," Donovan replied.

"Looks like Steven already is," Ryan added, and the entire group turned to watch Steven interact with the man in question.

"Jesus…" Donovan audibly gasped.

Steven turned from afar. "Good news, guys!" he yelled. "Same guy!"

Ryan smiled as Donovan shielded his face.

"I believe you now," Mike replied calmly as Steven returned to the group.

"Thanks for that, Steven," Donovan replied coldly.

"No problem," Steven answered. "Figured it'd help our conversation."

"Do you want to do your victory lap now?" Mike asked a still-embarrassed Donovan. "Do you want to tell us all how you're right?"

"Yeah," Maria added. "We all love hearing people tell us they're right."

"I think that's unnecessary," Donovan answered. "But you all know."

"But we shouldn't be surprised," Ryan interjected. "Correct? Wasn't that the whole point of your conversation? Coincidence is less coincidental upon the initial interaction."

Donovan ignored Ryan's comment. "Did he say he remembered me? Or just that he was in Oklahoma City?" he asked in a hush toward Steven.

"He remembered you," Steven replied as he sipped his iced tea.

Donovan's face dropped. "Seriously?"

Steven nodded. "Yeah. He said he remembered your purple vest."

"You wore a purple vest?" Mike asked as he looked up from his drink. "Why haven't we seen the purple vest?"

"Because none of you go to gay bars," Donovan replied matter-of-factly.

"There are gay bars in Oklahoma City?" Ryan inquired.

"There's gay bars everywhere," Donovan replied. "Sometimes masquerading as straight ones."

The group laughed over their liquor before Donovan sat upright.

"Should I go over there?" he asked. "I mean, I don't want to be too formal."

"Wait for a signal," Maria replied. "Eye contact or something. Then go over."

Donovan nodded. "I'm glad someone's here to help me out."

"I'll be your wingwoman," Maria replied as she sat coolly in her chair. "I got you."

It took only seconds for Donovan to receive the signal he desired. Standing slowly, he set his glass onto a nearby table before casually strolling over to the group in question. Ryan, Mike, Steven, and Maria all watched, breaths held, to see how the interaction would go, and after several questionable moments, all were relieved to see the two men move to a table away from the main group.

"He made that look really easy," Mike said after a moment.

"Yeah," Ryan replied. "That was well done."

"Probably because he had the right amount of nervousness and humility," Maria replied.

The three men looked toward her.

"Oh, come on," Maria replied. "You guys treat the approach like a newspaper headline. First words have to be a banger or else no one will ever care, and that's just stupid." She took a sip of her drink. "'Excuse me, miss, did your license get suspended for driving all these men crazy?' Or how about 'Good thing I got my library card because I'm checking you out.'"

"Someone actually said that?" Mike asked.

"I've heard it all," Maria replied. "'Are you a chicken? Because you're impeccable.'"

"I assume that one wasn't a winner?" Ryan asked with a smile.

"Mine was, 'Excuse me, miss, you dropped your glasses,'" Steven said with a shrug.

The three turned to him.

"She had dropped her glasses," he explained. "Leaving the grocery store."

Maria pointed in his direction. "You see, that's good."

"I was afraid someone would step on them."

"All women, be it in bars or wherever, they've already scoped the place out," Maria explained. "They already know who's getting a conversation and who's not. What you say on the approach means little unless you say something stupid or just plain cringy, and if saying something cringy or stupid worries you, then that's a *you* problem."

"So no pickup lines?" Ryan replied with a smile.

"Just say hi," Maria replied. "Tell them your name. Tell them you saw them from across the bar and hope you aren't intruding. It's that simple."

Ryan looked to Mike and Steven. "I guess I should be the only one taking notes," he said with a laugh.

"I'm sure that's all Donovan did," Maria replied. "And look at him now."

The three of them looked back to the table in the corner, where Donovan still sat with his companion.

"Wouldn't it be crazy if they get together?" Steven said after a moment.

"Huh?" Mike asked.

"Like what if this is their starting point?" Steven explained. "What if this is the first moment in a series of lifelong moments for them together? What if this is the beginning of their story?"

"Technically it began in OKC," Ryan said with a shrug.

"Shut up, Ryan," Maria replied with a laugh.

"Wouldn't it be cool?" Steven continued. "Knowing that we all got to see the start of something? That's pretty neat." He paused as he considered it. "What about the guy in the pickup who waited for me to pick up my future wife's glasses?" he explained. He turned to Maria and Mike. "Or whoever saw you two first meet?"

Ryan watched the color drain from their faces as Steven continued his talking.

"We could all be witnessing firsts for everyone, and we just never know it. That's awesome. What if, twenty years from now, we all look at our Facebook pages and see Donovan and that guy and we say, 'I remember when…'?"

The group remained quiet for a few moments.

"Jesus. Twenty years is a long time," Mike said.

"It is," Steven replied. "My kids will be into and out of college."

"I'll be in my mid-forties," Mike replied.

Maria sipped from her drink. "I'll be past that."

"I'll probably still be hearing about how I offended you," Ryan said to Maria as he sipped his own glass.

"Oh, most certainly," Maria responded with a chuckle.

"You think we'll all still know each other?" Steven asked. "Think you'll still be working at Central Plains?"

"God, that'd be depressing," Mike answered.

"Depressing?" Steven asked.

"The working part," Mike replied quickly. "Not knowing you." Steven smiled.

"You want to spend twenty years doing this?"

"It doesn't have to be this," Steven answered. "Could be anything, I suppose."

It was Maria's turn to inquire. "So you want to work for Central Plains for that long?"

"I don't know," Steven replied. "I remember my parents working for the same companies for a long time. I know it doesn't happen much anymore."

"I'd like to be out west, I think," Mike replied. "Hiking and fishing and all that."

"You're a regular man of the woods," Maria chided.

"You know it," Mike responded back smoothly.

"What about you, Ryan?" Steven asked.

The music changed overhead as Ryan considered the question. *Twenty years.* It seemed like a millennium. He could barely register where he had spent the last five.

"I'm not sure," he said. "I sometimes wonder how I ended up here, to be honest. Asking that far in advance seems…hard."

"I'm sure you'll be pissing off someone special in your life," Maria said to much laughter from the group.

"We can only hope," Ryan replied. "As long as it isn't jail, then I think I'll be fine."

"Hopefully we don't have to worry about the future too much tonight," Steven concluded, as though content with where the conversation had ended. "It's a lot easier to live in the present, I think."

"Agreed," Mike replied, raising his glass. "Here's to our merry band of travelers and all the success we have ahead," he said. He half turned toward Donovan as everyone else raised their glass. "Some sooner rather than later."

They each clanked glass, then sat back in their chairs and sipped from their cups.

Ryan found himself staring at each of his companions as they settled into their seats, and an immediate sense of appreciation warmed him.

He felt his phone vibrate in his pocket, and he reached for it. Staring at the screen, he saw a text he had been hoping to see.

I found Vertigo *on TV,* Emma had texted.

Ryan smiled as he read the text. *That's a good one,* he texted back. *What are you up to?* she asked.

Ryan sat back in his chair. *At some bar in Minneapolis. Donovan's idea.*

Having fun? I can leave you alone if you're busy.

Ryan looked around the group, finding comfort in their contentment as they each enjoyed the soulful music of the bar.

No, that's alright, he texted back. *I'm free to talk.*

***

"I enjoyed that," Steven said loudly as Ryan buckled his seat belt inside the rental.

"That's surprising," Ryan replied.

"Surprising?"

"Eleven-thirty on a Friday, and Mr. Jesus Christ himself enjoyed his time at a bar," Ryan said as he looked down to his watch.

"How about you leaving with me instead of waiting until last call? That's surprising too, isn't it?"

Ryan smiled. "You're cheaper than an Uber."

"That's not the only surprising part."

"Yeah I know," Ryan replied. "I'm also mostly sober, which is depressing, but still a plus, I guess," Ryan continued.

"Not really what I meant but it is true," Steven replied.

"And there isn't some waitress or bridesmaid with us," Ryan continued as he looked into the back seat. "Unless you got one stored somewhere."

Steven smirked. "That isn't funny."

"No judging," Ryan replied. "That's what you told me."

"You say that when someone's lifestyle makes them prone to judging."

Ryan attempted to process his words. "Maybe I'm not mostly sober."

"The surprising point I'm trying to make is that you're changing," Steven said as he ignored the response. "Especially since you came back from Florida."

Ryan did not immediately respond as his mind went back to that morning some months back.

"It's none of my business as to what happened, for the record," Steven added.

Ryan nodded. "But you want to know, don't you?"

Steven continued to grip the steering wheel. "I just know it was hard for you."

"The women," Ryan began. "Mel….it turns out that she has been married. She didn't tell me until *after* I woke up in a hotel with her."

"That had to be tough."

"It was," Ryan replied. "Pulled out a ring and everything." He paused. "So after some yelling back and forth, she told me never to contact her again and she left."

Steven did not reply.

"But it wasn't until the long drive back to Miami that I began to wonder why I had actually taken the trip in the first place."

"And?"

Ryan shrugged. "I don't know. I don't know what I was looking for. All I know is that it was tough to get over her."

"Well if it's any consolation," Steven began. "I don't think you're changing because you're getting over Mel, or anything like that. I think you're changing because of your time with Emma."

Ryan felt his breath leave his throat as he returned to his window glances.

"She's a lovely girl," Steven answered. "Julie and I both thought so."

"That's your response?" Ryan replied. "*She's a lovely girl?*"

"She is!"

"You're not subliminally judging me?"

"For?"

Ryan turned. "You know what for."

"I don't think-."

"She's engaged."

Steven took a deep breath. "She is."

Ryan gritted his teeth. "And you know I like her."

"I do. And I presume she likes you."

"And she's engaged."

"Yes."

"So, aren't you supposed to tell me to stay away? To not be a homewrecker?"

"Do you feel like you're a homewrecker?"

"No," Ryan replied honestly. "But the further I get into this, the more I realize there's no way this situation ends well for me. It'll be a repeat of Florida once again."

"So why do you respond to her texts?"

Ryan considered the question. He had no answer that made sense.

"You're staying at the Fairfield, right?" Steven said after a long period of silence.

Ryan sighed. "Yeah," he replied. "It's across from yours."

Steven nodded.

"I'm hanging out with her Sunday," Ryan said sheepishly after a moment.

"You all doing anything fun?"

"I don't know," Ryan replied. "I'll probably spend most of the time trying not to get attached even though, as you've clearly indicated, I can't help myself."

"I don't think I indicated anything," Steven responded.

"Yes, you did," Ryan said. "You know you did."

"Listen—" Steven attempted to say.

"Tell me the truth," Ryan replied as he turned fully toward Steven. "Tell me I'm an idiot for falling for this girl. Tell me there's no way this ends well. Tell me that I'm, I don't know, committing a cardinal sin for even considering this path."

"People like other people all the time," Steven replied. "There's nothing new there."

"I think this one's a bit different."

"So you want my advice?" Steven said as he moved the car off the highway and onto an off ramp.

"Please," Ryan replied.

"Fine," Steven said. "My advice is to do what makes you happy."

Ryan's eyes went wide. "What?"

"That's it," Steven replied. "That's my advice."

"Do what makes me happy?"

"Yep."

Ryan threw up his hands. "Where was that when I was drinking and whoring?"

Steven shook his head. "Did that make you happy?"

"In the moment, yes."

"And after?"

Ryan bit his tongue.

Two Thousand Miles from Omaha

Steven turned on his signal as he stopped the car at a red light. "Do you know why I believe in God? Why I do my volunteer work? Why I *really* go to church?"

Ryan took a deep breath. "I don't know, to see hot chicks in many layered sweaters?"

Steven glared at him.

"You believe so you go to Heaven," Ryan replied seriously. "You go to profess your beliefs and inspire your kids."

Steven shrugged his shoulders. "Sure, those are some of the reasons."

Ryan continued to stare at his counterpart. "And the main reason?"

The light turned green, but the car remained in place.

"I believe in God," Steven replied softly, as though the secret would wilt if heard too loudly. "I believe in God because it became impossible to believe in myself."

Ryan said nothing as the green stoplight reflected on Steven's face.

"I know, right?" Steven said after a second. The light changed to yellow and then red.

"That's heavy," Ryan replied.

"It is," Steven said. "But it's true. I found it exceedingly difficult to believe in myself. To see myself for who I was, especially in dark times. My relationship with God, and my commitments, it helped that. The foundation of faith is that your higher power believes in you, and that resonated with me. I figured if *He* could believe in me, then maybe I could try again too. So I did."

Ryan remained silent as the light changed back to green. This time, Steven edged the car forward and into the turn.

"My point is this," Steven said. "Faith is crazy. You believe in giant arks and burning bushes and all that stuff. There's really no logic in it at all. But, faith is a relationship, just like any other one. And we don't get to choose how most of our relationships start. Sometimes they just happen, and there's nothing you can do about that beginning or how it makes you feel. The only thing that does matter, however, is does the relationship make you a better person? Not to the world and not to me, but to *you*. Does it make *you* a better person? A happier person? Those are the relationships that matter. Those are the ones worth being in, even if you think, or you know, that they'll never last. So," Steven continued, "do what makes you happy, and if spending time with Emma makes you and her happy, then do it."

The car continued onward down the side road as Ryan continued to process the words that were just spoken. "I'll be honest," he said after a long while. "I don't think I could have ever prepared for that response."

Steven laughed. "Yeah, well, now you know a secret about me."

Ryan returned to looking out the window as the lights of the hotel came into focus.

"Hopefully it's good advice though," Steven added.

"Coming from you," Ryan replied, "I'm sure it isn't terrible."

"I guess that's something."

Ryan continued to think on Steven's words as the hotel grew closer.

"Since you're doling out assistance," Ryan said after a moment, "you got anything on confidence?"

"Confidence?"

"Yeah," Ryan replied. "I feel like I'll need confidence to keep from screwing up whatever I have with Emma."

"Why would you sc—mess it up?"

"Because it's a habit," Ryan replied. "I guess it just comes naturally."

Steven pulled the car into the hotel's overhang. "Well, let's see," he said after a moment. "I believe a great man once said to use 'Ignorance. Sheer ignorance. There's no confidence to equal it.'"

Ryan opened the car door and unbuckled his seat belt. "Ignorance?" He stepped out and shut the door as Steven lowered the window.

"Yep," Steven replied.

"That another Jesus quote?" Ryan asked as he leaned forward.

"No," Steven replied as he shifted the car into gear. "That one was Orson."

Ryan stepped back as the car bolted forward. Soon it was out of the hotel parking lot and onto the main road. Ryan watched it intently as a smile formed on his lips. Shaking his head, he managed one more glimpse of the car before it was lost in the night.

Chapter 19
In Omaha

"So," Emma began as she set her golf ball down on hole one of the miniature golf course. "Did you plan on attending half price kids day at the mini golf course?"

Ryan laughed as he looked around the course to see dozens of children running around chaotically. "I did not," he replied. "But to be fair I didn't even know there was a half price kids day."

She laughed in return as she lined up a putt. "All these parents look younger than us." She hit her ball and watched as it stopped short within a few feet of the hole. "I'm not the best mini golfer," she said with a chuckle as he stared at her ball.

"That's alright," he replied. "I'm not great either."

"Probably due to my lack of competitiveness," she said after a moment.

Ryan lined up his shot and stepped behind his ball. "Your lack of competitiveness?"

"Yeah," she replied. "I'm the least competitive person you'll meet."

"Seriously?" He moved back from his ball.

"Yeah!" she said with a laugh. "You haven't been watching me play?"

He shrugged.

"I'm terrible at most games or sports mostly because I just don't care about winning."

"You're serious?"

"I am."

"Then why'd you want to go to mini golf?"

She considered it. "It sounded fun."

"But now it's terrible?"

"No!" she said with a laugh. "I'm having a great time. I just like talking with you. Where my golf ball goes though…" She trailed off as she raised her hands as if to say *who cares?*

Ryan smiled as he returned to lining up. "Have you always been like this?"

"Dancing, cheerleading, ballet…. Yeah, pretty much," she replied.

"You were a cheerleader?" Ryan asked.

"I was," she replied as though catching the interest. "Though it was pretty much by default given the size of my school."

He swung and his ball careened down the green. "And even then? No competitiveness? You weren't going all *Bring it On* to the rival schools?"

"I was just happy to be there," she said with a laugh as she moved to her ball and took another swing.

"That's amazing."

"Is it?" she replied. "Does that mean you're super competitive?"

Ryan shrugged. "I don't know about super competitive," he answered, "but I think I'm a normal amount for a guy."

"You're probably super competitive."

He laughed.

"I don't understand it much either," she said as she walked with him down the green. "My dad and brothers are all big sports guys, and even though Jay isn't into sports much, he's big into competitions with dance and all that."

Ryan stopped. "Dance?"

She considered his question. "Yeah, dance."

"Like tangoing?"

"Yeah, and like break dancing. He's won a few contests."

Ryan thought about her words. "So he's about to be in the military, he's well educated, and he can break dance?"

She laughed.

Ryan moved behind his ball. "Jesus," he muttered softly.

"If it's any consolation," she said from across the green, "the face you made when I brought Jay up is the same one he makes when I tell him things about you."

Ryan felt his breath catch. Eyes fluttering, he stood upright, no longer concerned with his golf ball.

"Wait," he said after a moment. "You've told him...about me?"

She stood firm with her purse on her shoulder. "Yeah," she replied. "Was I not supposed to?"

Ryan could feel that his jaw had dropped slightly. "I'm not sure." He fumbled for words. "I mean...what did you say?"

"That you were my friend," she replied matter-of-factly. "That we hang out and usually get coffee. Is that not true?"

He closed his jaw and shrugged. "Yeah, that's true."

"I didn't think it was wise to lie about that," she added.

"Did he have a response?"

"A response?"

"Yeah," Ryan clarified. "Was he…okay with us hanging out?"

"You're my friend, so he should," Emma answered. "But to be honest, I don't think he's thrilled with it."

Ryan heard his own idiotic response before he knew what he was saying. "Why?"

There was a silence as she processed the question. "Well," she answered. "I'm sure he thinks that by hanging out, it will eventually lead to feelings and that could lead to me liking you."

Ryan stared at her from across the green.

"And" she added softly, "I'm pretty sure he's right."

He felt his palms grow sweaty. He no longer knew what to do.

"But what he doesn't know," she continued, "is that I think I liked you from the moment we first talked. I don't think I needed to hang out to realize it." She adjusted her shoulder strap on her purse. "The only question I have, though, is why?"

"Why?"

"Yeah," she clarified. "Do I like you because you're different? Someone other than Jay who has shown interest in me? Or do I like you because I know I can't have you? Or do I like you because I genuinely like who you are and who I am around you? And what about you? What if you don't like me?"

"Impossible…" Ryan interjected. He could feel his shielded cards falling rapidly onto the table.

She smiled in relief. "What does that mean then?" She took a deep breath as she stared across the mini golf course. "Do you like me because I'm a rebound for someone who you actually like? Or do you like me because you can't have me? There's a lot of whys to answer here."

"Excuse me," a loud voice said from Ryan's left. "Can we play through?"

Ryan turned to see a family of four staring at the pair midway down the next green. He blinked wildly. "Yeah," he replied as he picked up his ball. "Go ahead."

He looked across to see her laugh as she picked up her ball. He could tell his flustered nature was not well hidden.

"Thanks," the father said as he readied his family.

Ryan quietly followed her to a nearby bench where they sat down.

"Sorry to stop our game," Emma said after a moment.

"It's alright," Ryan replied, struggling to find additional words.

They sat in silence for several moments as the family moved past and onto the next hole. The sun began to set in the distance as the lights of the course illuminated.

"What if," Ryan heard himself say. "What if the *why* doesn't matter?"

"Excuse me?"

He watched as she turned. and seeing her waiting for his response gave him confidence. "I mean," he attempted to clarify, "what if it doesn't matter?"

"You don't think it matters?" She rephrased her response. "What if I just like you because you're different than my fiancé? Or what if you like me because I'm different from your ex?"

Ryan shrugged. "What if?"

"I think that's potentially a big deal."

"It is," Ryan replied with another shrug. "But we aren't going to answer it sitting on this bench."

She turned from him and looked out across the golf course.

"But on the flip side," he said after a moment. "What if *this* is the real feeling and the other stuff is just that? Other stuff."

He knew no answer could determine her mind. There was nothing he could say or do to change her opinions. He could only speak truthfully and from the root of his soul.

"I do know," he said, "when I'm with you, I'm happy."

She lifted her head and looked at him.

He shrugged. "I also realize that prior to you, I wasn't happy very often."

"I'm happy with you too," she replied.

"I also see your green headband pretty much everywhere I go," he added, staring at the beacon in her dark blonde hair.

She laughed as she felt for the token. "This thing? It's at least ten years old."

"It fits you perfectly," he replied.

"Are you calling me old?"

Ryan laughed. "I meant bright and vibrant."

She nodded as she leaned forward and looked at the ground. "So what do we do now?"

Ryan took a deep breath. The question had been rolling around in his mind for quite some time. His internal reactions were simple: *Say goodbye to Jay.* He knew, however, that no answer was that simple. "I'm not sure."

"Me either," she replied. "Though now's your chance to back out if you don't want to like me anymore."

"Why would I want to do that?"

"Because there's no telling how this is going to end," she replied honestly. "And as you can see, I'm a mess."

He laughed as he reached for her arm and then her hand. He could sense an initial tremble, but soon, her hand closed around his.

"You're not a mess," he said after looking at their enclosed hands. He couldn't recall ever touching her before, and he reveled in the softness of her hands and the warmth in her touch. What was once mere sparks with words was now a fully formed inferno.

"Plus," he said as he looked into her eyes, "no matter how it ends, it'll be worth it."

He could see the tears form in her eyes, and before he knew what was happening, she let go of his hand and wrapped herself around him, embracing him with a compassion he had never known. He exhaled as he wrapped his own arms around her. He interlocked his fingers, never wanting to let go. He could feel her breath against him, and he could smell her hair under the headband that he rested his cheek on.

No one said another word as they hugged tightly, never wanting to let go.

There were no past relationships. There were no fiancés in other states. There was only here, and there was only now. That was all that they needed. That was all that mattered.

No ending could ever ruin that.

S.D. Goldman

Chapter 20
In Omaha

Ryan knew there was something amiss the moment he walked into the corporate office. Ears perked at the hustle and commotion, he perceived a hurried energy that he had not seen any time before. It was as though everyone was moving throughout the atrium, but no one was saying a thing.

He moved up the large glass stairs and down the hallway until he approached the conference room they had frequented all the times before.

Looking down at his watch, he saw that he was on time, but there was no one else around. In fact, compared to the ominous hustle of the first floor, the second was a ghost town.

He contemplated moving past the conference room altogether and heading straight for the cubicles. Perhaps *she* would provide some sort of clarification on the oddities of the office.

He reached down into his pocket and pulled his phone upward. Immediately, more red flags went off. There were missed calls. There were texts. It was as though his phone was a concoction of notifications. Swiping upward, he unlocked and attempted to open the first notification, but he was halted.

"Hi, Ryan," Kim Anderson's voice said softly from the now-open conference room door. "Come on in."

Ryan felt the lump grow in his throat. There was no happiness in her voice.

He pocketed his phone and followed her inside. He looked around the large room but found no familiar faces. His team was not present. Emma was not present. There was no one besides him and Kim and one other, a male face he saw seated at the only table in the room.

Ryan reached the seat opposite Kim and the unknown man at the table, and looked around. Suddenly he saw the reality before him.

This was not a meeting. This was an execution.

"Ryan, it's no secret that the company is facing hard times within our industry," Kim began in an almost prerecorded tone. "Between the legislative failures and the oil industry, Central Plains has had a rough eighteen months, with the last four being the most difficult. Tough decisions must be made, and unfortunately…"

Ryan watched as the man remained expressionless. Finally, Ryan ignored the man altogether and turned directly to her. "Am I fired or laid off?"

Kim sat back, clearly unnerved that her difficult speech was being amended. She looked to the other man and then back at Ryan. "You're being laid off."

"Just me?" Ryan spoke matter-of-factly.

The man attempted to speak, but Kim beat him to the punch. "The entire team."

"Including here?" Ryan inquired. "The corporate team?"

Kim remained silent for a moment. "The entire team."

Ryan could feel his pulse quicken. He no longer cared to be in the room.

"Four hundred employees across the company are being let go," Kim added, speaking as though she was now off-the-cuff. "We also closed two plants."

"Ryan," the man interjected, "my name is Dean and I'm with HR. I'm here to tell you that today, Central Plains is providing you with a severance package as indicated in this packet." He slid across a premade packet. Ryan noticed that there were several more in the basket behind the table.

"Given the uniqueness of your role," the man continued, "your severance package is also unique. You'll be given insurance and your salary for the next eight weeks to bridge the time until you find your next opportunity."

Ryan looked down at the packet that the man had casually opened, but he barely read the words. He looked up at Kim. "Has everyone else already been let go?"

Kim closed her eyes and then opened them. "I can't tell you that."

"Ryan," Dean interrupted, "this packet is full of information for what you'll do next. But in order to receive it, you'll have to sign this form."

Ryan ignored the man in front of him as he continued to look at Kim. "Can you at least tell me if there's anyone in those cubicles?" He motioned in the general direction of the cubicles beyond the conference room walls.

Kim didn't answer, and Ryan could tell from her pained expression that the area was likely empty.

"Ryan, I'll need you to sign this form indicating that you understand this situation," Dean said confidently. "It comes with an agreement not to post on social media—"

"Did we screw this up?" Ryan asked, again to Kim.

Dean remained calm. "Ryan, I'm going to need you—"

Kim shook her head. "No, you didn't."

"The entire team?" Ryan asked as he leaned forward. "Not even relocating them within the company?"

"Ryan—" Dean interjected.

"Fire me," Ryan continued. "You can even keep the benefits. Just get rid of me. Not them. Not Steven. Not Maria." He shook his head. "Not Emma." He looked up. "They all deserve their jobs."

"Ryan, please sign this form."

"Isn't that an option?" Ryan asked imploringly.

Dean grew curt. "Ryan, I'll need you to focus."

"Sorry, *Dean*," Ryan retorted in a biting tone. "I'm not talking to you."

Dean sat back in his seat. "This process will go much smoother if you—"

"Smoother for who?" Ryan quipped. "Me? Smoother for *me*? I doubt that. Smooth would be me keeping a job with my team, and from the sounds of it, that's not really on the table. I think you mean that this process will go smoothly for *you* if I shut up and sign your damn form."

Dean sighed. "Ryan, I'm just—"

"I don't know who you are," Ryan continued. "I've never met you. Don't you think that's a problem, especially if you're human resources?"

Dean didn't reply.

Ryan shook his head, ire growing in intensity within. "I'm not trying to make a scene, but I've got questions, and if your plan is to get rid of me without even affording me some goddamn answers, then the lack of *smoothness* in this process is on *you*, not me."

"We legally can't answer some of your questions," Kim said after her long silence.

Ryan turned to her. "I guess that's all that matters then."

Dean leaned forward. "Ryan, this decision is the hardest the company has ever had to make. But this opportunity will only benefit you in the long run."

Ryan looked down at the packet. "I'm sure the *company* is really losing sleep over it," he said wryly. "I assume my role in Spirit Lake is no longer available."

Dean took a deep breath. "That was backfilled when you left."

Ryan shook his head.

"Ryan," Dean said, "I'll need you to sign this agreement."

Ryan stared at the form for another minute before grabbing a nearby pen and signing in the designated spot. He pushed the form back across the table and pulled both his company card and company ID from his wallet before setting them on the table.

"Further instructions are in that packet," Dean summarized as he rose to walk Ryan out.

Ryan stood as well. He turned toward the door before one glance back. "What plants were closed?"

"What?" Kim asked from her seated position.

"You said they closed two plants," Ryan replied. "What two?"

"Grand Meadow and Waterman," she replied.

Ryan could feel his heart sink. Without another word, he turned and walked out of the conference room with Dean close behind.

***

Ryan was outside of the building when he pulled his phone from his pocket. Ignoring the packet in his other hand, he quickly unlocked the device and began to scroll through notifications. He clearly saw a group chat between Maria, Steven, Mike, and Donovan, but he breezed past that in search of others. He saw voicemails from Steven and Donovan. He saw additional messages directed solely at him. He worked past them all until he found the one he knew he would find: a brief yet summarized message from Emma.

Meet me at the coffee shop.

Ryan closed his eyes as he pocketed his phone. Despite the past twenty minutes, he felt as though his headspace was calmed and reserved. His internal anger had peaked during the meeting before, but now he was past the shock and disappointment and on to searching for solid ground. He needed something, and thankfully she was already a step ahead and waiting for him. Perhaps that solid ground was close at hand. Perhaps the fall would not be as violent as it could be. Perhaps this moment would not turn catastrophic.

He stepped inside the shop after several minutes of walking and quickly looked around the half-empty space until he spotted her at a table on the near side of the café. She smiled upon viewing him, and hope grew within.

"You at least got a packet, I see," Emma said as he approached.

Ryan looked down to see the object in his left hand. "This and the memories, I suppose." He took his seat and watched as she sipped her coffee. "You didn't get a packet?" Ryan asked as he sat his own down onto the side of the table.

She shrugged. "Hourly," she replied.

Ryan was not sure he understood. "How did yours go?"

She gripped her coffee with both hands as though they were cold. Leaning upon her elbows, she attempted to maintain her composure. "It was tough," she said honestly. "We all cried. I cried a lot, which I'm sure isn't hard to believe."

Ryan remained unmoved.

"Kim just told me that it wasn't my fault, that I was a great employee, and that she tried all she could. And that was pretty much that."

"She seemed distraught to say the least," Ryan said. "Probably more for you than me." He smiled weakly.

Emma returned the smile as she looked down at her cup. "Did you have any indication this would happen?"

Ryan watched her watch the coffee cup. "None."

She shook her head slowly. "It's crazy, isn't it? Leave on Friday and everything's good. Come in Monday and you're gone."

Ryan didn't respond. He wanted more than anything to comfort her, to reach across the table and hold her hand, yet he remained stoic. He could only watch as her eyes filled with tears.

"It'll be OK," Ryan said as she continued staring. "These things…" He paused as he attempted to find the words. "These things happen, but it's nothing we won't overcome."

She brushed her eyes and smiled as she continued looking down.

"I'm sorry this happened," Ryan continued, hoping an increase in words would make the situation better. "I really am."

She looked up and her tears subsided. "Why are you sorry?"

Ryan shrugged.

She smiled. "This isn't your fault."

"Surprisingly," Ryan replied with a chuckle.

She continued her smile as she returned her gaze to her cup. "What are you going to do?"

"Do?"

"Yeah," she responded as she looked up. "What are you going to do now?"

Ryan sat back as he struggled to think of an answer. "I don't know, honestly. You?"

She shrugged. "My parents have already called me at least four times."

Ryan's eyes went wide. "They know?"

"My dad has company news sent to his phone," she replied. "When the news broke this morning, he practically knew before I did."

"How did they handle it?"

She huffed. "They were ecstatic. Now I get to return home and join 'the real world.' Their words, not mine."

"The *real world?*"

"It's like I've just been playing around out here."

Ryan didn't reply, but merely watched as she related her earlier conversation.

"I still don't think they really understand why I left, or why I've stayed out here. All they know is Tennessee."

"You don't want to go back, though, right?" Ryan heard himself speak before he knew what he had said.

She looked up at him, and he saw tears. "I don't have a choice."

Ryan felt his heart sink into his chest.

She looked upward as though attempting to control her emotions.

"I think," Ryan said in his calmest voice, "I think you have a choice." He knew he was standing on the precipice of their relationship, yet he couldn't back away. It was time to stand back or fall.

"Ryan," she replied after a deep breath, "I have to go back."

He wanted to fight. He wanted to say anything to change her mind. Yet he couldn't find the magic combination of words. What she said was right, and it would always be right. She had to go back.

"My mom," she continued, unaware of Ryan's internal struggles. "She's already booked the next flight out here so that she can help me pack up and head home. And undoubtedly on that ride home we'll talk about the wedding, and undoubtedly, she'll win me over and make me comfortable and then we'll plan a date and then I'll be married and then we'll move, and I'll raise our kids and life will be good." Tears welled. "Life will be good."

Ryan could no longer help himself. He quickly moved across the table and pulled his chair until he sat alongside her. He pulled her close and into the deepest of embraces that he could muster. Cradling her head under his chin, she wept into his shirt as he felt his own emotion grow.

"I'm so sorry," she repeated over and over. "I'm sorry, Ryan."

He shook his head. "Don't be sorry," he replied as he held her. "Don't ever be sorry. You have nothing to be sorry for."

"What I said last night—"

"You meant it," Ryan finished her thought. "And I did too."

She looked up at him and he could see her affection behind her reddened cheeks and watery eyes.

"I do too," he repeated.

He lessened his grip and she pulled away slightly as she rubbed her eyes with her napkin. He turned his chair slightly as he watched her calm.

"This sucks," she said after a moment.

He smiled, happy to see her humor through the tears. "Yeah, it does."

She looked around the coffee shop as though realizing where she was for the first time in a while. "I'm going to miss this place."

Ryan exhaled. "You can always come back," he replied slowly. "Bring your fifty kids."

She smiled as she took a sip from her cup.

"I take it that this will be the last that I see you then," Ryan heard himself say. "Right here, in this moment."

She did not readily answer.

"I mean," Ryan said. "I could always meet your mom and try to impress her with my lack of job, tattered suitcase, and storage unit that may or may not have been sold off."

Emma smiled, though he could see tears in her eyes. "I hope you don't think bad of her, or anyone in my family," she said after a moment.

"Of course not," Ryan replied with a smile.

"It's just…" She trailed off. "I guess I just haven't been honest with them about where my head's at in all this."

"They just want what's best for you," Ryan replied softly.

"Yeah," she responded. "Yeah, they do."

Ryan wished that he had more to say. He felt as though he needed to say more, to perhaps explain how her happiness was paramount to him, and how much he wanted her to stay right here. The idea rolled through his mind like a moss-covered stone, yet he couldn't interpret the thought into words that made any sense.

"I'm sorry," she said softly.

Ryan turned, suddenly realizing that perhaps his lack of words was contagious to her as well. "Sorry?" he asked, incredulous at the notion that she would have anything to apologize for.

"All of this," she replied. "For leading you on."

Ryan shook his head. "You have nothing to apologize for," he said, knowing that his words meant little now.

She began to stare at her cup, and he could sense that their time together was ending.

"Do you want me to walk you to your car?" he asked after a moment.

She looked up at him. "No," she replied. "I want to remember you here, in this place. Not some parking garage somewhere."

He nodded.

"I also don't want you to say goodbye," she continued. "How about instead, you just say something fun and witty? Something to have us leave here on an..." She considered her words. "Uplifting note."

"Fun, witty, and uplifting?"

She nodded.

"So instead of goodbye," Ryan turned his head, "you want a yearbook quote?"

She began to laugh.

"That's it?" Ryan replied with a smile. "You want me to say, 'Have a good summer'?"

"HAGS," Emma chortled.

Ryan rolled his eyes. "That's the most millennial thing I've ever heard you say."

"That was all the rage in our high school," Emma answered. "That and HAKAS."

"Whoa," Ryan replied. "What a rebel."

"I never wrote that," she countered. "But I know people who did, and it wasn't long before the Christian school teachers figured it out."

"Regular Morse code breakers, I'd say," Ryan said with a chuckle.

"Indeed."

Ryan stood upright. "Alright, fine," he began. "How about this for a yearbook quote." He paused. "You," he pointed directly at her as if to remove any confusion. "You didn't have to talk to me. You didn't have to hang out with me. To be honest, you probably shouldn't have, given my past."

She smiled and he did as well.

"I think that says a lot about your character choices, or lack thereof," he added with a wink. "But in all seriousness," he continued, "you didn't have to give me the time of day, and you did, and although we both knew it couldn't last, I can honestly say that knowing you has been nothing but perfect."

He could see tears well in her eyes.

"And I know," he said after a deep breath, "I know I'm better for it."

"Thank you," she said softly as she wiped her eyes.

He leaned forward and calmly embraced her.

It was simple and pure, and Ryan never wanted it to end. He gripped tightly, feeling her hold throughout his entire being. He closed his eyes and breathed in the scent of her hair and her perfume before opening them and seeing the bright headband below his nose. If the moment was to become a memory, then he knew it was one he never wanted to lose.

They let go, and she slowly stood up. He could feel his heart empty, yet his face remained stoic. He wondered if he had even breathed in the last minutes.

"You know," he heard himself say he stood as well, "if you ever do decide that fifty kids and life on a military base just isn't for you, I'll be here."

She looked up. "You say that as though I'll know how to find you."

He pulled his phone from his pocket.

"Don't worry," he said as he looked at the device and then back to her. "I won't text you or call anymore. But if you change your mind…" He considered his words as he spoke them. "Just text me 'hey.'"

"'Hey'? That's it?"

"Yep." Ryan nodded. "That's it." He knew it made little sense, and he wondered why he had said it. "Think of it as our secret code."

She smiled.

"Just text 'hey,' and I'll know what it means."

She nodded, as though considering the enormity of his words.

"Don't forget me, alright?" she said as she embraced him.

"Same," Ryan replied as he held her close.

She finally let go, and he did as well.

"Goodbye."

Ryan took a deep breath. "Bye."

She moved past him like a breeze, and before he knew what had happened she was out the front door. She turned and gave him one more smile from the window before she moved out of frame, and out of his life.

He took a deep breath as he sat back down at the lonely table and closed his eyes. He could still feel her embrace. He could still smell her perfume. A short time ago, he held everything in his hands, and yet now, nothing remained. It was all for naught. The hourglass had run out.

He opened his eyes to an empty window, and that was when it finally set in.

She was not coming back.

***

That evening, Ryan found himself sitting in his hotel room chair alone. The room was quiet, and the lights were turned low as he stared out the window to nothing in particular. He barely moved as cars passed by underneath, oblivious to the man above.

Dusk was creeping in.

He had felt it take hold soon after parting with Emma. It was at first a quiet anguish, discernible only by his increased heart rate. Yet as he drove away, the rage grew, first like a rolling pebble and then like a mighty boulder. The anguish was replaced by anger. The anger was replaced with seething contempt.

He hated that he was in this situation. He hated that he had fallen for her so fast. He hated that she cared for him and he for her. He hated that she had no other options.

She had other options, he thought. *He* was the other option. She could have chosen him. She could have turned away from her fiancé. She could be with him. She could do all those things. She had chosen not to. It was her fault. It was all her fault.

Except it was never her fault.

Perhaps he could have said more, he thought. Perhaps he could have given her a reason to stay. Perhaps he could have offered more. Perhaps if he'd had stability, a job, a career, a life. Perhaps if he'd had anything, it would have been enough. How could he compare to a perfect specimen of a human being? He had no ambition. Jay had ambition. He had no goals. Jay had goals. He had nothing to offer. Jay had everything to offer. He had no financial stability. No relocation opportunities. No perfect looks or dancing moves. Jay had it all. He had nothing. He could give nothing. Nothing compared to the relationship that Jay had with her parents. Nothing compared to the relationship he had with her. Nothing. In actuality, the choice on paper was the easiest choice ever. It was never her fault that he had nothing.

It was his fault.

Ryan stood from the chair. He needed a drink. He needed something, anything to quell the rising tide within him. He wanted to forget her. He wanted to bury his pain. He wanted anything but to be alone in a hotel room that he had to check out of tomorrow.

He walked to the hotel door and pulled it open. As he did so, he heard his phone ping.

His breath held in his throat. *Could it be?*

He pulled his phone out to see not a text, but another icon on his screen.

New Facebook Message.

Instantly, his senses became heightened. Opening the app, he quickly clicked onto the mail icon. His eyes went wide, and he felt a slight tingle on the back of his neck. He brought the phone closer to his face.

From Max Willis.

Ryan felt the lump in his throat grow, yet he knew there was no way to stop his actions. He pushed to read the message, and with sweaty palms, he sat down on the bed's edge as he read the words hurriedly:

Hey Ryan—Hope all is well. Just curious how it went with Mel. Did you find her in Florida? I haven't heard from her since, and when we last talked, she was excited to see you. She said she was going to wait around, so I hope you did. Hope you had a good time. Let me know how it went. Thanks, man.
Max

He stared at the screen for a long while as he attempted to process the words on the screen. Then, as though lightning struck his core, he bolted into motion. Quickly, he moved to his suitcase and rummaged inside, throwing clothes and toiletries onto the floor. Finding nothing to his liking, he moved to the outer pockets. Finding the main one empty, he quickly moved to the top zipper, and in seconds, he had discovered his query.

Moving back to the computer, he set the receipt onto the desk nearby and unfurled it until it laid flat. Then, without a second glance, he moved back to his laptop.

His heart began to race and sweat grew on his brow. None of these things deterred him, however. Nothing would discourage him now.

He had a message to respond to.

Chapter 21
3,819 Miles from Omaha

Ryan pulled his sunglasses down as he looked at his phone. Around him, the hustle of the airport was extensive, and as he waited outside for the shuttle, he could feel the heat from the Hawaiian sun bear down on his hair.

Casually, he switched the phone off airplane mode and held it outright in waiting, as though expecting the message he hoped would be coming. Perhaps that was all he needed, he thought. Just a message. Just the "hey" he was looking for. Perhaps then he could stop the madness that he had embarked upon. Perhaps then he could let Mel go.

It had been a long plane ride. Ryan looked at his watch then back to his phone, knowing it was well into the afternoon.

It had taken over a day to arrive in Honolulu, and between the delays at Chicago and the overnight layover in L.A., his confidence in his task was growing smaller and smaller.

He felt the phone vibrate in his hand. Quickly, he unlocked the screen to see a text message. His breath caught in his throat. Could it be? From Steven.

Do you really think this is a good idea? What if her brother was just mistaken? What if she doesn't want you to see her?

Ryan sighed as he briefly looked at the previous messages explaining his sudden absence. He thought that, of anyone, Steven would most understand.

She knew I was coming. He typed with fervor. *She could have left but didn't. I need to know why.*

Seconds later, Ryan felt his phone vibrate via a call. He looked down to see Steven's name.

"I'm not asking for your permission," Ryan said as he put the phone to his ear.

The voice on the other end was measured and calm. "Maybe we should just talk about this."

"Talk about what? How Mel isn't married?"

"The real reasons you are doing what you're doing."

"I told you. She knew I was coming. Her brother said she was *waiting* for me. No married person would wait for me like that."

"I meant the other reason."

"What other reason?"

"Ryan. What happened with Emma?"

The name hit him like a punch to the gut. "What about her?"

"Emma."

"I heard you."

"You can't say her name."

"What does she have to do with anything? She left and went back to Tennessee to get married and move to a military base and become a housewife and it's for the better."

"Who's better?"

"I don't have time for this."

"Why'd she leave?"

Ryan's voice grew. "*Why?* Maybe because she's engaged? Or maybe it's because there sure as shit isn't anything here for her with me."

There was silence at the other end of the phone.

"I'm not here because of her," Ryan replied coldly. "I'm here because I was lied to."

"Because you think this other woman who told you she was married isn't actually married."

Ryan nodded. "Exactly."

"And you know this how?"

"I told you. Her brother said that she knew I was coming."

"And?"

"What married person would allow themselves to engage with an ex-flame and carry it out for well over a day?"

"I don't know, Ryan," Steven answered. "But that logic hardly proves your thesis."

"I knew you'd say that," Ryan replied. "So I responded to her brother's message for more info."

"You asked if she was married?"

Ryan hesitated. "Not exactly. I asked if she was seeing anyone or if she was in a relationship because she seemed *off* during our encounter."

"So you lied?"

Ryan gritted his teeth. "Those weren't my exact words. I just wanted him to tell me what was going on."

"And did he?"

"He said, and I quote," Ryan paused as he pulled his phone down and opened the messenger app. "He said, 'Seeing anyone? Not that I know of. We don't talk very often, but she's never mentioned a boyfriend or even dating, honestly. Weird that it didn't go great.'"

Steven remained silent.

"You see?" Ryan asked as he put the phone back to his ear.

"What am I supposed to see?"

"What kind of person wouldn't tell their brother or father that they were married? Can you imagine?"

Steven sighed.

"She never told them about her *husband* even when she was dating him, although everything else about her life he knows—her job, her travel plans, where she lives. You mean to tell me she's maintained a secret marriage? I don't buy it. Plus, no married woman is going to knowingly subject themselves to the weekend we had, full of sparks and emotion, without telling me about their husband."

"But she *did* tell you."

"She was scared," Ryan reasoned. "It all probably moved too fast. She freaked out. She made up an excuse. It makes perfect sense."

"She had a ring, didn't she?"

"Yeah, it was a ring," Ryan replied. "Doesn't mean it was a wedding ring. I didn't even see it very closely, so who knows."

Another pause.

"You still think I'm reaching here."

Steven exhaled. "I think you need to leave this alone."

"Why would she lie?"

"Why does anyone lie, Ryan?" Steven said in an elevated voice "The *why* doesn't matter. She's clearly either married or wants to be away from you, and that's all that matters. I'd respect her wishes."

"I knew you'd say that."

"It is the most logical answer."

Ryan rolled his tongue over his teeth. "If she's lying, I need to know why."

"She doesn't owe you anything."

"I spent years trying to find her," Ryan replied. "*Years*. I think I'm in the right."

"To find someone who doesn't want to be found?"

"Then why did she wait for me? Why agree to spend time with me?"

"Ryan, you're searching for answers that you may never find."

"Well, I have to find them. If anything, it'll be closure."

"Closure?"

"Just like when you found your faith."

"What?"

"You finding your faith," Ryan replied. "That was your moment of clarity. Of closing one door. Maybe this is what that is for me."

"Ryan, finding my faith wasn't something that just happened miraculously."

"You know what I mean. You found closure to move on and build your life. Now I need mine."

"It wasn't closure that allowed me to move on," Steven reasoned. "It was realizing that I needed to stop hating the one thing that I hated most."

Ryan ignored him. "I need this," he replied. "I need these answers. I have to find them."

"How?" Steven finally asked. "How do you even intend to find her again?"

A long pause.

"Ryan," Steven began. "I know this is tough—"

"I know where she lives."

Steven's voice went soft. "What?"

"I-I have the receipt from the hotel," Ryan explained. "She used her card. She paid for it and apparently, they took her information from her driver's license. It's all right there on the receipt."

"Ryan," Steven attempted calmly. "You can't..."

"I need to ask her why," Ryan replied.

"Rip up the receipt and throw it away," Steven cautioned. "Nothing good can come from anything you're thinking about doing."

"I have to go ask her why," Ryan repeated. "I need to know why she lied. Why she's kept herself so far away from me." There was another pause.

"Ryan, I can't stress enough how that is a terrible idea."

"Why is that?"

"Because!" Steven answered. "Visiting her house unannounced? That's almost stalkerish!"

"*Stalker?*" Ryan replied. "Knocking on someone's door is stalkerish?"

"Do you want a court of law to decide that?"

"That's ridiculous," Ryan answered. "I'm going to knock on her door and ask her calmly what happened. Then I'll leave."

"And if she isn't there? You going to stay there until she comes back?"

"I'll leave a note or something," Ryan replied. "I won't hang around."

"I'd rather you just have her brother ask. Let him be the middleman."

"She'll ignore his questions," Ryan replied. "She may even tune him out. But if I meet her face to face, she'll have to answer."

"And what if you don't like the answers?" Steven asked.

"Anything is better than nothing."

Both men turned quiet.

S.D. Goldman

"I know it's stupid to you," Ryan finally said after a long while. "I know it sounds crazy, but you don't know her like I do." His voice sounded weak, almost defeated.

"Maybe you don't know her either," Steven replied.

"Maybe so," Ryan said. "Maybe you're right. But no one has ever made me feel like she does. The way we are together. The way we feel together. Nothing compares. If there's any chance that we can make it work, I have to take that chance. What's the worst that could happen?"

"A lot," Steven answered.

"It's nothing worse than how I feel right now," Ryan replied.

"I know you're in pain, Ryan," Steven reasoned. "I know you're upset."

"Upset is an understatement."

"Then let's address why you're upset."

Ryan's voice rose slightly. "I'm upset because I was lied to."

"You're upset because you couldn't give her a good life."

"Excuse me?"

"Or you're upset that she found one without you."

Ryan grit his teeth. "You still think this is about Emma—"

Steven sighed. "It was interchangeable," he replied.

Silence.

"Ryan, sometimes things come into our life we're not ready for, even if they seem perfect..."

"I need to let you go," Ryan replied as he saw a bus approaching.

"Come here," Steven responded. "Come back to Omaha and hang out at my place for a bit. We can work all this out."

"I can't," Ryan replied. "I need to see this through. And that's here in Hawaii. Not Nebraska. Not Tennessee."

"Tennessee?"

"I'm not a homewrecker," Ryan said indignantly. "I'm many things, but not that."

Steven remained silent, as though he had no further words.

"I'll let you know how it goes," Ryan said. "Wish me luck."

He hung up the phone without another word and got onto the waiting shuttle.

Sitting in the back row, he let his bag rest between his feet as he settled into the multicolored seat. He allowed the air conditioning to wash over his body as he attempted to make sense of his situation.

No one understood him. No one could understand why he had to make this journey. No one could understand why he needed to be here, right here, at this moment.

Answers.

That was the true root cause of his travels. He wanted answers. He *needed* answers. He needed to understand why Mel would lie to him, why those that he loved were so content to walk out on him. He needed to grasp how something so perfect couldn't be realized. He needed to understand something that he currently couldn't.

Mel had lied. He was convinced of this. There was too much supporting evidence not to agree, regardless of what Steven had thought. The secrets. The ring. The hurried need to leave a perfectly good Key West hotel. It was all too convenient.

But why? Why wait for him, then leave him? Why do it at all? Why break his heart over and over?

He pulled his phone from his pocket. No further texts.

Sighing, he pulled up his map app and retrieved a piece of paper from his pocket, carefully looking at one while transferring information into the other.

He knew it was her house. He knew it deep within his soul. Yet to be certain, he looked at the address online, and sure enough, it was a small yellow bungalow with a perfectly pruned yard. It was too perfect, Ryan had concluded. Even the house matched her personality. It was clearly where she laid her head at night.

Ryan finished typing the address and saw that it was twenty-five minutes away.

The air conditioning was beginning to revive him, while his belabored thoughts were beginning to sway toward his initial conviction. Despite his mid-journey trepidations, he was growing in confidence now.

He needed answers. He needed to hear her reasoning. He needed to understand why.

Minutes later, he got off the shuttle and into a waiting rental car without further delay.

Nothing would stop him now.

***

The house looked exactly like it had online.

Ryan parked along the suburban street and sat for a moment in the car as he took in the scenery.

The yellow bungalow was older, but still well maintained, complete with a variety of tropical plants and small trees adorning both sides of the front walkway. In the driveway, a black SUV sat idle.

He took a deep breath. She was home.

The sun continued to bear down on him as he opened the driver door and stepped out onto the street, taking in the view. Casually, he looked at himself in the window's reflection and saw that despite many hours of air travel, he still looked presentable in his button-down and khaki pants.

He took one more deep breath from the car. It was now or never.

Cautiously, he began the walk past the fenced yard and towards the front door. Stepping around the SUV, he quickly glanced inside, as though looking for any further clues, yet there was nothing discernible to his roving eyes. Slowly, he approached the front overhang.

His hands felt empty as he walked. He should've brought flowers or a gift, he thought.

But no, this was not a reunion, he knew. This was a trial.

And yet, what if she was happy to see him? What if she was waiting just for this moment, just to see if he'd chase her down? Is that not what anyone would want? To be pursued cross country? To be shown that level of love? Perhaps this was exactly her plan, and he was merely actualizing it. How would he ever turn her down? How could he resist the flame they'd once had? How could he ignore the feelings that sprung inside of him? Perhaps this was a reunion after all.

A million emotions welled through his body, yet as he knocked on the large wood door, everything faded by the wayside. He was here. He was about to see her. That was all that mattered now.

He heard the door unlock. He could feel her presence on the other side. The moment was now.

"Holy shit," the voice said as the door was pulled open.

Ryan felt his breath catch as he stared into the shadows of the house. He had heard the voice before, but it was not Mel's.

Quickly, he pulled his sunglasses from his head as he saw the figure before him.

Tall, slender, and every bit the picture of masculinity, the man he had once seen on a Chicago rooftop stood in front of Ryan.

Dru's face remained frozen in shock as Ryan saw Mel appear at his side.

"Holy shit," Ryan replied.

Chapter 22
3,829 Miles from Omaha

"What are you doing here?" Dru's tone remained astonished as he stood smiling. Next to him, Mel's eyes remained transfixed in abject horror.

Ryan could feel as his brain attempted to explain the situation in real time. His palms immediately grew sweaty as he stood unshielded. "I—" Ryan paused as he attempted to process his setting. "I wanted to drop by to…" His mind was roving. *Think,* he told himself. *Think.* "I wanted to see how you're doing," he stammered. "I was in the neighborhood."

"You were in Makakilo?"

Ryan could sense the hesitancy in the response. He racked his brain for signs he had seen along the way to the house. "Pearl City," he replied calmly. "For work."

Dru stared at him, but it was Mel's gaze that most haunted Ryan. The moment felt like an eternity.

"Well come in," Dru responded as he held the door open with a huge smile.

Going in was the last thing Ryan wanted to do.

"You sure?"

Dru immediately softened. "Yeah, of course," he replied. "I'm sorry, I'm just in shock to see you. I didn't mean to give you the third degree."

Ryan smiled, and his gaze caught the unremittingly startled face of Mel. He swallowed the lump in his throat and followed the pair inside, knowing he had no other options.

"You have a wonderful home," Ryan said as he stepped inside and shut the door behind him. It was small and quaint, with minimal tropical décor, and despite the size, an open-air feel courtesy of the large sliding-glass windows separating the main living room from a large backyard porch.

"Thank you," Dru replied. "Please come and sit." He sat down on a large three-person sofa while Ryan slowly sat upon a loveseat nearest the entry corner of the room. "It's our first home," Dru continued. "And it's a bit small, but it's nice for what it is."

"Yeah," Ryan replied as he attempted to calmly look around the room, noting that Mel was nowhere to be found, though he was certain she was listening from wherever she was.

"So Pearl City," Dru replied. "Quite a journey for you, I imagine."

Ryan smiled. "Yeah," he answered. "This is a far cry from Nebraska."

"What is it that you do again?"

Ryan was not altogether sure their first encounter had included such details, but on the off chance it had, he didn't want to further a lie. "Sales. For an ethanol company."

"Ethanol?"

"Yeah," Ryan replied as he continued to survey the room. From the uncluttered furniture to the white, colorless walls, it seemed like a space completely devoid of Mel. He would never have expected her to own such a living room.

"I didn't realize there was ethanol in Hawaii."

Ryan's eyes returned to Dru, and he could tell the questioning was far from over, despite the jovial nature in his tone.

He smiled. "Well, not yet," he replied. "Though I wouldn't be surprised if one day they try with pineapples."

Dru laughed.

Ryan leaned back in the loveseat, doing his best to show complete calm. "No, to be honest, this is a retreat for the company. Typically, when harvest season begins in the Midwest, we get a few weeks off since the farmers are all in the fields. So here we are."

"Not a bad retreat," Dru said with a laugh.

Ryan smiled as his wits continued to roll. "I think my boss just wants to earn a lot of those American Airlines points."

Dru's laughter increased as Ryan settled a bit in his seat. "So," Dru said after his mirth died down, "I have to ask—how on earth did you find our house?"

Ryan shrugged, knowing the question was coming. "Well, it was kind of a fluke." He could feel the pressure of the answer, and he knew he had to deliver. "I was talking to my friend Steven, who still talks to one of the guys you were in Chicago with. You'll forgive me if I don't remember his name."

"Was it Pete?" Dru replied. "Or Nick?"

Ryan shrugged. "Maybe Nick? I'm terrible with names. Anyway, Steven casually mentioned that we were out in Hawaii and Nick had said, 'Oh, say hi to Dru for me.' Now Steven didn't remember who you were because I'm pretty sure you didn't meet, but I certainly did."

"And he told you I was in Makakilo?"

"God's honor," Ryan replied. "Didn't quite know the address, but he said it was a yellow house and pretty much was spot-on in location."

"That's crazy," Dru replied with a laugh. "Nick's never even seen this place outside of a photo I sent him."

"Well, he knew somehow," Ryan responded with a chuckle. "I was nervous when I approached because there's a few yellow homes out here, but I figured what the hell. Let's see if it's really you."

Dru laughed, and Ryan could sense that somehow, inexplicably, his story had been bought.

"I can't believe he got you to the right house based on a picture," Dru said. "That's wild."

"I agree," Ryan replied with a laugh. "Maybe he stalks you or something, who knows?"

Dru laughed harder now. "Maybe!"

Ryan took the opportunity to peruse the house via his sightlines, and he quickly spied down the length of the couch to the other end of the room, where he saw what appeared to be the edge of a child's playpen peeking around the edge of the hallway. He stared at the item intently, knowing he was more in over his head than he'd ever thought possible.

Mel's voice rang out behind him. "A drink?"

She stepped into the room, carrying three glasses of lemonade. Ryan watched as her gaze was transfixed on him.

"Sure," Ryan replied with a catch in his throat. She continued staring as she handed him the drink.

"Forgive my rudeness," Dru said as he accepted a second glass. "This is my wife, Melanie."

Ryan nodded toward her, though the tension in her gaze made him wildly uneasy.

"How," Mel replied as she sat next to her husband, "do you all know each other?"

Dru laughed. "Well, to be honest, this man here is the reason I was able to get married altogether."

Ryan put his glass to his lips and held it there as the words hit his ears.

"This is the guy," Dru continued toward Mel. "The guy I met in Chicago who kind of set me straight on everything."

Ryan knew he had been part of a conversation that had occurred long before his arrival.

"Really?" Mel replied, eyes roving between her husband and Ryan. For a moment, Ryan could sense that she, too, was confused.

"Yeah," Dru continued. "He was there with his work group, and I was there with the guys, and we met outside and talked for a good length of time, right?"

Ryan nodded as he sipped his lemonade with shaking hands.

"This man…" Dru pointed to Ryan. "He's got a way with words."

"Does he?" Mel replied.

"He really does," Dru continued. "He told me that marriage was sacred, and that the way I talked about you showed how much I cared, and he made me see that nothing else really mattered when we were together. It was impressive, especially coming from a stranger."

They both looked at Ryan, and as he sat his glass down, he shrugged. "You were conflicted," Ryan replied. "You'd have done the same for me."

Dru smiled as he sipped from his glass. "He's here on a business retreat," he said toward Mel. "And apparently got our address from Nick."

"Nick?" Mel replied.

"I know," Dru said with a laugh. "I didn't even realize Nick knew where Oahu was."

Ryan sipped from his drink to keep his nervousness on edge.

"So, Ryan," Mel said after she sipped from her glass and set it down. "Are you married, or have kids?"

Ryan felt his hand shake slightly. He moved his leg across his other knee in an attempt to look comfortable. "No, actually," he replied politely as he attempted to turn on the charm. "Still haven't found that special lady quite yet. And as for kids, none that I know of." He laughed in a manner more unsettled than humorous.

"Well, it's impressive to have that range of advice," Mel responded calmly. "I'm happy you set Dru here straight."

Ryan nodded with a smile as the married couple exchanged a quick glance. He reached down and picked up his glass as Dru did the same.

"So I'm curious," Dru said after he sipped from his drink, "how does my wife know your name?"

The room went cold.

Ryan looked up from his glass as he saw Dru staring at him, the smile no longer present.

"Excuse me?" Ryan said softly.

Dru leaned back against his sofa, and another smile appeared. This one, however, lacked any sort of friendliness. "My wife. How'd she know your name?"

"My name?"

Dru turned to Mel. "How'd you know his name was Ryan?"

"You said it," Mel stammered. "When I walked in. You said, 'Ryan was in Pearl City.'"

"No, I didn't."

Mel looked at Ryan, who remained riveted to his spot on the loveseat.

"I didn't," Dru continued. "I couldn't remember it. I felt like an idiot this whole time. But you knew it. You knew it was Ryan."

Ryan set his glass on the table. His voice trembled. "I think it's time for me—"

"You stay right *there*," Dru replied. His voice was tinged with kindling.

Ryan swallowed the lump in his throat as his eyes roved the room, though this time, it was for the most accessible exit.

"I'm going to ask again," Dru said dangerously toward Mel, "how'd you know this man's name?"

"Dru." Mel set her glass down.

"Is this the guy?" Dru replied, clearly continuing a conversation Ryan had never heard before.

"Dru, please."

"*This* guy?" Dru replied as he quickly glanced at Ryan. "Seriously?"

"I have no idea why he…" Mel trailed off as Dru stood up.

"I can't believe this." Dru moved to the picture window and leaned against it, his back to the room. He turned to Ryan before returning to the window. "This *fucking* guy?"

Mel approached but was quickly rebuffed.

"Get away from me," Dru scolded as he remained against the glass. "Don't fucking touch me."

"Dru, I had no idea…" Her voice trailed off.

Ryan's hands trembled. He could see the muscles in the man's back tense. He could feel his rage growing. He knew that there was no way this ended well.

Like a missile from a cannon, Ryan sprang upward and leapt over the arm of the loveseat. In seconds, he was to the front door without a backward glance.

"*Get back here, asshole!*"

Dru's voice was thunderous as Ryan ripped the door open and sprinted through the lawn. Behind him, he could hear the heavy steps of the man in quick pursuit.

Ryan reached the front yard fence in stride and leapt upward, hoping he had enough clearance to cover the wood pickets. Surprisingly, he sensed clearance, and he lowered his shoulder as he landed ungracefully onto the sidewalk in a heap.

"*Don't you run away from me!*"

Ryan was upright in less than a second and he fumbled for his car key as he bolted to the front door of the vehicle. As he yanked the door open, he quickly saw Dru at a full gallop as he leapt the fence with ease.

"Holy shit," Ryan muttered as he fell into the car and heaved the door closed.

"*Get out of there,*" Dru roared as he approached the driver door.

Ryan's hand convulsed as he moved the key to the ignition as quickly as he could. Yet as it hit the edge of the ignition slot, Dru rammed into the driver's door with his full body. Ryan watched in horror as the key fell to the floorboard.

Ryan looked to his right as both he and Dru realized that the passenger window was down.

As quick as lightning, Dru leapt the hood and was at the passenger door. With one hand fully extended, he reached inward and grabbed ahold of Ryan's shirt. *"Get out of there,"* Dru screamed.

"Get off of me!" Ryan wailed as he was pulled across the console. His feet kicked wildly as he attempted to reach the key beneath him. Yet all his strength paled in comparison to the military grip and enraged ego that held him tightly.

Like a ragdoll, Ryan was pulled through the window of the passenger door. Appendages flailing about, Ryan punched and scratched at the arm that held him tightly before it let go, causing him to fall out of the car and onto the cement curb, back-first.

"Stop it!" Mel's voice boomed behind him, but Ryan was too far into his flight-mode to respond. Screeching in agony, he made the best of his temporary release and rolled directly under the car, hoping that its shield would buy him more time.

"Get out of there and face me like a man!" Dru roared.

"Fuck you!" Ryan shrieked from underneath. His eyes darted as he watched Dru's footsteps move to each side of the car. He rolled his body one way and another to escape the proximity of the feet.

"You fucking weasel," Dru taunted. *"Get out here."*

"Stop this now!" Mel yelled. "The fucking neighbors are out here!"

Ryan did his best at dodging, but it was to no avail. From the back of the car, Dru latched onto Ryan's right leg, and despite some well-placed kicks, Ryan screamed as he was dragged across the asphalt.

He tried to scramble away, but Dru quickly disarmed him with a rough push, causing Ryan to fall sprawling into the grass. Immediately, Dru was on top of Ryan with his full body weight.

"You fucked my wife?" Dru seethed, though his tone remained strong. "Even after Chicago?"

Ryan wheezed under the man's stout weight. "I…didn't know…"

"You didn't know what?"

Ryan could feel his chest grow heavy. Sensing this, Dru moved his knee lower.

Ryan gasped. "I didn't know…she was married!"

"Bullshit!" Dru countered. "Did you have this plan when we talked? *Tell me!*"

Ryan knew his answers were pointless. "I didn't know anything," he yelled. "I'm as confused…as you are!"

"You expect me to believe this?"

Ryan's eyes grew wide. "I don't…even know if…we had sex!"

He felt the weight of a sledgehammer hit his cheek as Dru lowered his right fist square. "*Tell me the truth!*"

Ryan spit a mix of blood and saliva. "*I am!*"

Another blow across his temple.

"*Stop it!*' Mel screamed. Ryan could sense she was close.

"*Tell me!*"

Another blow. Ryan could feel his nose crunch under the weight of the well-trained fist.

"I didn't know…" Ryan muttered as he continued to cough up his own blood.

"*Stop lying to me!*" Dru's rage only grew as his sweat and spit rained down on Ryan alongside the fists. "*Stop lying to me!*"

"*He's not lying!*" Mel roared.

Ryan could feel the fists stop, though his eyes were already grayed over.

"He's not lying!" Mel repeated from nearby. "I didn't tell him I was married!"

"What?" Dru's tone turned from rage to confusion. "What? What do you mean?"

"I didn't tell him," Mel repeated. "He didn't know I was married."

Ryan could see nothing of the conversation, but he felt as Dru shifted off him.

"You didn't tell him?"

"Not until the morning," Mel explained. "When I left him."

Ryan coughed loudly as the blood continued to flow down his face. He closed his eyes and opened them as the color began to return.

"How could you?"

"I don't know," Mel replied. "I had no idea you'd met each other. I had no idea he was coming here. Dru, please."

The sound of departing footsteps brought Ryan back to a full reality.

"Dru, please!"

Ryan turned his head to see Dru stomp up the driveway back toward the house with Mel in close pursuit.

"Dru, stop, please!"

Ryan waited until he heard the front door to the house open. Then, with all the effort he could muster, he clambered to his feet.

Legs shaking, he fell against his rental car before he was able to brace himself into a standing position. In the window's reflection, he could see a sea of red across his face.

His mind was spinning. His face was numb. His back was enflamed in agony. Yet somehow, despite the injuries, he managed to stumble his way to the driver's door.

"Are you OK?" an old woman neighbor said as Ryan pulled the door open. Ryan turned to her, realizing that he could only see through his left eye.

"No," he replied curtly.

He fell into the driver's seat and reached down to fumble for the key. Finding it, he groaned in agony as he pulled the driver's door closed. Hand still shaking, he managed to insert the key and turn the engine on.

He turned to the house to see Dru exit the front door, with Mel close behind. The scene was muffled as Ryan watched from the car window and one good eye. Nevertheless, he could see her face flooded with tears as Dru moved toward the driveway, car key in hand. He no longer acknowledged Ryan.

Ryan turned back to the steering wheel to see his own bloody handprints. Without another thought, he reached down and shifted the car into drive.

Seconds later, he was gone, away from the promise of what might have been, and away from the reality of the anguish that was.

Chapter 23
3,819 Miles from Omaha

Ryan's body ached as he pulled himself into the bathroom. Dropping his bag to the ground, he moved to the mirror and noticed just how swollen his eye and cheek were. By now, all the blood had dried and his makeshift napkin bandages from the car were stiffened. He looked as though he had gone ten rounds, but even he knew he had barely survived one.

He pulled the tissue from his nose and turned on the water, taking care to be gentle as he rubbed the cool water onto his wounds, wincing each time he did. He looked like hell. He felt even worse.

He looked down at his shirt to see a variety of bloodstains. Gingerly, he stripped off his button-down shirt. He discarded it in the trash and tucked his undershirt into his jeans, no longer caring about formalities. He pulled his overcoat from his suitcase and set it on top of his luggage.

Stepping outside the bathroom, he took a deep breath as he looked down at his phone for his boarding pass. He barely had enough energy for the task.

"Sleep on the plane," he said to himself softly, knowing he was close to needed rest.

He walked slowly, giving no care to any of the tropical décor or happy travelers around him. He only cared about getting through security. He only cared about making it onto the plane.

He spied the security line ahead, some distance off. He could feel his pace increase slightly. It wouldn't be long now.

As he walked, bag rolling behind, he spied movement to his right, standing up from a row of chairs along the wall. At first, he ignored the form, but as it began moving to him, he couldn't help but turn. His breath caught into his throat, and he froze in the middle of the terminal.

Mel had been waiting for him.

Surprise turned to dread as Ryan watched her approach.

"Mel," he began once he knew she would hear him. "Mel, I've got a plane…"

"I don't care," she replied coldly. Her eyes were puffy from a mixture of rage and sadness, and her cheeks were red from the pressure of her emotions.

"How did you…?"

"You fly American," she said bluntly. "This is the only American terminal. You see, I listen to you when you talk."

"I could have gone to a hotel…"

"Your bag was in your car," she replied. "Plus, after your ass beating, there was nowhere else you would go."

"Well," he replied, knowing he was not going to win any verbal sparring, "if it's okay with you, I'd like to continue my plan."

"And what exactly was your plan?"

"Excuse me?"

"I want to know what your plan was. Why are you here? Why did you come to my fucking house in broad fucking daylight?"

"Was I supposed to come at night?"

"Don't you dare…" Her tone was dangerous, almost lethal.

He looked around the terminal, noting that so far, their conversation had remained without any onlookers.

"Why are you here?" Ryan asked. "Isn't there someone else who needs your attention now?"

She stared at him with nothing but disdain. "That's none of your business."

"It's interesting what you think is and isn't my business, isn't it?" Ryan replied, voice attempting to measure her tone. "Especially given just how well you divulge your own business."

"Why are you here?"

"Where is he?" Ryan ignored her question. "And why aren't you with him?"

"Why are you here?"

"How about you answer mine and then I'll tackle yours?"

She continued to glare but remained unmoved. "I don't know."

"You don't know?"

"No," she replied, voice clearly resonating how little she wanted to share. "I don't know where he is, or where he goes."

"He goes places?" Ryan replied mockingly. "How mysterious. Seems like something you'd tell your wife."

"I don't know because I don't ask," she seethed in retort. "Believe it or not, marriage doesn't mean you open your entire book to someone. He's got his outlets, and I let him have them."

"Funny hearing marriage advice from you."

"Fuck you."

"That's what I thought." He grabbed his bag and moved past her on the way to security.

"Why did you come here?" she asked from behind him. Her voice became elevated, and he had no choice but to stop.

"Why does it matter?" He turned and let go of his bag.

"It matters."

He shook his head. "You know why I came here."

"I assure you, I don't."

He bit his tongue.

"The last thing I remember," she replied coldly as she took a step forward, "is me telling you to never contact me ever again. That's what I remember. What I didn't say was to come to *my* house and do the exact fucking opposite of that."

Ryan exhaled. "I didn't think you were married."

Shock registered across her face. "You what?"

"I didn't think you…were actually married." He paused. "I wanted to prove myself right."

"You've got to be kidding," she replied. "That's the dumbest thing I've ever heard you say, and that tops a long list."

"I'm sure it does," he said. "I'm sure it *is* the absolute stupidest." His voice began to rise on its own. "But do you want to hear the dumbest thing I've ever heard? You'll love this. How about a married woman who *knowingly* waited for an old flame to show up despite being married, and, oh yeah, not even telling her fucking family about the marriage? That's pretty dumb, right? I mean, can you imagine someone actually doing that? To their husband? To their family?"

She stared at him, and he knew he was going too far. Nevertheless, he couldn't hold back.

"You knew I was coming," he continued. "You knew, just like I knew you'd be there. Your brother knew. Everyone knew, and yet only one of us knew that they *shouldn't* have been there. And yet that person, for some reason, stayed. *You stayed.*"

"I told you not to contact me."

"Yeah, I know," Ryan replied sarcastically. "My mistake. But knowing what is true and what is false with you is next to damn impossible."

She shook her head. "I've never lied to you," she replied. "I've never lied. Unlike you."

He rolled his eyes. "Not telling the truth is just as bad as lying."

"Maybe that's how you justify it," she said curtly. "But not me."

"Well, thanks for clearing that up," he replied. "I'm glad we've had this talk."

"So was that your plan? Find out I wasn't married and then what? Woo me again? Because we've worked out so good in the past?"

He didn't respond. In truth, he had no good answer.

"How did you know he was my fiancé?"

"What?"

"In Chicago," she replied. "You met in Chicago. Were you stalking him? Did you find him online? A photo of us or something? How did you possibly know?"

He took a deep breath. There was no way she would ever understand.

"If you're going to turn my life to shit," she said after a moment, "I should at least get to know how long it was planned."

"I didn't want to turn your life to shit..."

"Did you know in Miami? Of course you did. You've had to know all along. Do you realize how much I tried to stay away from you?"

He stared at her. "I didn't know."

"What?"

"I didn't know he was your fiancé. I didn't know who he was," he replied truthfully. "I thought he was some guy. He *is* some guy. I had no idea he was marrying you, and I had no clue he would be opening your door. Trust me, I was just as surprised as you were."

"You expect me to believe that?"

Ryan sighed. "To be honest, I don't really care if you do or don't. But I'm telling the truth for some reason. I have no idea how or why we were both there, but I guess it's just some sort of sick coincidence."

"You're seriously going with that? Do you know what the chances of that happening are?"

"Not offhand," he replied coldly. "But as I was getting my ass beat, I did think, *Wow, what are the odds?*"

She stood stoically. There was no mirth in her face.

"You didn't really convince him to marry me, did you?" Her voice turned softer.

He looked around the terminal as he considered his response. "I don't remember what I said." He stepped back to his bag and gripped the handle. "And it doesn't matter now."

She was silent, and he wondered if the conversation was over. He half turned, hoping to escape.

"Why don't you ask the question you've been wanting to ask?" Her voice was now even.

"Excuse me?" He dropped his grip as he turned back around.

"Go ahead," she replied bluntly. "Ask it."

"Ask what?"

"What you've wanted to ask all this time. Since Shannon. Ask what you've been dying to know."

He stared at her. "Mel, I don't know what you want me to say."

"You want to know why I didn't wait for you."

The words leveled him.

"That's right, isn't it? That's what you've wanted to ask me all along? Maybe that's why you're here."

"I don't really care…"

"Bullshit," she replied. "Even you can't play that off."

He closed his eyes and took a deep breath.

"Do you want an answer?" She paused. "Do you want *the* answer?"

He felt his heart rate increase. He was not prepared for something he'd had all the time to prepare for. His mouth opened. His brain struggled to process. Maybe he didn't want the answer after all.

"I didn't wait for you," she replied, "because there was nothing to wait for."

He could barely maintain his eye contact with her, but he knew that despite his trepidations, he needed to hear this.

"Do you know what happened after you left Shannon in handcuffs? After the news crews and reporters and everyone in that shithole town came by? Do you think things returned to normal? Not by a long shot." Her voice grew in rage. "Every day, people were pointing. There were whispers. 'She's the girl whose heart was broken.' 'She's the girl who's waiting for him.' 'She's the girl who had a gun pointed in her face.'"

"It was pointed in my face too," Ryan interjected.

"And maybe you accepted that, but I sure didn't," she replied. "I'm not the girl whose heart breaks over a man. I'm not the girl who waits for a boy."

"Clearly," he said.

"You're damn right," she continued. "Especially not a boy who's *completely* unable to become a man. Do you remember what you said to me as you were being dragged away?"

Ryan remained silent.

"You said, 'The things that you hear about me, they're *not* me. *I know you*,' you said. 'I know the *real you*.' That's what you said." She paused. "That's exactly when I knew. It wasn't with the whispers. It wasn't with the stories. It was the exact last moment you saw me. That's when I knew you weren't worth waiting on. Do you know why?"

Ryan again stood silent.

"Because you still don't get who you are. Who you really are. The good and the bad, they're all the same person. The same *you*. We don't get to choose which parts we ignore, and which parts *aren't* us. It's all us. It is *all* us."

She took a deep breath. "A *man* understands that. And that's what I need, Ryan. A man. A man who understands his faults. A man who understands who he is and what he is. A man who knows that he has good parts and bad, yet is able to accept himself for who he is. Dru is that man. And he makes me a better person. A person who also reasons with their faults and tries to be better. He is the man I need. You? You think your faults are the result of someone else. A Mr. Hyde to your good Dr. Jekyll. But I can't blame you, Ryan, because that's exactly how a boy thinks. A boy can never reason with who he is because he can't. He's just a boy." She paused. "For years I was fine with that," she continued. "I accepted where we both were and moved on. It wasn't hard. It just needed to happen. But you're right. I screwed up in Miami. I waited for you. I wanted to see if you had changed. I wanted to see if perhaps you had grown and matured. And God, your charm. It's always been indescribable. I *almost* believed it. I almost fell again. I can only imagine how many impressionable women you've taken to bed just because they believe the shit that you say."

He continued to stare at her.

"People believe what you say, Ryan." Her voice turned to a whisper. "But at the end of the day, even you can't hide the simple fact that you're still a boy."

He nodded, raw from an internal anger and sadness that gripped his being.

"There was nothing to wait for, Ryan. There never was."

He looked around the terminal, knowing he had little rebuttal. "I suppose that's why you've removed yourself from family and social media and all that, right? Because it was easy to accept all that and just move on, right?"

"Some things just aren't about you."

"I'm sure they're not," he replied, voice almost breaking. "And maybe you're right. Maybe I'm just an asshole. Maybe I am just a boy. If that's what you need to think, that what we had didn't matter, then so be it. I'll be whatever you need."

She stared at him, and he could sense pain in her eyes. Such pain, however, would never be vocalized, especially by her.

"I don't ever want to see you again," she said after a lengthy pause. "I mean it. I don't want to hear from you. Don't talk to my family. Don't ever come back to find me."

He scoffed softly. "Trust me, you have nothing to worry about there."

"I'm serious."

"As am I," he replied, voice now cold. He looked around the terminal. "You can have your paradise," he said as he grabbed his suitcase handle. "I'm just fine staying out of it."

He had nothing else to say. His voice and his body had both been defeated from fatigue and emotion. He looked her in the eye and sensed that she, too, was done with words. They had said all they had to say. He shook his head and turned away. Pulling his suitcase behind, he took one step away, and then two. Before long, his pace had increased, and soon he was far away from the battle site.

He didn't know how long she watched him go. Perhaps it was only a minute, maybe two, but he knew she didn't immediately leave. Something had made her stay and watch him walk away. Something had made her think about the words that she had said. Regardless, he knew she would not walk out without some hesitation.

He pulled his luggage into the security line. If she had stuck around, he was not about to turn around and check. He didn't need confirmation. He didn't want to be wrong. He had already been wrong enough for one day.

Chapter 24
In Omaha

"How's this look Mr. Keller?"

The voice caused Steven to peer up from his own canvas located at the first of a series of tables parallel to one another in the large rec room.

"I think I messed up the nose a bit," the man continued, "but it's kind of funny."

Steven approached the man's canvas and saw a crudely imagined version of a much more detailed artwork located at the front of the space. He continued to stare at the canvas before turning to view the source and then returning back to the man's canvas.

"Why is the nose weird?"

The man shrugged. "I was using the wrong side of this brush-,"

"No," Steven interjected. "Story-wise. Why is the nose weird?"

"Huh?"

Steven took a step back as the men surrounding the main artist and the other tables all looked up.

"Your painting makes you the artist, and as the artist, you get to tell the story that flows freely within you, and so you Kevin, you made this piece. What does your piece say?"

Kevin shrugged as he stared at his image intently. "I just thought I used the wrong side of the fucking brush."

"Don't say fucking," another man several persons down said. "Show this man some fucking respect."

Kevin rolled his eyes.

"Think about it," Steven replied. "It can be anything you want. Maybe he had plastic surgery and it went wrong?"

Several of the men laughed.

"Maybe he, I don't know. Maybe he got punched."

Another man at an opposite table spoke up. "Maybe he threw one to many bows out on the court Kev."

Kevin smiled, but his eyes didn't move from the canvas.

Steven stared at the man opposite him clad in a light blue jumpsuit, similar to all the other men around him. He once felt out of place in his polo and kakis, but having been in this space so often now, his attire was an afterthought.

"Maybe he was just born that way," Kevin finally said after a moment. "Just a messed up nose. And people made of him and told him to fix it and all that shit, but he didn't give a fuck." He looked up. "Sorry man," he said.

Steven urged him onward.

"Yeah, maybe he didn't care. Maybe he just owned what he had and that's why he looks so....content."

"Content?"

"Yeah. He's ready for anything. He knows who he is."

Steven nodded.

"How's that?" Kevin asked.

"I think," Steven replied as he looked down to the canvas. "I think that's a great story."

***

It was nearing dusk when Steven finally began packing up the mini canvas and painting supplies that he had brought with him. Looking at each of the images, he found the usual mix of eclectic details and variety in quality. One thing remained the same in all of the images, however; they were all unique.

Packing his items delicately, he finally moved out into the hallway before following the guard through a cavernous maze of hallways to a check-in station.

"Same time tomorrow?" the man behind the glass asked.

"I'll see you then," Steven replied as he signed the clipboard and set his clip-on badge on top. "Have a good night David."

"You too Steven."

Steven waited for the door to unlock before he moved out of the facility and towards his car. He loaded up his materials in his trunk before sitting down in the driver's seat. Rubbing his hands, he then opened his center console and pulled out his cell phone before peering at the text that displayed on the front screen. It was a picture that clearly read "Omaha Eppley Airport." Beneath the image was a text message:

I'm here.

***

"I expected you to be waiting here," Ryan said from a chair near the airport exit door.

Steven smiled as he approached from across the large space.

"I figured you'd have a tent pitched or something," Ryan continued as he stood slowly.

Steven said nothing, and instead gripped his friend tightly in a hug.

Ryan winced as he was squeezed, and he half returned the embrace.

"If it means anything," Steven said as he released, "I had parking prepaid."

Ryan smirked, knowing his wit was not lost on the man. "Got to get those discounts."

"Let's go home," Steven said after he stared at Ryan for a moment.

Ryan didn't reply, and instead struggled to grip his luggage, a move that was quickly rebuffed as Steven took over instead.

Ryan attempted to regain his control, but it was no use. He was much too tired, and it was much too late.

***

"I know I look like hell," Ryan said as the car proceeded down the highway.

"You do," Steven replied from the driver's seat.

"There was a baby who wouldn't shut up like two rows up."

Steven considered the statement. "Did that baby beat you up?"

Ryan squinted his eyes as he looked over to his counterpart. "That's why I didn't sleep on the plane."

Steven smiled. "I understand." He attempted a few glances at his companion, but could only see shadows in the darkened car. Nevertheless, every time they passed a streetlight, he could see a brief glimpse into the bruises and cuts.

"It looks worse than it feels," Ryan said in an attempt to downplay.

"That's not saying much," Steven replied.

Ryan sighed from the passenger seat.

"Do you want to talk about it?" Steven offered.

Another deep breath.

"We don't have to."

Ryan turned. "I'm sure you don't need an explanation."

Steven shrugged. "Not really," he replied. "But if you'd like to talk about your feelings…"

"I'd rather not."

"Fair enough," he replied. He wanted to know more, especially regarding just how his friend was doing mentally, but he knew he couldn't seek answers now. There would be plenty of time for that later. For now, he must be content with knowing that Ryan was alright. Time would tell what would happen next.

"Did you have a good flight otherwise?" Steven asked.

There was no answer.

Steven half turned to see that Ryan had already fallen asleep against the passenger window.

One hand on the wheel, Steven leaned back in his seat, more relaxed in the silence. He pressed the gas pedal down a bit more as the car left the glow of the airport and returned back home.

Chapter 25
In Omaha

Ryan forced his eyes open despite his body's exhaustion. There was silence around him, and for a moment, he lay still, soaking in the quietness and enjoying the feeling of the high thread cotton he lay upon.

Turning his face toward the window, he could see the bright sun cascading through, and in the stillness, he could see the occasional dust particles in the rays. It was peaceful and serene. It was everything his body was not.

Dragging his head up off the pillow, he turned to see bits of dried blood in his wake. Taking a deep breath, he pulled the covers off his body and examined the remainder of the sheets to make sure there were no additional stains left behind. Seeing that there were none, he shook his legs awake and slowly proceeded into the on-suite bathroom, where he examined his wounds.

Walking back into the bedroom, he spied a clock on the nearby nightstand that read 1:18 p.m. To the right of that was a hook with a robe hanging idly. He shook his head, attempting to disrupt the overnight cobwebs as he reached for the robe.

Quietly, he pulled the bedroom door open and investigated the hallway before stepping out. As he proceeded down the corridor, he was enamored with the home's high-quality finishes and design. The hallways were coated in a pleasant light gray color, and as he continued down the stairs and past the collage of pictures he once stared at, he found himself in the kitchen, a space that was decent-sized, well maintained, and tasteful.

"Good morning," Steven said from behind the kitchen island.

Ryan leaned against the counters on the opposite side. "Afternoon, more like it," he replied.

Steven looked at the clock on the microwave. "I guess you're right."

Ryan could sense that he was examining him.

"There's coffee in the pot if you'd like," Steven offered. "Wife made it a few hours ago, but still."

Ryan nodded as he saw the pot to his right. For now, however, he didn't move.

"Did you sleep well?"

He considered the question. "I did," he replied. "I might have gotten some blood on your pillowcase."

Steven looked down at a tablet that was in front of him. "That's fine," he said. "I would have been surprised if you hadn't."

Ryan nodded, not knowing what else to say. Awkwardly, he moved to the coffee pot and grabbed a nearby mug. Pouring himself a small cup, he brought it to his lips, revolting in the initial taste but swallowing it nonetheless.

"Probably a bit cold," Steven said as he looked at Ryan over his glasses.

"A little," Ryan replied as he attempted to mask his displeasure.

For a moment, neither of them spoke, and instead, Ryan held his mug while Steven continued to look over his magazine.

"Where's your wife at?"

"Took the kids to the zoo," Steven replied. "Lucky her."

Ryan smiled weakly, and silence ensued.

"I still don't feel like talking about yesterday," Ryan said after a few moments.

Steven looked up. "That's fine," he replied. "I understand."

Ryan continued to stand idly by, unsure of what to say next. "You have a nice house," he muttered.

Steven smiled as he continued to read. "Do I?"

"Yeah," Ryan replied. "I'm not sure I told you that the first time I was here."

"Well I appreciate that," Steven replied. "Luckily we've owned it for a few years so the mortgage isn't terrible. Otherwise I doubt one salary would keep us here."

Ryan nodded. "Yeah," he said. "I take it you haven't found anything yet?"

Steven looked up. "It's been three days."

Ryan lowered his mug as he smiled. "Jesus it has hasn't it."

Steven returned the smile.

"Feels like ten years," Ryan said as he ran his fingers through his hair with his other hand.

Steven returned to his magazine. "Some days I suppose it does."

More silence.

"I know it's only been a couple of days," Ryan finally said. "But do you miss it?"

Steven considered it. "Sometimes. But it is nice to be home."

"I think that's surprising," Ryan replied.

"Oh?" Steven looked back up.

"I just thought you loved it."

Steven looked upward. "Parts of it, sure. But I think I realized that I needed a refocus, and this helps me achieve that."

Ryan smiled. "That's pretty optimistic."

Steven shrugged with a smile.

Again, more silence.

"What about you?" Steven asked after a moment. "Did you love the job?"

Ryan took a deep breath. "Did I love selling ethanol?"

"Yeah," Steven replied. "And the traveling and all that?"

Ryan considered his words. "I liked parts of it."

"Parts?"

"The traveling. The rewards points." Ryan smiled as he looked down toward the floor. "The people." He thought for a moment before raising his glance. "The selling part is whatever. I can take or leave that. But there are parts I liked."

He could sense that Steven wanted to ask additional questions, yet for some reason, he remained restrained.

"So what's next? Are you just going to be home every day?" Ryan said after another pause.

Steven chuckled again. "I'm sure I'll find another opportunity somewhere," he replied. "But for now I'm good with my volunteer work."

"Doing?"

"Arts and crafts with some less fortunate folks."

"Did I know you did that?"

Steven shrugged. "I don't know, did you?"

"I don't think so."

"Well then, you learned something new."

"You've gotten a lot more...different...since I last saw you."

"Different?"

"Content? Confident?"

"Maybe I'm just getting wiser."

"I doubt that's it," Ryan replied.

Steven smiled as he stood from the island. Casually, he moved to the window where he peered out into the surrounding landscape. "Have you seen any good movies lately?"

"Movies?"

Steven turned. "Yeah, movies. You're the cinephile, aren't you?"

It was Ryan's turn to chuckle. "I don't think I've seen a new movie in a long time."

"No?"

"No," he answered. "Though to be fair, I'll have plenty of time now."

"Maybe your next job should be something involving that."

"Movies?"

"And traveling, since you liked that."

Ryan shook his head. "I'm sure I'd be the only person looking for a job where you can travel and watch movies."

Steven smiled, as though understanding the sarcasm. "Yeah, probably not. Good call."

Ryan thought on the subject for a moment. "Maybe I'll go see a movie or two while I'm here. That'd be nice."

"You should," Steven replied. "Get caught up."

Ryan reached for his mug again. "I won't wear out my welcome though."

Steven turned from the window. His face was rigid. "You can stay as long as you like."

"I know you have to say that."

"Not really," Steven replied. "I could say 'get out now,' but I'm serious. The room is yours."

"Well, I won't stay too long."

"Why?"

"*Why?*"

Steven stepped back toward his island chair. "Yeah. Why not?"

"Because it's your house. You have a wife and kids."

"Do you have somewhere else to be?"

Ryan considered the question. "I'm not sure."

"Not sure?"

Ryan shrugged. "My cousin is having an engagement party in Florida that I'm supposed to go to next weekend." He was surprised that he even remembered.

"Oh?" Steven replied. "Are you going?"

"No," Ryan answered.

Steven laughed. "Why not? Why bring it up?"

Ryan pushed away from the counter as he moved around the kitchen, eager to find anything to look at. He stopped at the refrigerator and the assortment of magnets on it.

"Do you want to go?"

"Not really," Ryan replied. "It's nothing against my cousin. It's just that…I don't know…I'd feel weird."

"Weird?"

"You're analyzing me again," Ryan replied as he peered at Steven from around the fridge.

"I've been analyzing you since I picked you up yesterday," Steven replied with a smile.

Ryan returned to the magnets. "I should go to the party."

"You probably should."

"But that's just not my life, I guess."

"It's not?"

"I haven't been home for something like that in five years," Ryan replied. "What would I say to them? How would it look?"

Steven shrugged. "You don't have to say anything. If they invited you, they want you to be there."

"You sound like my mother."

Steven laughed. "I'm just offering logic."

"We'll see," Ryan replied. "But it's most likely going to be a no."

Steven nodded and reopened his magazine. "If you ever get bored here, you're more than welcome to help me out with my art classes."

Ryan moved to the island across from Steven.

"It's just an offer."

"Do I look like I'm good at ceramics or whatever it is your doing?" Ryan reasoned. "I can barely keep myself together."

"It's painting stills mostly," Steven replied. "It's kind of hard to fit a kiln in my car."

Ryan smiled.

"I was just merely offering," Steven replied. "You can also just sit in the back and do nothing but listen."

"Listen?" Ryan replied. "Listen to what? And why?"

"Listen to other people, I guess," Steven replied. "I don't know."

"You're offering because you think I need to *listen* to other people?"

"I offered because it's what I'm doing this afternoon," Steven corrected. "And I figured you could either spend time with me or sit here alone."

"I'll take that second one."

"I forgot how frustrating you are in the flesh." Steven took off his glasses and rubbed his eyes.

Ryan laughed. "Not the first time I've heard that this week, and it likely won't be the last."

"That's pretty presumptuous."

"Maybe *I'm* just getting wiser too," Ryan replied. "And speaking of wise, I think it'll be wise for me to go get a shower and some ice so that I don't look like a punching bag when your wife and kids get back."

"Smart," Steven replied. "I'd hate to have them scared."

"Me too," Ryan responded. "It's rude to scare your hosts."

With that, Ryan left Steven alone in the kitchen and proceeded back up the stairs to his room.

Chapter 26
In Omaha

"This shit looks like garbage," a man said from the table in front of Ryan.

"Watch your fucking mouth," a guy to his right said as he hit him in the arm. "Sorry Mr. Keller."

"I'm just saying," the first man continued. "I can't draw this pot."

"It's a vase brother," another man said.

"More like vasé," the second man said.

"It's a pot," the first replied. "And I can't paint it."

Steven approached and looked at the canvas before looking over his shoulder at the flowers sitting upright on a stool. "I think you're doing just fine."

Ryan wordlessly stared down at his canvas with its sketched re-creation before looking up at the men in front of him.

He could not believe he was back in jail.

Upon driving in, he immediately had a feeling of paralysis. Despite the Omaha Correctional Facility being latitudes away from his Florida jail memories, he could still feel the cold saturated colors and harsh lighting that dominated memories he tried hard to forget. He wasn't even inside and yet it all came rushing toward him like a failed dam.

He tried to return his body to normalcy, but his pulse would not respond. It was then that he considered bailing altogether. Steven didn't need a reason. Steven wouldn't care. He could just say that he was sick, or tired, and that he didn't want to go in. Yet his mouth would not open, and soon enough, he found himself carrying in a bag to the check-in station.

Surely his ID would give him away, he thought. Could he even visit a prison? Yet before he could fully develop all his questions, the guard issued him and Steven a badge and unlocked the large steel door.

"It's a rec space," Steven replied as they entered the room, "but it works well for painting."

Ryan did not say a word.

"I think they do town halls or something in here as well," he continued as he moved to a table and set down his bag. "You can unload your stuff on this table."

Ryan could feel his palms sweat as he pulled out fifteen blank canvas and sat them on the tables under Steven's direction.

"Obviously we're limited in what we can bring in to paint," Steven continued explaining despite Ryan never asking. "But I figured flowers might be nice for today." He pulled out a vase and a grouping of fresh cut plants before arranging them at the front. "I think that will work."

Ryan wondered if he had said any words since the car entered the parking lot.

Soon enough, the men in light blue jump suits entered the room, and after a brief introduction, Ryan found himself staring at his own blank canvas, wondering if any of the surrounding men could sense his apprehension, or if any of them could sense that he was more like them than they'd ever know.

"Man I think I found a new career," a man said from the front table amidst all the other ongoing discussions, cursing, and paintbrush swishes.

"You couldn't draw a dog last week, but suddenly your van Gogh," another man said.

"Who the fuck is van Goah?"

"Jesus Christ Jimmy, stop saying fuck."

"Who is van Goah?"

"It's van Gogh," another man interjected. "He's the dude who cut off his ear."

"Why the hell did he do that?"

"Jimmy!"

"I said 'hell', not 'fuck'."

Thirty minutes later, the class ended and Ryan found himself removing the canvas and replacing them for another round of artists.

"Hey Ryan, this look familiar?" Steven asked.

Ryan looked up to see Steven in a far corner of the room standing behind a podium not unlike the ones they'd find in the assortment of hotel conference rooms across the Midwest."

"*My name's Ryan,*" Steven mocked as he gripped the podium. "*I can sell ice to an ice fisher.*"

Ryan smiled weakly and returned to his task.

"Everything okay?" Steven asked finally as he moved away from the podium.

"I'm fine," Ryan replied bluntly.

Steven nodded. "I know it's kind of a weird place, but I promise it's safe. The guards are well trained and-,"

"Why did you bring me here?" Ryan interjected as he stared coldly at Steven.

"What?"

"Why did you bring me here? Why am I here?"

"To help me out?"

"Why did you bring me to a prison?"

Steven stared back with hands to his side. "What?"

"Am I supposed to be seeing something here? Am I supposed to be learning something from this?"

"Ryan, not everything is-,"

"What's the message? That my life could always get worse? That I could be one of these guys? Is that it?"

Steven remained still.

"If that's the message, then it's pretty fucked up. It's pretty fucked up to use these men to prove that point."

"That's not what this is."

"Then what is it? Why am I here?"

"You're here because I'm here, because this is what I do-."

"Steven. Cut the *bullshit*. Tell me why you decided-."

"Because *they're honest!*" Steven finally yelled back.

It was Ryan's turn to be silent.

Steven looked down at his hands, which rested on the table in front of him. "This is the most honest place I've ever been, and it's one of the reasons I keep coming back. It's refreshing, you see? These men have nothing to lose, and so they live their life honestly. They say what they feel and they react the way they want to react. It's all honesty. Nothing to hide."

Ryan stood rigid as Steven spoke.

"I guess," Steven continued. "I guess I just felt like you needed a place like that." He looked up, as if his eyes were grasping for his next words. "It sounds ridiculous, but I don't know, I guess I was just trying to help."

"What do I need an honest space for?" Ryan asked evenly.

Steven shrugged. "I don't know. It just seems like you are running a million miles a second." He paused. "I just wondered if maybe you didn't need a safe space to breathe for a minute. Breathe and do some art."

"You think *this* is a safe space?"

"It's dumb, I know," Steven replied. "I-I'm not sure I even know what I'm doing."

"I don't need your help," Ryan replied. "I don't need help."

"Ryan, you just flew to Hawaii on a whim because of-,"

"Stop."

"I think we need to-,"

"I don't need your help!" Ryan replied, voice rising. "I don't need you, or this place, or honesty, or anything else." He could feel his pulse elevated and his heart rate rise. "Fuck this," he finally said as he set down the canvas that he was previously working with. Without another word, he turned and walked out of the room. Steven did not follow.

Moments later, Ryan was out though the giant steel door and into the parking lot where it was quiet and still.

Breathing deeply, he turned and looked back toward the building, not knowing what else to do. Somehow, he could still feel the Steven's eyes on him, even though he was as alone as ever before.

He knew he had lost his temper. He knew he had been a disappointment. Yet in the stillness of the night, he almost felt a calm in his thoughts, as if he had become exactly what he had set out to be.

He wanted a drink. He wanted to forget this night. He wanted to find someone at the bar and throw his body into oblivion. He wanted all these things, and yet somehow, his feet never moved.

Hanging his head, he sat down onto the sidewalk. Disappointing felt calming. Disrupting was a relief. How did that make sense?

Ryan sighed, understanding for the first time that maybe, just maybe, he had a problem after all.

***

Steven splashed water on his face and quickly dried it off with a paper towel. Taking a deep breath, he shook his head as he examined his image in the mirror before stepping out of the bathroom and into the long prison hallway where his box of art supplies greeted him on the floor.

Ryan did not come back for the second class.

Knowing he had another art session, Steven could do little more than watch him leave the room, though he had little idea where he would go to. Perhaps he'd catch a bus? Or walk down to the train station? Or maybe even hitch a ride? He had no idea what his friend was capable of.

Gripping his box in his hand, he stepped back into the middle of the hallway. As he began walking to the check-in desk, he saw that his rec space light was still on. As he passed. he stepped inside and reached his hands around the corner for the light switch.

"I was in Hawaii this past weekend."

Steven's gaze shot upward. Ryan stood at the front of the room, directly behind the podium with hands gripping each side.

"This story would probably be better with the lights on," he said with a shrug.

"You didn't leave?"

Ryan shrugged. "It's frowned upon to leave and come back in the same day, but I convinced him to let me back in."

Steven dropped his hand from the switch and stood, perplexed, at the back of the room.

"You can take a seat if you'd like," Ryan said nonchalantly.

Steven stood for a moment before slowly walking to the second table on the opposite side of the podium. Wordlessly, he took a seat onto the table as he sat his box nearby.

Ryan nodded from the podium. "I was in Hawaii this past weekend," he began, as though the words had been considered but not rehearsed. "Which is kind of crazy to think about since, you know, it's pretty fucking far away."

Steven nodded.

"But I wasn't there for vacation," Ryan continued. "Not the beaches or the nature or the resorts. That's what *normal* people would do." He paused for a moment. "I was there to see if a woman who I had feelings for was married like she claimed to be." He paused. "Saying it aloud sounds pretty ridiculous."

Steven smiled weakly.

"Spoiler alert," Ryan said louder. "She was." He rubbed his scarred cheekbone. "But of course, I didn't just go out there to figure out if she was married." He scratched his brow. "I also went to figure out why she didn't marry me. Or why she didn't want me. Not to hear the reasoning, because I think deep down, I knew the reasoning, but I went to *hear* the reasoning, to have it played for me so I could feel that pain once more."

Steven continued to listen.

Ryan's eyes turned to him. "I'll be honest," Ryan said after a pause. "I'm not really sure what to say next." His voice had lost its confidence.

Steven leaned back in his chair. "You can say whatever you want," he replied. "This is your space."

Ryan bit his bottom lip as he looked down to the podium, hands still gripping the sides.

"This used to be my specialty," Ryan said softly, looking at the lectern before moving his gaze out into the room. "This podium. This room." He paused. "The open space full of chairs or tables and the dim, centrally focused lighting. The eyes of the people all looking up at me, waiting for me to talk; to be witty, to be controlled and focused, to sell." He drew his breath in. "You're always selling when you're up here. Always. Selling ethanol. Selling a project. Selling an idea. Podiums and auditoriums are just huge forums to sell." Another pause as he exhaled. "And man, I could sell."

"I don't think it was ever even that difficult for me," Ryan continued, words growing in intensity. "As you know I'd throw a line in about their wives or the president or something that I could riff a joke from, and it was done. They were mine, and I knew it. Selling was…easy…" He looked down at the podium. "Because I've been doing it my whole life." He shook his head slowly. "Selling electronics. Selling my parents. Selling ex-girlfriends. Selling everyone the version of me that I wanted people to see." He looked up from the podium. "The charming version. The calm and collected version. The version that can talk his way into any bedroom or hotel room. The version of me that's successful. That's the version I try to sell. I even try to sell it to myself. And I do it…"

Steven leaned forward.

Ryan shrugged. "I do it because it's the version of myself I like. That version feels good. That version feels alive." He paused. "And because I hate the other version."

Steven inhaled and leaned back on the table.

"I hate him," Ryan continued. "I hate how he looks. I hate how he feels. I hate how insecure he is and how he always screws everything up. I hate who he is and how he fails." He gripped the sides of the stand. "I hate that he isn't who I wanted him to be when I was younger." He bit his lip.

"But most of all," Ryan said softly, almost inaudibly, "I hate the fact that despite how much I try to run from him, how much I try to drink him away or cover him in dust, he *is* me. It's *all* me. The version I love and the version I hate—it's all me, and no matter where I go, it all still remains. The same failure who ran out on his life and family in Florida. The same disaster who's already been to jail once before. The same guy who lied to a girl he cared about. It's all me, Steven. I've spent years trying to put it in the past, but I can't do it. No distance from Clearwater or exiles in Iowa can change that fact. It's all me." He looked up and into Steven's eyes.

"And to be honest with you," he said more angrily, "I'm really fucking tired of trying to find new places to bury me."

Steven could see the pain radiating from his friend's eyes. He could almost see the hint of tears present, and that alone ripped his heart in two. He could only begin to sense the anguish that he felt, yet the pain of self-hatred was one he knew all too well.

"Ryan," Steven said. "I'm sorry that Emma left."

Ryan looked up, and his pain broke within. "I can't keep doing this," he wheezed as a flood of tears rolled down his cheek. "She...accepted me. She knew...my past." His voice continued to break as he cried openly. "She cared about me. She accepted me. She knew who I was and still cared about me."

"She loved you."

Ryan continued to grip the podium as the tears fell downward.

"She loved you," Steven repeated. "She accepted you and cared for you despite all the flaws you think you have. That's love. But Ryan..."

Ryan looked up through his watery eyes.

"She couldn't have accepted your faults if you hadn't first shown them."

Ryan swallowed and wiped his eyes.

"You showed her who you were. *You* did that," Steven continued. "And she loved you, and you loved her. And unfortunately, it ended. And I'm so sorry that it did."

"I don't understand..."

"And you probably won't." Steven stood from his seat. "And that's okay. Ryan, sometimes you have to let something you love go. Sometimes you must walk out of someone's life. Sometimes the relationship doesn't continue. And it hurts. But in time, that pain goes away, and one day, maybe you'll be able to focus on the good of that relationship, and hope that your presence gave them happiness and peace. You hope that you bettered their life, just like they did for you. And once you get to that point, truly get there, you'll realize that you impact people more through good than you ever could with bad. And when you see that, you'll see that people do the same to you as well." Steven gripped the table in front of him as he looked up at Ryan. "And from then on, it's like no one ever really leaves at all."

Steven could see that Ryan was attempting to control his tears. Carefully, he moved into the aisle and up to the podium.

Ryan pulled back slowly, unable to move any further away. "I'm sorry I'm a shitty friend," Ryan said as he breathed out. "I'm sorry I've been…"

"You're here now," Steven replied. "And you're far from a bad friend." He embraced Ryan, knowing that the action likely meant more than any words.

He smiled upon feeling a return embrace. Half expecting a joke or a witty comment, Steven was pleased to hear only silence.

While the rest of the room remained silent and empty, Steven continued to embrace his friend, knowing that, for once, there were no words left to say.

Chapter 27
In Omaha

"It's a good day for flying," Steven said as he gripped the steering wheel with his eyes focused ahead.

In the passenger seat, Ryan sat leaned back, head rested on his hand with his elbow propped on the door. "That's the most *old man* thing you've ever said," he replied with a smile.

Steven quickly cast a searing glance over. "I'm sorry to make conversation."

Ryan continued to smile from the passenger seat. "You going to ask if I printed my boarding pass too?"

"A week is much too long to spend with you directly." Steven shook his head as his indignation turned to a smile as well. "Have I ever told you that?"

"It's on my phone, by the way," Ryan continued. "Like it is for everyone not ninety years old."

"Can I request that they put you under the plane?" Steven replied.

Ryan chuckled as he looked out the window.

There was silence for a moment as the car continued down the road.

"Are you nervous?" Steven asked.

"Nervous?" Ryan turned his head. "For Tampa?"

Steven smiled. "To see your family again."

"Oh." Ryan faked his realization. "I don't know, maybe."

"I think that's okay," Steven replied. "You'll have plenty to tell them."

"Yeah," Ryan replied. "Tell them about how great the unemployed life is."

Steven shrugged. "You could tell them about how a Hawaiian guy beat you up."

Ryan considered it. "I could tell them how I volunteered at a jail."

"How noble of you," Steven replied with a smile.

There was silence.

"Would you tell them about Hawaii?" Steven asked. "Or all your travels across the country with your friends?"

Ryan eyes perked at the word *friends*. He was unsure why, but the word sounded different, as if it were truth instead of fiction. "I don't know," he finally said.

More silence as Steven continued to drive onward.

"I have so much to tell them," Ryan finally said. "I don't think I'd know where to start."

"Start wherever you like," Steven replied. "When it's your story, you can tell whatever you want."

Ryan smiled as he leaned against the window and remained silent for a long while. "So, what are you going to do after this?" he asked after a moment.

"Me?"

"Yeah," Ryan replied.

Steven judged it. "Well, I'll need to get some gas, I think."

Ryan turned. "I meant generally."

"Ah," Steven replied. "My apologies."

"Have you thought about it? Will you keep volunteering?"

Steven considered the matter. "I don't know," he replied.

Ryan rolled his eyes.

"Fine," Steven replied. "I have thought about it." He paused as he changed lanes. "Truth is that I'm not sure. It's a great question." He paused. "I guess like you, my slate is pretty wide open."

Ryan nodded. "Look at us. The world is ours for the taking."

"Maybe I'll just use my severance time and spend the days with my kids." Steven replied. "Maybe I can become a stay-at-home dad. Or I can start my own non-profit."

"That's quite a change."

"Yeah," Steven responded. "I guess it is quite a steppingstone to go from corporate traveler to Mr. Mom. But we'll see."

Ryan smiled as he turned to look out the window. "I guess this means my next steppingstone is Tampa."

"Two thousand miles for a steppingstone is quite a jump," Steven replied. "You think you're ready for that?"

Ryan chuckled. "Not at all," he replied as he saw the airport come into view. "But there's only one way to find out."

It was soon after that the car arrived at the terminal. Carefully, Steven navigated the lanes of traffic while Ryan stared out the window at the many passengers disembarking from their cars. Soon he felt the car stop near the curb, and Steven shifted into park.

"Airport doesn't look too busy," Steven said as he leaned to look out the passenger window.

Ryan smiled. "You're right, Grandpa."

"Shut up and get out," Steven said with a chuckle. He, too, stepped outside.

Ryan waited at the curb as Steven unloaded his suitcase.

"Let me know when you land," Steven said. "Or if the plane blows up."

"Probably be a bit preoccupied on that last one," Ryan replied with a smile. "But it is nice to see my humor rubbing off on you.

Steven smiled before his face turned serious. "Come back and visit sometime."

"I will," Ryan replied, matching the seriousness. "Thanks for everything."

"Anytime."

Ryan hesitated. "And I'll work on being a better friend too."

"Work on what you want to," Steven replied. "Do it for you."

Ryan nodded, and Steven embraced him.

"Have a good flight," Steven said.

"See you later," Ryan replied. He gripped his bag and turned as Steven returned to his car.

Ryan stopped inside the automatic door and turned around. Giving a small wave, he saw as Steven returned the gesture from the driver's seat. Exhaling, he turned back around and proceeded inside.

Chapter 28
Leaving Omaha

Ryan pulled his suitcase onto the electric walkway and proceeded to lean onto the railing, allowing other passengers to pass him by.

Glancing out at the bluffs across the Missouri, he absorbed the setting for a moment before pulling his phone from his pocket. He slowly unlocked the device and pulled up a group text that he had ignored for many days.

Hey guys, he typed. *Sorry I haven't responded to anything in a few weeks. It's been an interesting couple weeks. But I'm good—*

He paused and looked up. He deleted the last word he'd typed.

I'm better now. I'm heading to Florida for a few days, but I promise I won't leave you all hanging anymore.

He considered his words and then shrugged off further suggestions.

Let's set up some time to talk. I'd love to hear what you've been up to. Whenever you want.

His finger hovered over the send button before he pulled it back. He didn't want to send a group text. It didn't seem nearly apologetic enough.

He copied the message and personalized the introductions. Then, one by one, he sent it, first to Mike and Donovan, and then finally to Maria.

Exiting the app, he pulled off the first electric walkway and moved onto the second. Anxiously awaiting a reply, he found himself pulling up an old app he had not used in many months.

His LinkedIn notifications were far too numerous to address, but the message icon caught his eye. Opening the folder, he saw a variety of bolded unread communications. Reading through the list, he saw several ads, but also several more that caught his attention.

Hi, Mr. Collins—I heard your presentation last night in Lincoln. You have a knack for public speaking, and I'm just curious if you've ever considered a career change.

His eyes moved to the next down the line.

Mr. Collins, my name is Doug Randall with Global Trainers Inc., and your name reached our hiring manager regarding an opening we have.

Line after line, he saw personalized career inquiries ranging from training to speaking to communication. Looking at locations, he saw everything from the Northeast to the West Coast. Smiling, he slowly closed out of the app, happy for a moment simply knowing that, for once, options were available.

Staring at his home screen, he felt a vibration as a response came through. The first was from Donovan. *All good, brother. Glad to hear you're good. Talk tomorrow?*

Ryan smiled.

Another text, this time from Maria. *Ryan! Jesus, we were worried. Don't fucking go AWOL anymore. But seriously, so happy to hear from you! Mike and I are on a road trip (long story). We'll be back in Omaha next weekend, though, so we'll talk then.*

Ryan's smile increased as he read through the message. Another message.

P.S.

He opened the photo to see her hand with a ring on it.

Ryan could feel emotion well within him as he read through the texts. Stepping off the walkway, he proceeded toward his gate with one hand on his suitcase and the other texting feverishly. First to Donovan, then his excitement to Maria and Mike.

Congrats! Thanks for responding. I'm sorry for the worry. It was pretty crappy of me.

He reached the gate moments later and found a seat near the far wall, where he sat alone, silently waiting for more responses.

Maria came first.

No need to apologize. Always here for you.

Ryan smiled as he read the message. *Good to know you never give up,* he texted.

Moments passed. Another vibration.

I never give up on friends.

Ryan kept his emotions in check, though it became difficult as the messages flooded in. He attempted to reply as fast as possible, and he eventually settled the conversations with the promises of phone calls soon. As the vibrations subsided, he leaned back in his chair, a smile still on his face.

He then scrolled up on his messages to find one conversation from months back that he had left unread.

Sorry I've been so unresponsive, he typed. *I know it's been awhile, but I'd like to catch up when you can.*

He looked up to see the name "Bo" on the top of the messages. Hovering his finger over the "send" button, he finally pressed down.

It took only a moment before his phone pinged again.

Can I call you later on tonight?

Ryan almost felt the relief wash over him.

Sounds good, he responded.

Casually, he glanced toward the monitor overhead to see that his plane was delayed. None of that mattered, however, as he leaned back in his chair in the waiting area.

For the moment, all was well, and that was all he needed. Not even a flight delay could change that.

***

Late afternoon sunlight cascaded into the airport terminal as Ryan continued to sit in his same waiting area chair. It was several hours into the delay, but somehow, he was content alternating between the magazine in his hand and the overhead television.

"Ladies and gentlemen," the overhead page called out after a long while. "Flight 982 with service to Tampa will begin boarding shortly. We apologize for the delay today and hope to have you aboard shortly."

Ryan exhaled as he laid his phone on top of the magazine in his lap. Legs sprawled around his suitcase, he allowed himself to lean back and close his eyes as he contemplated his trip ahead. The seats around him were empty, and overall the entire gate area was quiet, as though everyone was content to ride out the delay in silence. The calming air allowed Ryan to fall deep into his thoughts.

How would his family respond to his arrival? What would his cousin say after these years? Or his parents, whom he had barely spoken to?

Ryan considered all these questions, but knew that regardless of the trepidations, returning was the right thing to do. He had been without family for so long.

Other questions rolled through his mind, chiefly, how long would he stay in Florida? In truth, he had no return plans, just a one-way ticket with a question mark at the end. Eventually, he knew he had to return to Omaha and Spirit Lake, but after? Where would he go next?

He tried hard not to overwhelm himself with the unknowns. For now, he had a place to go, and that would have to be good enough. Tomorrow's problems would come later down the line.

He took another deep breath as he attempted to clear his mind in the quiet gate area. Closing his eyes, he allowed the serenity to wash over him.

He felt his phone vibrate in his lap.

Dropping his head down, he opened his eyes and looked curiously to see a new text message. Slowly, he lifted the phone from the magazine. Unlocking it, his eyes grew wide as he pulled the message up.

Hey.

It was the only thing Emma said.

Ryan's eyes stared at the message for a long time as his mind attempted to process the sole word on his screen. He felt a lump grow in his throat. He felt his eyes begin to water as he stared at the word. He felt his mouth open, first in shock and then in a hint of a smile, and he felt his hands begin to shake.

It was so simple and yet in that moment, it was everything he could ever have wanted.

Wiping his eyes, he typed in the only thing he could think of.

Hey.

He held the phone in his trembling hand as he continued to feel tears stream down his face. He didn't care who saw him cry. He didn't care if his plane was about to board or not. All that mattered was now. All that mattered was this moment. All that mattered was this text.

Ryan closed his eyes and wiped his tears. Opening them, he could see three little dots on his screen that told him she was typing a response.

Smiling from the very core of his soul, he sat the phone back down onto the magazine and waited for her reply.

THE END

Also Available from S.D. Goldman:

A THOUSAND MILES FROM SPOKANE

"There's a lot to love here. A THOUSAND MILES FROM SPOKANE is a gripping and interesting story offered by an obviously strong storyteller."
- *Judge, 29ᵗʰ Annual Writer's Digest Self-Published Book Awards*

"An interesting character study told with a clear and satisfying voice."
- *IBPA's Benjamin Franklin Awards*

"Goldman writes with an impressive hand, using clear, descriptive text that provides a full picture and engages the reader."
- *The Booklife Prize*

See how Ryan's story begins. Available in paperback and eBook at SDGoldman.com